The bar fell silent.

In the darkest corner of the room, the man keeping to himself felt the hair on the back of his neck stand on end. Straightening, he looked over his shoulder to see what was wrong.

In the doorway he saw impossible high heels, delicate-looking ankles, trim thighs that seemed to go on forever beneath a sinfully brief excuse for a skirt. The woman's whole midsection was exposed, the skirt barely covering her belly button, the top more or less covering her breasts. He saw honey-colored skin, imagined it must be smooth as silk, covering a body toned like an athlete's.

Or a spy's?

The man who called himself Alex Connor nearly groaned aloud. This was the dirtiest trick yet. If someone was sending a woman like her after him, he just might get caught.

Dear Reader,

It's summertime. The mercury's rising, and so is the excitement level here at Silhouette Intimate Moments. Whatever you're looking for—a family story, suspense and intrigue, or love with a ranchin' man—we've got it for you in our lineup this month.

Beverly Barton starts things off with another installment in her fabulous miniseries THE PROTECTORS. *Keeping Annie Safe* will *not* cool you off, I'm afraid! Merline Lovelace is back with *A Man of His Word,* part of her MEN OF THE BAR H miniseries, while award winner Ingrid Weaver checks in with *What the Baby Knew.* If it's edge-of-your-seat suspense you're looking for, pick up the latest from Sally Tyler Hayes, *Spies, Lies and Lovers.* *The Rancher's Surrender* is the latest from fresh new talent Jill Shalvis, while Shelley Cooper makes her second appearance with *Guardian Groom.*

You won't want to miss a single one of these fabulous novels, or any of the books we'll be bringing you in months to come. For guaranteed great reading, come to Silhouette Intimate Moments, where passion and excitement go hand in hand.

Enjoy!

Yours,

Leslie Wainger

Leslie J. Wainger
Executive Senior Editor

Please address questions and book requests to:
Silhouette Reader Service
U.S.: 3010 Walden Ave., P.O. Box 1325, Buffalo, NY 14269
Canadian: P.O. Box 609, Fort Erie, Ont. L2A 5X3

SPIES, LIES AND LOVERS

SALLY TYLER HAYES

Silhouette ®
INTIMATE™MOMENTS®

Published by Silhouette Books

America's Publisher of Contemporary Romance

SILHOUETTE BOOKS

ISBN 0-373-07940-0

SPIES, LIES AND LOVERS

Copyright © 1999 by Teresa Hill

This edition published by arrangement with Harlequin Books S.A.

Visit us at www.romance.net

Printed in U.S.A.

Books by Sally Tyler Hayes

Silhouette Intimate Moments

Whose Child Is This? #439
Dixon's Bluff #485
Days Gone By #549
Not His Wife #611
Our Child? #671
Homecoming #700
Temporary Family #738
Second Father #753
Wife, Mother...Lover? #818
Dangerous To Love #903
Spies, Lies and Lovers #940

SALLY TYLER HAYES

lives in South Carolina with her husband, son and daughter. A former journalist for a South Carolina newspaper, she fondly remembers that her decision to write and explore the frontiers of romance came at about the same time she discovered, in junior high, that she'd never be able to join the crew of the starship *Enterprise*.

Happy and proud to be a stay-home mom, she is thrilled to be living her lifelong dream of writing romances.

With gratitude to Michael, on *La Femme Nikita*,
whom I did find wonderfully inspiring.

Prologue

The cursor blinked annoyingly amid a mass of letters and symbols that would be nothing but gibberish to the masses. But Alex Hathaway understood them all, just as he understood that something was desperately wrong.

He tore off his headphones, silencing the hard, fast strumming of the guitar that kept him company hour after hour in the lab. Eyes scanning the room, he found it empty, everything just as he'd left it two hours ago when he'd gone to brief the brass on his progress.

Pulling his watch from a pocket in his faded jeans, he saw that he'd been working almost continuously for fourteen hours. Maybe he simply couldn't see straight anymore. That made more sense than what his eyes were telling him.

At a nearby sink, Alex cupped his hands under a steady stream of cold water, letting it pool in his palms. He drenched his face in the water again and again before reaching for a towel and returning to the computer.

"Come on, sweetheart," he coaxed, tapping lightly on the keyboard. "It's Alex. Don't scare me like this."

The screen filled once again with an incredibly complex chemical formula. But Alex knew the symbols and numbers like the back of his own hand, and they simply weren't right. He'd booby-trapped the thing. If anyone but him tried to access it, the computer automatically scrambled the formula, and he was definitely looking at a scrambled one now.

Alex mumbled a few choice phrases, all of them profane, and shut off the computer so quickly it howled in protest. Long, angry strides took him to the front of the windowless lab, to reinforced steel doors that he flung open.

Two fully armed military guards snapped to attention. Alex looked up one side and down the other of the corridor separating him from the outside world, finding it empty, as it should be.

Nose-to-nose with the biggest, beefiest guard, he announced, "Someone's been in my lab. In my computer."

The young man blanched, but met Alex's stare dead-on and said nothing. Alex could tell the guard couldn't have been more surprised if Alex had just announced he was Papa Bear, and Goldilocks was sleeping in his bed. It made as much sense as someone prowling through his computer—something Alex had been assured couldn't happen here.

"No one's gotten past you?" Alex demanded. "No one's gone in there?"

"No, sir."

Alex had given up trying to explain to them that he didn't need to be addressed as "sir." Raking a hand through his hair, he started issuing orders.

"Call your commander. Tell him I'm leaving. Tonight."

It was less than two full days later when the hit came. Alex was alone in a new, supposedly safe place. It was very, very early, and his two assistants were asleep, when he sensed more than heard someone else's presence in the lab.

He closed the file he'd been working on, shut off his notebook computer and slipped it into a small leather duffel bag he'd taken to keeping within arm's reach. He had money, a few clothes, a bit of a disguise, and he could hotwire a car with the best of them. All he had to do was get out.

He could bypass the security system on the front door—not easily, but he could do it. He'd made sure of that. There was an armed guard at the door, two more outside. At least there had been two hours ago when he'd last checked in with them. If someone had gotten past the guards…

Damn.

Alex pulled a small vial of liquid from his pocket, took a breath and held it. He emptied the vial onto the counter next to the desktop computer, thinking it would be the first place anyone looked. Then he crept around the corner and hunched down close to the floor, covering his mouth and his nose with a chemically treated mask. It would buy him a few extra minutes.

It wasn't long before he heard someone moving in the lab, heard him fall heavily to the floor. The urge to go back and see who had done this to him was strong, but so was the chemical that was buying his way out. When he got to the door, it was open and the guard was slumped over on the floor, bleeding heavily. Alex stopped to check for a pulse and, finding none, paused for a moment of regret over the havoc wrought so far by this thing he'd created.

He would trust no one now. He was truly alone.

Shortly before midnight, Geri Sinclair walked into a staid, utterly respectable-looking four-story brick office building in Georgetown where she reported for work when she wasn't away on assignment. Passing through a series of checkpoints, she finally found herself face-to-face with a deceptively sweet-looking gentleman who'd once been a

Navy SEAL. He tipped his hat to her and smiled as he punched in a code that opened the final reinforced-steel door.

"How's the arm, ma'am?" he asked politely.

After three months of physical therapy, Geri suspected her arm and shoulder were as good as they were going to get. To the security guard, she simply said, "Better, thanks, Harry. What's up?"

"No idea, ma'am."

She'd glanced at the TV as she dressed. There'd been no special news bulletins, either. Sometimes those held a clue to where she was headed.

Geri was the last agent to arrive at the briefing room. She took her seat and nodded to her boss, Martin Tanner, a former CIA operative who'd gotten his start in the military, as Geri and many of the other agents had.

Tanner stood at the head of the table, dimmed the lights and flicked on the slide projector. The smiling face of a boyishly handsome man filled the screen. He had dark eyes and light brown hair that he wore cropped close to his head. In his arms, he held a little girl of three, maybe four. She looked up at him as if she were simply dazzled by him and delighted to have him so close.

Hostage rescue, Geri thought absently, feeling a little queasy at the thought that they might be heading after the little girl, as well.

Then something had her studying the man once again. She'd seen his face before in a profoundly different situation. Methodically, she stripped away the details—the beautiful little girl, the sunshine—his open, honest look and even his smile, reconfiguring his features as she went.

The first real sense of excitement she'd felt since the shooting slammed through her.

It was *him.*

She'd never seen him in person—just a very serious-looking likeness of him at a hasty briefing much like this one, three months ago. She'd seen the same grainy photograph again when he'd made it to the top of the FBI's Ten Most Wanted list. He'd been inside the fortress-like safe house the entire time that she and her partner, Dan Reese, were on duty that disastrous night, and had been in the agency's custody for less than sixteen hours before he'd disappeared. His fingerprints had been found on the weapon that killed Doc—a man she'd known and worked with for years—and Geri blamed him nearly as much as she blamed herself for her partner's injuries and her own.

Despite her security clearance, up to this point she'd known little about the man. His existence had been veiled in the kind of secrecy Geri had seldom seen in her time with the agency and her previous experience in military intelligence. Right now, a joint task force of the FBI and the CIA were after him—for killing a federal agent. But that was merely the tip of the iceberg, the only crime the government was willing to publicly admit had taken place. Judging by the anxiety level in Washington, D.C., something much bigger was at stake. Geri wanted in on the hunt, but the agency had been yanked off the case by the president himself, as punishment for having lost the man in the first place.

But now, it looked as if they were back in the game.

Geri smiled for the first time in months.

Tanner quickly ran through the man's background—a near genius-level IQ, degrees in engineering and computer science, as well as a Ph.D. in chemistry. The little girl was one of his nieces.

Tanner tapped his pointer against the boyishly handsome face. "I'm sure you all recognize Dr. Alexander Hathaway. I don't have to tell you how badly I want to bring him down."

Geri gazed up at the man's face again. He was laughing,

damn him. Smiling. Happy. And Doc was dead. Dan was still in a wheelchair. Geri, herself, was a mess. All because of this one man—a man she hated.

"Dr. Hathaway worked for a government contractor doing research in security systems, particularly in their abilities to detect plastic explosives. He was trying to develop the next level of surveillance equipment to be installed in the nation's airports when he stumbled upon an interesting anomaly. He found a chemical compound that, when added to plastic explosives in use today, rendered them virtually undetectable to the security systems now in use.

"You can imagine," Tanner continued, "the kind of people interested in acquiring Dr. Hathaway's formula and what they'd be willing to pay for it."

Oh, yes. Geri could imagine all too easily.

"This man is a traitor, willing to betray his country for money," Tanner said. "We believe he slipped away from the government's protection to sell his formula on the black market. I hold him responsible for the death of one of my agents, the loss of the services of another. The FBI and the CIA have been looking for him for three months without any luck, but he's ours now."

Ours? No, Geri decided, sweet anticipation running through her veins. He was *hers*.

Chapter 1

The bar fell silent, except for a peculiar creaking, crackling sound.

In the darkest corner of the room, the man hunched over the only freestanding video game within forty-five miles felt the hair on the back of his neck stand on end. Straightening, he gave up all pretense of playing the game and looked over his shoulder to see what was wrong.

In the doorway, he saw impossibly high heels, delicate-looking ankles, trim thighs that seemed to go on forever beneath a sinfully brief excuse for a skirt. The woman's whole midsection was bare, the skirt barely covering her belly button, the top more or less covering her breasts. He saw honey-colored skin, imagined it must be as smooth as silk, covering a body toned like an athlete's.

Or a spy's?

The man who called himself "Alex Connor" nearly groaned aloud. This was the dirtiest trick yet. If someone was sending a woman like her after him, he just might be caught. Whoever she was, she was trouble. Young, good-looking, scantily dressed women didn't show up alone in seedy bars in the Texas panhandle without causing trouble.

She took three steps into the interior of the bar. Red leather strained and creaked with every step she took. He had a feeling the sound would come to haunt his nights, if the sight of her didn't kill him right away. Alex didn't think he'd ever had a fantasy about a woman in red leather, but he was an open-minded kind of guy. And he hadn't been near a woman in months—something he now could see might prove to be a fatal flaw in his plan.

The woman paused at the edge of the room, as if she were on the end of a runway in Atlantic City, flashbulbs popping all around her, the Miss America song blaring from the sound system. Either she didn't have the brains God gave a goose or she was here for a reason. *For him.*

The bartender's look said he knew she'd be trouble. The other six reprobates in the room might as well have had their tongues hanging out of their mouths, panting and stumbling over themselves like overeager puppies with no manners at all. They were going to pounce on her any minute.

Oblivious to the danger, the woman strolled into the room, selected one of the stools at the bar and sat, the motion hitching the miniskirt up even higher on her thighs.

From the right came a sound that might have been one of the men keeling over onto the floor. Eventually, stunned silence gave way to catcalls and whistles.

"What'll you have?" Buck, the bartender, drawled.

"A shot of tequila and a tall glass of ice water."

She picked up a cocktail napkin, using it to slowly dab at the sweat on her forehead, her cheeks, her neck. Alex started to sweat, too. As her hand dipped lower, to the hollow between her breasts, a decrepit-looking man to her right drawled out a curse, its pronunciation unlike any Alex had ever heard until he'd come to Texas. Silence reigned once again in the bar, until a drunken cowhand named Willie sat down beside the woman.

"You lost?" he asked.

"Car broke down," she purred. "About a mile from here. I was hoping someone at the garage could fix it. But I needed a drink first. It was so *hot* out there."

Hot? Alex swore softly. How dared she utter that word?

"Sal's is closed," the bartender told her. "Won't be open till Monday morning."

She pouted prettily. "Surely there's someone around here besides Sal who can fix a car."

Alex winced, because there wasn't. There was next to nothing to this town, which he thought made it a damned good place to disappear. Now, he wasn't so sure.

As he sat there on the stool in front of the video game, a weakness of his that he indulged from time to time in this seedy little bar, Alex wondered who had found him, how they'd found him, and how many more of them were waiting for him outside, or at his cabin. Then he heard another curse and turned back around.

The woman had her drinks—tequila in a shot glass, ice water beside it. She picked up the glass of ice water, condensation rolling down its sides, pressed it to her forehead and sighed. Alex watched her breasts rise and fall, straining against that sorry excuse for a top with every breath she took. Then she held the cool, wet glass to the side of her cheek and practically purred with satisfaction.

Alex considered begging her to stop right then. He could turn himself in, let her put the handcuffs on him. Maybe she would sit beside him in the back seat of the car and put on another little show like this one for him as they took him away. He'd be caught, but what a way to go.

His brain was short-circuiting as she fished a piece of ice from the glass. When she brought the ice to her lips, then let them close around it in what looked like a gentle kiss, Alex closed his eyes and started reciting the elements of the periodic table. The men in the room were so hot, she could have taken an ice cube to any one of them, Alex included, and it wouldn't just have melted; it would have given off steam.

From there, it wasn't long before a couple of cowboys were ready to come to blows over the woman. Alex was torn between the certainty that she'd come here after him and deserved whatever trouble she found in the process—and a damnable sense of honor that told him he ought to save her from herself.

As intelligent as he was, Alex made incredibly stupid decisions when it came to women. He had an innate need to try to fix whatever was wrong for them—something that had gotten him into trouble more than once. He wondered if the person who had decided to send her here knew that about him.

Angry, Alex let the woman sweat it out for a few moments. If she was really scared, she might be in the mood to talk by the time he got her out of here—if he wasn't picked up the minute he stepped outside. Besides, he wondered just what she could do to defend herself. If she was a trained agent, she shouldn't have any problem getting away from a couple of middle-aged drunks, one of whom had just grabbed her by the arm.

"Let me go," she demanded.

When Willie didn't, she drew up her right knee and jammed her shoe—stiletto heel first—into his shin. It was nothing flashy, nothing requiring a great deal of training, but highly effective.

Alex winced, almost feeling the pain in his own leg, as all hell broke loose and he charged into the middle of it. He was fighting his way toward the woman when she fell to the floor. The sound of breaking glass, followed by a spray of bits of glass, brought the room to silence. Another cowboy named Hawkins swung the jagged edge of the bottle in a semicircle around him and the woman on the floor.

"Back off," Hawkins warned him.

Alex thought the jagged end of the bottle was too close to the woman for him to try anything at that moment, but Willie, on his feet again, didn't care. He charged toward Hawkins. With a growl, Hawkins crashed to the floor, lashing out with the broken bottle as he toppled.

The woman gasped. Alex made it to her side, shoved three other drunks away, then turned back to her and saw a trickle of blood form a thin line down the woman's mostly bare chest. Damn. He'd waited too long to step in.

Out of the corner of his eye, he saw Hawkins coming back for more, Willie rushing in from the other side. Alex shoved his foot into Hawkins's big, puffy belly, took the heel of his hand and let Willie run into it with his nose.

A gunshot blasted through the seedy bar. "That's enough!" yelled Buck.

Willie swore at Alex. "You broke my damned nose!"

"Get near me again and I'll break something else," Alex told him.

"Enough," Buck said. "You boys get back to your seats."

The woman still lay on the floor. The long, thin cut on her chest was bleeding, but not heavily. Relieved, Alex decided it probably stung like hell but wasn't serious.

"Do me a favor, Connor," the bartender warned. "Get her out of here."

"Come on," Alex said to her.

She put her hand on the floor to brace herself, then gasped.

"What?" Alex asked.

"Glass," she replied, her voice tight with pain as she stared at her hands.

"Hold out your arms," Alex said.

Gripping her forearms, he pulled her to her feet. She swayed a bit on those ridiculous heels, looking scared and not ready to trust any man now.

Buck gave Alex a hearty recommendation. "Believe me, honey. You're safer with him than anybody else in this room. And if you left by yourself, you wouldn't get half a mile before one of these guys caught up with you."

Through impossibly thick lashes, she stared up at Alex for the longest time. Finally she grabbed her purse from the bar and turned to follow him.

"Do me a favor, honey," Buck called out as they left. "Don't come back any time soon."

The woman glared at Buck, then followed Alex outside into the near-blinding sunshine and oppressive heat. Alex was surprised and relieved that no one jumped them right away. He scanned the area and saw nothing amiss.

Could he have been wrong about her? Or were her friends simply lying in wait for him? Maybe waiting for him to lead the way to his cabin? Assuming they weren't already there, digging through everything he owned. Alex wasn't worried that they'd find what they were looking for—at least, not without his cooperation. But he had no idea *who* had found him. Some possibilities were definitely worse than others.

"Come on," he said to the woman, leading her around the corner of the building where he'd parked his bike. Cocking his head to the south, he asked, "Your car's that way?"

She nodded. "About a mile from here."

"Maybe I can fix it," Alex said, wondering if she did indeed have a broken-down car, wondering if she would drive off and leave if he managed to fix it. Alex doubted it.

Then he wondered if someone had somehow reached inside his head and sifted through his brain cells trying to come up with the perfect way to get to him. Or to tempt him. Whatever the intent, it had worked. The woman definitely had his attention.

Alex held out his helmet to her, then remembered the damage she'd done to her hands. He put the helmet on her himself, his hand brushing against her chin when he fastened the clasp, her eyes huge and wide and dark, the kind a man could drown in.

Damn, her skin was soft.

She was wearing too much makeup and had fussed too much with her hair, doing that Texas big-hair thing. Hers was dark and didn't even reach her chin, but it was all...puffy. Alex didn't understand big hair. Still, there was something delicate about her—her eyes maybe, or her mouth. How she managed to look delicate with the makeup and the hair and the leather, he couldn't understand. But she did. He wondered what the real "her" looked like.

Alex thought about all he'd given up in the past year of work without end. Until today, he hadn't realized how much he missed being close to a woman. And she could be just that, he argued with himself. She could be nothing but a sexy, soft-skinned, sweet-smelling woman whose car had broken down in the middle of nowhere. It was unlikely, but still a possibility.

Gently, he took her injured hand in his and checked her palms. Somehow, he managed not to let himself think of how soft her hands were or how angry it made him that anyone had hurt her this way, no matter who she was or why she was here. As a last-ditch effort at self-preservation, he decided he couldn't let himself look into those pretty eyes of hers again or do anything more than glance at the vulnerable look on her face.

Oh, she was good at this, he decided as he finished with her injured hand. "How's the rest of you?"

"I think there's some glass in my back."

Great. He gritted his teeth and walked in a half circle

around her. The tight skirt stretched across her bottom just
as enticingly as he'd imagined it would, and from this side,
the top exposed even more creamy soft skin. It also revealed
angry-looking scratches on her right shoulder. He brushed
his hand across them, and she tensed. Looking lower, he
saw jagged tears in the tiny skirt, where it swelled against
the curve of her hips.

Alex groaned, wondering if he'd somehow offended the
entire universe to deserve this kind of torture.

"That bad?" she asked.

When he thought about his options, he decided it was
indeed "that bad."

"Hold on," he grumbled, putting one hand on her waist,
remembering too late that that part of her was bare, as well.
She sucked in a breath, the motion sending her skin retreat-
ing from his touch. He was suddenly fascinated by every
little move she made, every indrawn breath, every inch of
exposed skin.

Determined to get this over with, Alex ran his other hand
along the tears of the skirt, then thought of the tortures still
facing him. If he took her back to his place, he was going
to have to play doctor. There was no way she could reach
some of these cuts herself. Alex had one very disturbing
image of her lying naked across his bed, of his hands skim-
ming up and down her body as he made sure he'd gotten
all the embedded glass out of her skin. The periodic table
didn't stand a chance of numbing his senses to that kind of
temptation.

Or he could leave her here, he thought. If she followed
him, she followed him. If she put a bullet in his back, he'd
die. At this point, he'd done all he could to protect his work
and to see that it didn't fall into the wrong hands.

But when Alex turned to face her, the look in her eyes
was enough to slay him. He saw a faint sheen of tears glittering in her brown eyes before she lowered those luxu-

riously long lashes to shield herself from his gaze, saw the faint trembling in her pouty little bottom lip before she curled it over her bottom teeth and bit down hard on it. She'd lost all that arrogance and sophistication he'd sensed in the bar and looked like a scared, lost woman on the edge of losing control.

Giving in to the impulse to stop her before she inflicted any real damage to herself, Alex came closer still and let the tips of his fingers softly stroke her lower lip. "You're going to hurt yourself."

She didn't even breathe, just gazed up at him, studying every inch of his face, obviously wary that he'd come this close, that he'd touched her this way. Alex still had his hand on the side of her face. His thumb traced the line of her bottom lip once again, and he tried very hard to ignore that way she smelled and the way she suddenly seemed so fragile, so feminine. She had narrow shoulders and hips, stood maybe five feet three inches without those ridiculous high heels, had a neat and trim body, yet was still obviously all woman.

She stayed still for what could have been five minutes or five seconds. Alex had honestly lost all touch with reality and the passage of time. And then she merely stepped back, leaving his hand to fall to his side, and said nothing, merely looked at him. Strange, he thought. She looked more wary now than she had when she'd ended up on the floor of the bar.

What kind of woman would be more frightened by the gentle touch of his fingers on her lips than the threat of a half-dozen drunken men dragging her into the back room of a bar and tearing off her clothes? Alex was intrigued by her now, which was likely every bit as dangerous as his urge to save her from this mess.

"Lady," he muttered as he pulled the hem of his T-shirt

from the waistband of his jeans, "if this is an act, you're very good at it."

As he advanced toward her, she paled—because of what he'd said, or because she thought he was going to strip off his clothes right in front of her? It only made him more curious.

"The cut," he explained, taking two steps forward for every one she took in retreat.

"What?"

Alex pointed to the cut running down her chest. "It's bleeding."

She finally stopped backing away. He had to get much too close in order to use the hem of his shirt to dab at the cut. To make matters worse, the injury extended all the way down to the point where her skin swelled against the neckline of her top. His T-shirt was so thin he could feel the warmth of her flesh, could easily imagine having his hands on her bare breasts. He watched them rise and fall with each breath she took, felt the movement as well. By the time he was done, he wasn't sure he could breathe.

"Thank you," she said.

At least her voice sounded a little strained—not that it came close to giving him the satisfaction he now craved.

Alex stepped back. "We need to get out of here."

He climbed onto the bike and started the engine. He faced straight ahead as he told her to climb aboard. Her weight settled onto the bike. Alex felt nothing more than the vaguest impression of her body behind him as she slid as far back on the seat as she could to avoid touching him, something he truly appreciated. Still, he couldn't let her stay there, because he could tell by the awkward way she seated herself behind him that she'd never ridden a bike before.

Hanging his head, he muttered, "What's your name, angel face?"

She hesitated for a moment. "Geri."

Geri. It fit, he decided. Even if it wasn't her real name, it fit.

"I'm Alex," he said, having long ago realized people were less likely to remember a man named Alex than one using some other name to which he couldn't remember to respond.

"Is something wrong?" she asked softly.

"You're going to have to trust me on this, Geri. If you don't get a little closer to me and hang on tight, you're going to fall off this bike before we go ten yards."

"Oh."

She eased herself against him, her bare thighs pressed against his buttocks, her leather-clad breasts against his back, her hands on his shoulders. He took her hands, pulled them around his waist, and pressed her palms flat against his abdomen, a move that brought every part of her that much closer to him.

Only a mile, he told himself. Her car was a mile away. If there was any compassion left in this world, the car would start and she would be gone.

A moment later they stood frowning down at a sleek, flashy, very expensive convertible. Geri claimed it was stalling and sputtering, so she'd pulled off the interstate. Before she could find a garage, the car had died.

Just for the hell of it, Alex tried starting it, to no avail. He checked the most obvious things he knew, and the next time he tried the engine, the car locked up on him totally. Nothing happened when he turned the key.

"Does this thing have a security system?" he asked.

"Yes." She was standing by the side of the road looking nervously toward town. "Won't those men come after us?"

"Maybe." Resisting the urge to cuss at the car, Alex explained, "That's the only bar within a forty-five-mile radius, and most men don't want to have to drive that far for a drink. Buck, the bartender, owns the place, and he's known to hold a grudge. Most everybody understands that if they make him mad enough, he won't serve them again for a long, long time. That should be enough to make Willie and Hawkins think long and hard about coming after you."

"Oh."

Alex tried the car one last time, setting off an annoying blast of the car's horn that continued at three-second intervals. Shouting, he said, "I don't suppose you could make it stop!"

She pressed a series of buttons on the oversize key, and the car quieted. "Sorry," she said. "It's a little temperamental."

Alex frowned, truly annoyed. She could have shut down the car herself—there were security systems capable of that—if she had reason to want to be stuck in this godforsaken town with him.

He weighed his options, which were few and far between. Leaving her to fend for herself was one he discarded right away. He wouldn't be able to live with himself if she was telling the truth and something happened to her because he was too paranoid to help her. He could take her someplace, if she'd go. Or he could keep her with him. If someone knew enough about him to have sent her here after him, sending her away now wasn't going to save him. Neither was taking off. She wouldn't have come alone. Someone was probably watching every move they made. *Damn.* Alex couldn't outrun them. Hopefully, he could outsmart them eventually. First, he had to know what he was up against. He had to find out who she was and whom she worked for, and his best chance of doing that was to keep her with him.

He turned to the woman who might well be his downfall and asked if she wanted anything from the car. She retrieved an expensive-looking leather tote bag from the trunk. Curiously, the car let her do that without the slightest sound of protest.

"Where are we going?" she asked, looking wary.

"My place." She started to protest, but Alex cut her off. "Look, you can stay right here on the side of the road if you like. But you should know there's no place in town where you can rent a room. And in case you haven't noticed, there isn't a lot of traffic on this road."

"I noticed," Geri said, managing to look quite troubled and more than a little vulnerable, despite her outrageous outfit.

Alex had been curious as to how much of a fight she'd put up about going with him. It seemed most women would be worried about their own safety, and she had nothing but a stranger's word that she was safer with Alex than with anyone else in that bar, which wasn't saying much, considering the crowd.

"How 'bout this," he offered, strapping her bag to the back of the bike. "Let's get you cleaned up, find something to eat, and then we'll talk about where you can go from there, okay?"

She agreed. Too easily, Alex thought.

"There's a motel in Red Rock, about forty-five minutes from here. If you like, I'll take you there tonight," he said. If she accepted, he'd be rid of her. If she refused, well…that should tell him something.

Geri said nothing, simply nodded her head. He hopped on the bike and braced himself for the moment when she'd climb on as well. He didn't flinch, didn't so much as breathe when her arms gripped him tightly around the waist and her body was once again pressed against his. Then he revved up the bike and they took off.

Chapter 2

I could always kill him, Geri told herself.

If she was honest with herself, she'd admit that she'd already been tempted to do just that. Even before the agency had been given the task of hunting him down, she'd considered extending her medical leave and taking off on her own to find him. *And kill him.*

There was an annoying little voice inside her head saying that it wasn't the way she was brought up—to be judge, jury and executioner for anybody. She was a soldier, first, last, and always. Her superiors gave her orders and she carried them out, and no one had told her to kill him. But he deserved to die, and she knew a half-dozen ways to kill a man with her bare hands alone.

Another nagging voice took over and asked, What if he wasn't Hathaway? If she could actually kill a man in cold blood, on no one's orders but her own, and she got the wrong man, she'd never be able to live with herself. If blaming herself—nearly as much as she blamed him—for

Dan's injury was this hard, killing an innocent man would drive her right over the edge. Not that she hadn't come close to it on her own in the last three and a half months.

Geri sighed, trying to keep her mind on the business at hand. *Him.* One look and she'd been fairly certain he was the man she sought, despite the fact that he wasn't what she'd expected—a dangerously intelligent, selfish, greedy, conscienceless, murdering man. She would have felt better if she'd loathed him on sight, if the evil inside him had resonated throughout his body, like a tangible thing. So often over the years, she'd felt evil in people, recognized it right away. But in him she had not.

Which meant what? That he was simply better at hiding his true self than most of the people she'd encountered?

Geri calmed down and went over what she knew. He used Hathaway's given name. In all published material, he was the most respectable-sounding "Dr. Alexander Hathaway," but to friends and family he was simply "Alex."

The physical characteristics were strikingly similar. The height was dead-on. Weight and build were trickier. Photographs showed him looking quite lean. This man certainly wasn't heavy, but there was more bulk to him; his arms and shoulders were clearly delineated beneath the T-shirt he wore. She couldn't help but feel his muscles, plastered against him as she was on the bike.

His hair was longer, enough so that he'd drawn it into a disreputable-looking ponytail at the nape of his neck. His skin was sun-browned all over, his face leaner, harder, and somehow...different.

The surprisingly few photographs available showed Dr. Hathaway in casual snapshots taken by family members, most often with his nieces and nephews, looking young and happy and carefree, as if he didn't have a sinister bone in his body. She cringed every time she saw him with those smiling children. The man was a murderer, after all.

Walking into the bar, she'd focused on him right away. Hunched over a video game in a pose that showed not much more than his backside in a pair of well-worn jeans, he'd seemed quite boyish to her. It was hard to imagine the man playing theatrical war games with such fervor on a video-game machine wielding the kind of power Dr. Hathaway did. When he'd finally turned around, she'd seen that there was something not quite right about his face, something throwing it off-balance just enough that she wasn't sure if he was the man whose photographs she'd seen. His nose or his chin, perhaps? She wondered if he'd had plastic surgery, something very subtle to alter his appearance. But then, if he'd had surgery, why would he have been subtle about it?

Then there was his age. Geri would have a hard time believing she and the man calling himself Alex Connor were the same age. She'd always felt older than her age and probably looked it, whereas he seemed impossibly young to her—maybe because Geri had been shooting at people and blowing things up since she was twenty-one, which tended to age people quite rapidly. So her perspective on aging was probably skewed.

Which left only one problem—Alex Connor didn't seem like an evil person. If anything, he'd been kind to her. Even worse, for a second, back there, when he'd been so close, she'd almost found him...attractive.

Geri gagged a bit.

"You all right?" he called out, turning his head to the side.

"Great," she lied, wishing above all else that she wasn't plastered so tightly against him.

He'd had his hands all over her, brushing the glass from her cuts and scrapes, and there'd been a strange heat that seemed to explode between the two of them when he touched her. She simply hadn't been able to stop it.

When he'd looked at her as if he could devour her right

there on the street outside the bar, it had scared her half to death, mostly because for one reckless instant, she'd been blinded by it, her mind erased clean of everything that mattered. She hadn't been able to think about anything else but letting him do what he'd imagined, what he'd telegraphed to her with nothing but a look.

"God," Geri muttered softly.

She'd lost it. Totally. She was thinking about killing a man, thinking she could take some pleasure in it. She was also riding on the back of a bike with the same man, her skirt hitched up to her fanny, her body flat against his. The engine was rumbling through her entire body, the noise and the wind blocking out everything in the world but the two of them. She'd discovered, much to her dismay, that he was a living, breathing human being, and that somehow she was both attracted to him and wishing him dead.

It was crazy. *She'd* been crazy, for months now. Just crazy.

At the moment, she wanted to be anyone but who she was—an agent tracking down a killer, holding his life and probably her own in her hands. If she killed him in cold blood, she might as well kill herself while she was at it. If she didn't, guilt would probably take care of it for her eventually. Not that it would matter so much—not to the life she'd led up to this point. One utterly unpleasant side effect of the shooting was that she'd learned there wasn't much to her life at all. That maybe she'd been missing something vital, and she should probably try to fix that, if she could. She honestly didn't know how, didn't know where to start, and the whole thing had her scared to death.

Little things, insignificant things she should have been able to put out of her mind, were piling up on top of each other. The cuts on her chest and her palms and her back stung, and she was so tired, her head so heavy. Memories of the night she'd been shot wouldn't leave her alone, and she was clinging to the back of a sinfully attractive, smiling man she'd actually considered killing the first moment she had a chance.

Life on the edge, she thought cynically. She'd always wanted to be here.

Somehow, it just wasn't working anymore.

The bike roared on, eating up the distance. There was no other sound, no other sensation but the wickedly enticing warmth of his powerful body and the rush of the wind. She was supposed to hate him, she reminded herself.

But she was so tired of it all, and the ride was somehow hypnotic. It was simply too easy to cling to him, her head turned to the side and resting against his shoulder, the strangely reassuring warmth of his body against hers. Under any other circumstances, it might have been relaxing, even enticing. He could just keep driving, she thought. She wouldn't have to face any of this if they simply never stopped. Geri caught herself about to fall asleep and jerked herself back to consciousness in what she would have sworn was just a moment later when all sound ceased. So did the motion of the bike and the feel of the wind. Blinking, she tried to clear her vision, to figure out where she was when, from somewhere very close by, a man swore.

"Lady, you need a keeper."

She felt herself being lifted high off the ground, into someone's arms, her body sagging against the unyielding muscles of his chest, her head on his shoulder, and she fought back every reflex in her body that would have sent her tearing out of those arms.

"Where are we?" she asked, as the world tilted on its axis.

"My place."

She choked back an oath. She couldn't have been nodding off for long—she would have fallen off the bike. And true sleep—how unlikely was that? She hadn't slept soundly since the shooting. Had months of sleepless nights finally taken their toll? Now? At the worst possible time? God, he could have killed her and dumped her body in the desert. She would have been buzzard bait, and no one would have been the wiser.

Equally bad was the fact that she had no idea how they'd gotten here. How the hell was she going to escape if she didn't know where they were?

Still in his arms and struggling for calm, Geri said, "I can walk."

"Sure you can," he muttered, kicking open the door and carrying her inside.

"You don't lock it?" she asked.

"Why would I? The place is about to fall down around me. It's not like it would be a big challenge to break in. Besides, I don't keep anything here I can't afford to lose."

She swayed a little when he set her on her feet. He kept his hands on her forearms to steady her. She stared down at them for a moment and asked herself how that felt. His hold was easy, firm but gentle, threatening only because she believed he'd shot and killed her friend and because on some level, she liked having his hands on her.

Damn.

When she looked up, he was watching her intently, trying to catalog every nuance of expression on her face. Slowly, deliberately, he took his hands away and said, "Why don't you sit down for a minute while I get your bag and take care of the bike?"

"Okay."

Sitting, Geri gave the cabin only the briefest of glances. She was still struck by the fact that she ought to be dead by now. She'd given him ample opportunity. Shaking her head in amazement, she told herself to get it together. She was alive, even if she didn't deserve to be, and she had work to do.

Then there was the door. He didn't even lock his own front door, claimed there was nothing here he couldn't afford to lose. Was that nothing but an offhand remark? Or did he somehow know who she was and what she was looking for? Had he figured he might as well go ahead and tell her it wasn't here? As if she'd take his word for anything.

Looking around the cabin, she had to admit he would be a fool to keep something valuable here. Of course, he could have been counting on no one finding him.

When Alex returned, he carried her leather bag. Geri wondered if he'd searched it in the time he'd been outside. She carried no official ID, no weapon, just some sophisticated electronic equipment, but it was so tiny she doubted he'd find it, no matter how long he looked.

He set the bag down at her feet. "I should have asked you earlier if there was anyone you needed to call. Anyone who's expecting you who might worry if you don't show up."

"No. There's no one."

He nodded. "About the motel in Red Rock—"

"Is it just off the interstate?" she interrupted.

"Yes."

"Going toward El Paso?"

He nodded.

"I can't go there," she claimed.

He surprised her by not even asking why. Instead he said, "We need to clean those cuts of yours and make sure all the glass is out."

"I know."

She didn't want to think of what that process would entail—her nearly naked, with his hands all over her. She shivered. With dread, she told herself. She absolutely dreaded having his hands on her.

Alex went to a door to the right and pushed it open.

"Why don't you get in the shower? Maybe that'll wash most of the glass out."

Geri accepted. If necessary, she would have begged for a shower. She was hot, tired, sweaty, and eager for a few minutes alone, for cold, bracing water and a chance to pull herself together before she died of sheer stupidity.

The bathroom was tiny but clean, and Geri thought about searching it. She imagined them furtively searching each other's things in turn—her bag, his bathroom. What next? She knew—her own body.

Geri cursed again and decided the search could wait. The sound of the water would surely cover any noise she made, but she didn't want to rush. It would be better to wait until he was asleep tonight and do the job right.

Turning, she caught sight of herself in the mirror, still surprised by what she saw. She'd expected to look ridiculous in the leather miniskirt and minuscule top. But all in all, she hadn't looked bad before the fight in the bar. Showing all this skin made her uncomfortable, but it had been exciting, too, in a strange sort of way. Men had noticed her in this. Not just the red leather, but her. Her legs, her hips, her breasts. It had given her a wicked thrill, a strange sense of power, appearing to be someone she was not.

Two days ago, when she'd realized what Tanner expected of her, when he'd pulled out the tiny skirt and top, her first impulse had been to laugh. Her next had been to insist that he send someone else. Finally she'd wondered how he couldn't have realized, when looking for a woman to play this part, that she should have been his last choice.

There wasn't anything feminine about her, except her height—or lack of it. She was a short, plain, no-nonsense woman. Men did not lust after her. They seldom even noticed her, and she was fine with that. It probably helped her in her work in a male-dominated field. The men around her found it easy to accept her simply as a co-worker, with none of that messy, distracting sexual interest to gum things up. Her sexual experiences had been thoroughly uninspiring, thoroughly forgettable, and she was fine with that. Which was why this assignment had thrown her, particularly this outfit.

No slave to fashion, Geri had an extensive wardrobe of camouflage and basic black. She dressed to blend into the jungle or the night, not to call attention to herself. Never had she worn red leather. When other little girls had been putting on their mother's nightgowns, pilfering pearls and lipstick and high heels, Geri had been traipsing through the woods with her father while he taught her to track an animal through the forest, to shoot a gun without flinching and to defend herself against someone bigger and stronger than herself.

Daddy was on the Joint Chiefs of Staff now, a career army man with a distinguished combat record and a string of medals Geri couldn't hope to match. But she still hadn't figured out how to stop wanting to please him.

She'd done a lot of dangerous things for the agency over the years—done them willingly, without complaint or protest. But why, she'd wondered, upon hearing about this mission, couldn't Alex Hathaway have hidden away in the jungle? The agency would have given her a big knife, some explosives, and a semiautomatic with enough ammunition to blast away a small army. She could have handled whatever problems she encountered along the way—snakes, bugs, wild animals, crazy men who chased her with guns of their own. No problem. But this... Geri sighed. She'd never expected the agency to give her red leather and want her to use her own body to get the attention of a traitor and murderer.

All she had to do was catch his attention, find out where he was living, search the place, plant her bug and get out. At first, she'd balked at showing up in a way guaranteed to attract so much attention to herself, but as Tanner had explained, the town was so small, any stranger would be noticed. Tanner was betting that if Hathaway was there, he wouldn't be expecting an agent to show up in what might as well have been a flashing neon sign. Hathaway, they'd learned, had a chivalrous streak where women were concerned; he couldn't ignore a woman in trouble. Plus, Tanner's reports indicated Hathaway hadn't been seen with a woman in the entire three months he'd lived in Texas.

"Believe me, Geri," Tanner had quipped, "when the man sees you in this outfit, he won't be thinking about covering his back."

Standing in front of the mirror in Alex's bathroom now, she couldn't help but be surprised at the heat that flared between them. She tried to analyze it in a purely professional way. They were both adults, both had been alone for a long time. They'd been thrown into close physical proximity. He'd had his hands all over her, and she was wearing next to nothing. If she ignored the fact that she was supposed to hate him, it wasn't surprising that a little sexual tension had reared its ugly head.

And she sensed that he didn't like it any more than she did. One quick look had told her he didn't want to want her, but he couldn't quite help it. Fine. She could handle it. She'd consider it nothing more than an unpleasant complication. She'd deal with it.

A nagging little voice inside said it wouldn't be that easy. With Dr. Alexander Hathaway, the traitor, the murderer, she could easily hold her own, but with Alex Connor, the sinfully sexy man, she was entirely out of her depth. Geri sagged against the wall, thinking that was a pathetically sad commentary on her life to date—that she was more comfortable with a homicidal traitor than a smiling, attractive man.

Disgusted with herself, she peeled off the red leather that

clung like a second skin. Stepping into the shower, Geri found the water cold. She sucked in a breath as the spray hit her skin for the first time. When the water dug into her injured shoulder, she gasped and turned away.

She'd had far worse injuries on the job. In fact, she still carried bruises from some trouble she'd run into in Mexico a week ago—a bungled dead-end search for Hathaway. She'd been tired in Mexico, too, doubting herself, scared of walking into another disaster, and the combination of things had made her sloppy. She'd started off this mission with even sloppier mistakes—letting things get out of hand at the bar, nearly falling asleep in his presence, feeling something inside her just melt when he touched her.

Deliberately, Geri angled her body toward the cold spray and stood there, letting it sting and burn—her shoulder, her hip and then that long scrape on her chest. She did it because it hurt, because the pain sobered her up and made her think about what was at stake here.

He was a killer and she was an agent on a mission. Nothing else mattered, she told herself. Nothing she felt. Nothing she wanted. She could bury it all far beneath her duty, her orders, her training.

"Geri? You okay?"

She tensed. His voice was so clear and so close, he was either in the room with her or had opened the bathroom door, which had no lock. She cleared her throat, but still her voice wasn't quite steady when she told him, "Fine. I'll be out in a minute."

"I brought you a dry towel and an old shirt of mine to put on until we get those cuts covered."

Geri went hot and cold at the thought of going into the other room and letting him tend her wounds, of having his hands all over her.

Shaking her head to rid it of those treacherous images, Geri finished her shower and dressed.

This was an act, she reminded herself. Nothing she said to Alex, nothing she did, nothing she felt was real. Geri had a gift that served her well in her profession. She studied people, dissected their movements, their expressions, the inflections in their voices. And she stored all the memories inside her, drawing them out when it suited her purpose. The walk she'd used as she'd made her entrance into the bar, the attitude, the play of her hands over her own body, had come from a high-class call girl she'd seen in Monte Carlo years ago.

She could be a hundred different women, a thousand. There were so many stored inside her, she found it hard to remember what was real, what was her. But this woman who wore skintight red leather and trembled so easily beneath a man's hands wasn't real. She was simply an agent on a mission. Feeling marginally better, Geri slipped behind her mask and went to find her quarry.

He glanced her way when she stepped into the main room of the cabin. His eyes might have narrowed, his body might have tensed a fraction, but he didn't take his eyes off her.

Geri knew what he saw—bare thighs, his own shirt hanging loosely around her, wet hair that fell to the bottom of delicate-looking earlobes. Could he tell she hadn't bothered with a bra? She figured women in red leather didn't wear bras, but as his gaze lingered on her breasts, she was no longer sure that standing in front of him like this was a good idea.

Alex poured her a generous shot of tequila that burned all the way down her throat. She downed it without so much as a grimace.

"Let's get this over with," he said, then led her to his bed.

Chapter 3

He motioned for her to sit on the side of the bed, then sat down himself in a chair he'd pulled alongside. On the nightstand, she saw gauze pads, bandages, antiseptic, some sort of cream and a pair of tweezers.

He obviously took his first-aid duties quite seriously. Odd, Geri thought, her mouth twitching. He'd invented something that could blow up thousands of people, but he wasn't going to let her die from an infected cut she'd gotten from a broken bottle in a bar fight.

He pulled a lamp to the edge of the bed, snapped it on, then tilted the shade so the light fell directly on her. Geri closed her eyes and turned away, tried to forget she wore nothing but a pair of panties and his old shirt.

"This is going to hurt," he warned.

"I know," she said. The littlest of cuts often did.

Closing her eyes might have been a mistake. Every one of her other senses kicked into high gear to compensate. She heard a wonderful voice, low and soothing and sexy.

Her skin felt his presence, made her aware that he was very close, every part of him within inches of every part of her. He smelled of dust and wind and heat—something she found quite pleasant—and for some odd reason, she couldn't help but think of the way he would taste, that sun-browned skin....

"Oh, please," she breathed.

"Please, what?"

Geri blinked, the light blinding her for a second, and then she saw his face, saw that wry smile, something between amusement and a deep curiosity that scared her. She must have spoken those last words aloud, when she'd meant to keep them entirely to herself.

She'd been aiming at sarcasm. *Oh, please.* But obviously, it had come off sounding like something else entirely. Like a breathless plea. To him. What did he think she was asking for?

"It was nothing," she said too quickly, too harshly, with a combination of nerves and impatience.

Before she could come up with an explanation or an apology, he touched a gauze pad soaked in antiseptic to her collarbone. She bit down on her lip to hold everything inside her as ridiculous tears sprang to her eyes.

She was tired, she told herself. Frustrated. Angry. Confused. More than a little scared. That was the reason she couldn't find the distance she needed for this assignment. He shouldn't be able to get this close to Geri, the woman. No one touched her heart. Or her soul. At least, not before the shooting.

Since then, her feelings had been raw and frighteningly powerful. It seemed as if every emotion she'd swallowed over the years and pushed down inside her had come roaring to the surface all at once. And ever since then, Geri had been out of control, on edge, so unsure of herself. She didn't recognize the woman who had surfaced after the shooting.

She'd given so much of herself to the job over the years, and she now wondered if that had been a mistake—if there was simply nothing left of her.

And now this man, this dreaded man, kept showing her something new, something totally unexpected. She looked up at him, realizing Alex hadn't moved or said a word for the longest time. Geri found quiet concern that she simply didn't understand etched on his face. He let his hand settle on her left shoulder and stay there, in a touch that comforted her, reassured her, reached her in a way that had nothing to do with hands and skin.

It was as if he could touch her heart. Geri stared back at him, thoroughly puzzled.

"All right?" he asked.

She nodded, telling herself it was an act. He was very, very good, and this was an act. He was not concerned about her. He was not kind. He was likely playing some demented game with her, but...he was so good at it. And if it hadn't been for the shooting, she'd be totally immune.

"For a minute, you were a million miles away," he said.

"More like a thousand," she said, thinking of D.C., where it had all started.

"A thousand?" he repeated.

Geri felt every drop of blood drain from her face. How could she be so stupid as to tell him that? If he was Hathaway, he knew what had happened in the District of Columbia three and a half months ago.

"A friend of mine," she said, stumbling on, thinking of other cities a thousand or so miles away, reminding herself that sticking as close to the truth as possible always helped in remembering the lies she told. "He lives in Virginia. Ran into some trouble this past year. And I was thinking of him."

Alex nodded. Thankfully, he didn't press for details.

Armed with a cotton ball, he asked, "Are you ready for me to finish this?"

Geri nodded and told herself not to flinch. As he pressed the cotton ball to her skin, she sucked in another ragged breath.

"Sorry," he said softly, his touch infinitely gentle.

Geri watched him, mesmerized by the way he moved, the smile on his face, the rambling commentary he kept up, she suspected, in an effort to take her mind off the pain. And she found herself liking this man he was pretending to be. Maybe they were simply alike, she thought. Maybe he could put on an act as well as she could, for all the world seeming to be a tender, caring man.

It occurred to her that she had never known tenderness from a man. Or quiet concern. Or kindness. Her father loved her. But he wasn't a kind man. Or a gentle one. He was gruff and impatient and busy. There had always been matters more pressing for him to attend to than her. She was closer to her former partner, Dan Reese, than anyone, but there was nothing between them but friendship and respect.

But this... She'd never been disarmed by kindness, seduced by tenderness, confused by desire. She wanted to yell at him, *Don't be nice to me. Don't.* Alex was so close she could feel his breath against her shoulder. It was quiet here, his voice the only sound she heard. They were far from anyone, absolutely alone. She flinched as he hit a particularly tender spot on her chest. He gave her a tight smile and gentled his touch even more.

This was unlike any other time she'd been injured on the job. First aid had been highly skilled, brisk and efficient, usually administered on the run, sometimes in a helicopter in midair.

Never had it been intimate. Never had anyone made such a fuss over a few scrapes. She wanted to tell him that, to yell at him. This was nothing compared to what she'd been through over the years, and especially in the last few months, because of him. So how could it feel like so much?

Opening her eyes, Geri saw hair, more blond than brown, saw his gaze intent on her as he worked over her injuries, as he touched her so gently.

The frustration and the burning pain gave way to something else entirely. Her body was responding shamelessly to his nearness, to the sound of his voice, the feel of his breath on her skin. She felt heat gathering low in her belly, felt her breasts swell and start to ache. She liked his touch too much to let him continue.

"Don't," she pleaded.

Geri saw the knowing look in his gorgeous brown eyes as he pulled away, fighting against the smile forming on his lips. *Damn him.* Then he reached for her, smiling sinfully now. She was ready to shove him across the room until she realized he'd done nothing but pull the collar of her shirt open a little wider.

"You want to get the next button for me?" he asked.

Geri tried. Angry, she found her hands were shaking. The simple task of undoing a button was nearly too much for her. His hands, when he reached for her, were perfectly steady. Maybe he made a habit of rescuing women from bandits in bars. Maybe there was nothing unusual about him finding a total stranger half-naked in his bed at night. Maybe she simply didn't have the power to make him tremble. But dammit, he could certainly do it to her.

Alex pulled one side of the shirt aside, baring the beginnings of her right breast. She felt the antiseptic burning. How could it burn so much? It was a tiny cut. She didn't understand, just felt the air leave her lungs in a rush, felt what seemed to be every bit of her strength, the protective shell that she'd honed to perfect hardness over the years, simply dissolve. Utterly drained and unable to fight anymore, she felt tears running down her cheeks.

"I'm almost done," Alex promised.

Bewildered and angry at herself, Geri swiped at her tears and decided to concentrate on just how much her chest hurt. It was certainly safer than listening to him try to soothe her and tease her both at the same time.

It had to be about seduction, she decided. Seduction with kindness. With a teasing grin and a cool impersonal touch that could turn wickedly sexy in an instant. The man had turned first aid into foreplay. Geri wondered if he'd been one of those little boys who was constantly trying to con the girl next door into playing doctor with him, wondered if he had some unfulfilled fantasies that he was counting on her to make come true.

Finally, Alex sat back and dropped his weapon—his cotton ball. Then he warned, "I need to make sure there's no glass in the cut."

"I know."

Her mouth went dry and she fought to control her breathing. His hands were wonderfully warm and unfairly steady, his touch, if possible, even gentler than before. Too easily, Geri remembered the sensation of having her body pressed against his on the bike, her breasts against his back, her hands against the hard muscles of his abdomen, her thighs spread wide with his between them. The bike had rumbled at times, bounced around at others, until it had seemed that someone was intent on fusing their bodies together.

She'd been tortured before, of course. But not like that.

Alex looked over her injuries slowly, carefully, then picked up one of her hands, checking her palm, then the other, and announced, "All done here."

He gave her a devilish grin, one that had her cheeks burning again, and held up a tube of ointment. "This should take away the sting. It has an antibiotic, too."

"I can do that."

"Be my guest." He handed over the ointment, offered her a box of bandages. "You want to handle this part, too?"

"Yes," she said tightly. With hands that were still shaking, she managed to cover the worst of the damage.

When she was done, Alex suggested, "Why don't you lie down while we do the other side?"

Sighing, Geri rolled over, putting her back to him, undid two more buttons and hitched the shirt up so he could pull it down to bare her shoulder. The bed gave beneath his weight as he sat down beside her, then leaned over her shoulder.

"These aren't nearly as bad," he said.

The antiseptic still burned. His breath was still cool and comforting as he leaned close, inspecting the damage. His touch was as gentle as ever as he brushed the cuts with ointment and bandaged them. Geri sighed as he tugged her shirt back into place on her shoulder. She couldn't say his hands were anything but impersonal as he pushed her shirt up and pulled aside a minuscule scrap of lace to expose one hip.

Burying her face deeper into the pillow, she sucked in a breath and wondered how long it had been since anyone had touched her like this. Honestly, she wasn't sure if anyone ever had. No one touched her so intimately, so tenderly. And touch was, after all, a basic human need. She'd read studies on it at some point. People felt a deep-seated need to be touched, to be held.

She hated his gentleness and yet was inexplicably drawn to it.

"Don't, Alex," she said, reaching her limit.

"Don't what?"

"Don't be nice to me."

"What?"

"You heard what I said. Don't do this. Don't try to be nice. Don't try to make me like you. Just get this done."

She was desperate now, desperate for it to be over. Into her head came the image of her and him locked together in an embrace. Her body positively ached at the thought of how it would be, how good it would feel.

"You're one of those women who gets off on pain?" he asked, laughter in his voice.

Maybe that was the answer, Geri thought. Maybe she had some weird sadistic streak she'd never known about.

"Maybe I am," she said, her sarcasm missing somehow and the words sounding weary beyond belief.

"I don't believe that," Alex said. "Not for a minute."

Geri didn't, either. The truth was, there was nothing sensual about her. She was an altogether-practical woman, a determined one, a woman focused on nothing but her career. And in the space of one bizarre evening, he had her thinking she liked this man he'd invented for her, the one that wasn't any more real than she was. He had her wondering what she'd been missing all these years, wondering if everything would somehow be different with him, the imaginary man playing the white knight to a wounded woman in red leather.

He went back to work. She was starting to relax when he slid his hands up under her shirt and started kneading the muscles in her back.

"You're so tense," he said. "Are you afraid of me, Geri? Afraid to be here alone with me?"

She wondered if this was some sort of test, wondered if she'd done something to make him suspicious, so she willed herself to relax and take it. His hands... He had wonderful hands. They were at the small of her back, seemed to have found the spot where every bit of tension in her body had gathered. He took his knuckles and worked the tension away.

Was she afraid of him? *Desperately.*

But what about the other *her,* the one she was pretending

to be? Would she be afraid? Surely she would. After all, they were strangers, alone here in the middle of nowhere.

"I…" As his hands slid higher, midway up her back, she had to stop and breathe, to think. "I feel safer here with you than I did in town. Do those men know where you live?"

"I don't think anyone in town knows where I live. You were nodding off through a lot of the ride, but it's more a dirt trail than a road. I haven't had any visitors in the time I've been here, although that doesn't mean someone hasn't found the place while I've been away."

"Why?" she asked. "Why do you live this way?"

"I like my privacy," he said easily, his hands sliding higher, onto her shoulders now, then her neck. "Why can't you go to Red Rock, Geri?"

As she lay there, as relaxed as she could possibly be and half-naked on his bed, he made his move, flipped her over like a rag doll and pushed up her shirt until it was bunched just below her breasts.

Geri didn't make a sound, told herself not to panic, not to react too quickly, because then he would know that her training in self-defense had been extensive. The trouble was, if he wanted to kill her, he might act so quickly that nothing she did in response could save herself.

But Alex didn't hurt her at all. He wasn't undressing her, either. Instead, he was staring at her right side, at her rib cage. He touched her lightly there, and she flinched, then knew what he had found. She'd covered her side with some body makeup, because the leather outfit showed so much of her midriff. The makeup must have come off in the shower, but it wasn't a problem. She had a story to tell, after all. This fit rather nicely.

"Is it the bruises?" he asked, his voice cold with fury. "Is that why you're out here by yourself and would rather take your chances with me than in some little town along the interstate where the man who did this to you might be looking for you?''

He sounded like he was ready to go to war for her, if that was what it took to protect her, which surprised her. She wasn't the kind of woman who normally brought out a protective streak in men. In the field, what she lacked in strength and height, she made up for in quickness, cleverness, agility and sheer determination. The men she worked with saw her as an equal, not someone to protect.

"Tell me," Alex said. "Who beat you?"

"A man," she said. That wasn't a lie.

"What else did he do to you?"

"Just bruised my ribs," she claimed.

He took her arm and gently placed it above her head, then fitted his hand to the faint bruises there. It was a near-perfect match. "And grabbed you here and wouldn't let you go?"

Geri nodded.

"What else?" he insisted.

He gave an entirely credible picture of concern, laced with an undertone of anger she truly didn't understand. They were just bruises. She'd certainly had worse.

"What else?" Alex demanded, sounding as if he could tear somebody limb from limb quite easily.

"You don't even know me," she complained, knowing she was dangerously close to forgetting all the lies. She was so tired of them. She just wanted to know who he was.

"And that's supposed to make a difference? I get mad at the idea of any man hitting a woman."

Geri frowned and took a breath. He was driving her crazy, refusing to be what she expected, refusing to fit into that neat little picture she'd painted of him—traitor, murderer, all-around rotten guy. Why the hell would he care if she'd been beaten up in Mexico while trying to find him? Why in the world would that make him mad?

"I don't understand you at all," she complained.

He shook his head. "I guess we're even, then. I sure as hell don't understand you."

She stared at him mutely, her breathing agitated and refusing all efforts to slow and deepen. She was too aware of the fact that she was lying on his bed, wearing next to nothing, and that he'd had his hands all over her. Tender hands, soft touches, gentle concern—what she could only think of as fierce protectiveness coming out at the idea that she'd been hurt.

"What else did he do to you?" Alex asked one more time.

Geri opened her mouth to tell him—to lie—and found herself nearly choking on the words. She didn't like this man, she told herself. She didn't know him. He could probably be ten different men, just like she could be ten different women, and none of this meant anything. So why did she feel so lousy about lying to him? She lied nearly every day of her life. It was as easy as breathing, and so far it had kept her alive. It was not a bad thing.

"Alex," she replied wearily, "what's the point?"

"The point?" He swore.

She actually flinched.

"What about the next time?" he asked. "When he grabs you again? When he hits you? What if he doesn't let go that time? What if you can't get away?"

She thought about her own life, not the pretend one. Somehow with him, she couldn't stick to the role. Everything was about her. The real her.

Next time? If she couldn't get away? Then she'd die. If she didn't get out of this mess with him, she'd die, and if this case didn't kill her, the next one might. She thought she'd dealt with that long ago, accepted it. But maybe she hadn't. Maybe the shooting had taught her that. Or seeing Dan in the wheelchair. Maybe she understood the price, as she never had before. Because of him—Alex Hathaway. The man standing in front of her? The one so concerned about something as mundane as a few fading bruises on her body?

How could he create something as evil and destructive as the next generation of plastic explosives, then go ballistic over a few bruises on her ribs?

"Geri?" he prompted, and she realized she was lost. Lost in him, in the terrible, conflicting feelings she had for him.

"I don't want to talk about this with you," she said. "There's no point."

It was all a lie, after all. Everything she told him would be a lie.

"Are you going back to him?" he asked, ignoring her and going right on, trying to learn what he wanted to know.

"Not unless he finds me and drags me back," she said. If that was what he wanted to hear, she'd tell him. She'd do anything to get him away from her right now. But he didn't go away. The damned man didn't go away. He put his hand to her side, over the bruise he'd uncovered moments before, his thumb sliding back and forth over her rib cage, almost reverently.

She sucked in a breath, surprised by the warmth of his hand soaking into her skin. It was just his hand, she thought. Over that bruise. As if he could take it away, erase it clean. As if he cared. In all her life, she would swear that no one had ever touched her with such genuine concern.

"It wasn't the first time, was it?" he asked, as if it hurt him to think of her being hurt that way.

She shook her head back and forth, feeling worse with every lie she told.

He shook his head. "How could you let someone hurt you like that? How could you let him do it again and again?"

"Alex." *Dammit.*

He just didn't understand. She'd been hurt so many times. Her whole life, if something had hurt her, it just didn't matter. It was simply the way things were. She'd accepted that, hadn't she? So why couldn't he? Why couldn't he leave it alone?

Something twisted loose inside her; the awful fatigue that seemed to have seeped into her bones was now crying to get out. Frustration. Uncertainty. Fear. Anger. A flood tide of emotions he seemed singularly capable of drawing out of her in vivid detail. She was so angry at him for refusing to be what she expected, for making her doubt what her own eyes told her—that he was Alex Hathaway—and that she was going to absolutely destroy him.

She thought about the order that might come once they had his formula. To terminate him. Could she do it, she wondered? A few hours ago, she'd been tempted to do it all on her own. For months, she'd dreamed about exacting revenge on him, and now she wasn't sure if she could, even if ordered to do so. She would look at his face and see him like this, touching her so tenderly, outraged that anyone dared hurt her.

No one took care of her. Not ever.

"Oh, baby. Don't," he whispered.

His face softened even more, and he looked at her the way he'd looked at his nieces in those photographs that disturbed her so very much—tenderly, sweetly, almost lovingly. His hand cupped the side of her face for a moment, and it was only when he brushed his thumb across her cheek and she felt a trail of moisture that Geri realized she was crying.

She took a breath—a great, straining grab for air where there was none. Crying was such a foreign thing to her, and she'd done more of it in the last three and a half months than she had in the nearly thirty years she'd been alive.

Dammit, she couldn't cry now. Not in front of him. Not over him.

"I hate this," she said. "I hate to cry."

But despite her resolve to stop, her tears merely fell faster. From somewhere deep inside her, she felt the emotions she'd held in check for years shaking loose, flooding up inside her, choking her, scaring her.

"It's all right," Alex said as he pulled her into his arms.

She sat there stiffly in his embrace, bewildered and confused and so very angry, because she liked it here, right here in his arms. It was as if her traitorous body had decided to rebel against the years in which she'd ignored the part of her that was simply a woman and to take its revenge right now with the most unlikely of men.

Groaning, she wondered if this was what it felt like when someone cracked under pressure. They used to joke about it in training, in those times when they were figuring out if they could cut it, either in the military or in the agency. Cracked. Cracked up. Lost it. Freaked out. Gone AWOL. Gone off the deep end.

That was how she felt—as if someone had thrown her into the deep end, and she was sinking fast. She didn't even recognize herself. If she could have peeled off her skin, stepped out of her traitorous body and left it behind, she would have, with an open invitation for Alex Connor to do anything he wanted with her, to get it over with and be done with it. He could have sex with her. He could hold her and stroke her back and pretend to care about her, for reasons she'd never understand, and then it would be over. Then she could deal with him, rationally, calmly, competently, like the agent she was supposed to be.

If only she could do that... Geri fought unsuccessfully for air. She was smothering, crying harder. "I can't do this."

Alex pulled back, cocked his head to the side, and then

smiled a bit. "Baby, I don't think you have a choice tonight."

He tucked her head against his chest, so solid and strong. His arms locked around her, and she had the insane sensation that here in his arms, no one could get to her. No one could hurt her.

"I never cry," she told him, simply unable to give in to it.

"All women cry," he countered, and again she sensed that hint of a smile on his lips—an indulgent, all-knowing smile.

"I guess you know all about us," she said between her tears.

"With three sisters, I had no choice but to figure out women. It was pure self-preservation on my part."

"Three?" she asked. Alex Hathaway had three sisters.

He nodded.

"Were you close?" she asked, because it was much easier to talk about anything except the fact that she was falling apart, right here in his bed, with his arms tightly around her. She was absolutely losing it.

"Not always," he said. "Not as close as I would have liked. It's not…something that comes easy to any of us, not with the way I grew up."

His mother, he meant. His mother died when he was very young, and his family life had been a bit chaotic after that, as Geri's had been.

"I've always wondered what it would have been like to have sisters," Geri said wistfully.

"You don't have any?"

"No."

"No brothers?"

"No. Just me and the General."

"The General?"

Another slip. *Dammit.*

"My father," she explained, then knew what she had to do. "My mother died when I was very young, and he never married again. So it was just the two of us."

"Mine, too," he said, stroking his hands across her back. "My mother, I mean. She died so young, I don't have any memory of her."

Of course not. He'd been two.

Geri sat there, huddled against him, trembling and crying like some kind of weak, idiotic female—a woman she'd never been before, had never even remotely resembled. He'd done this to her, she thought. He'd torn her life apart, and now he was going to kill her with kindness, smother her with warmth and concern.

"Oh, damn," she cried, and he only held her tighter.

She'd never been like this, she wanted to tell him. She'd never needed anyone like this. Until him. Until he'd ruined it all, just like he was ruining everything now.

"Please don't be nice to me," she said ridiculously.

"What do you want me to be, Geri?" he asked indulgently.

"Nothing," she replied. "I don't want you to be anything at all to me."

She didn't want him anywhere near her, didn't even want to be on the same planet as him. Because he was so very dangerous. Even more dangerous than herself, because he made her want to believe in him—in all the lies, all the tenderness. Even knowing what she did about him, she wanted to believe.

"Just go away," Geri said miserably, weakly. She absolutely abhorred weakness, especially in herself. She could have sworn the General had drummed every ounce of it out of her, and yet here it came, charging to the surface when she could least afford it. All she had to do was hate him, she thought. *Alex. Hate.* Even as she sat here with her face buried against his chest, shaking so hard she could scarcely breathe, her tears streaming down now, she was trying to convince herself. *Just hate him.*

"Why don't you just let me hold you until the worst of this is over," Alex said. "And then I'll go. I'll do anything you want, Geri, and if you want me to leave you alone then, I will. But don't ask me to let you go right now. I don't think I could."

"You don't understand," she said, shaking her head back and forth when he was trying to hold her still.

"Make me," he said. "Make me understand."

"I'm always alone," she said, anger shooting through her words. "And I'm just fine that way. It's better that way."

"'Better'?" He finally backed away, letting her go, seeing those awful tears running down her face. "How is it better?"

"Safer," she replied.

She'd done it again—forgotten all about the woman she was supposed to be, the story she was supposed to tell. She'd forgotten all the lies. This was all about her—painfully, honestly about her. And he hated it. He hated the way she lived. She could see it in his face.

"How long have you believed that?" he asked. "How long have you lived it?"

"Always," she said.

Alex just shook his head. "You can't do this forever, Geri. I know you think you can. I know you think you're better off this way, because I used to be a lot like you. But things happen. You're going to need somebody someday. You'll regret what you've done to push everybody away. You'll find yourself alone, and it's no longer by choice. It's just the way your life is, and you might not be able to change it."

"I don't want to change," she claimed.

He reached out with a finger, tracing the path of one

wretched tear. "And what you're doing is really working for you? So well that you can't stand to give it up?"

No, it wasn't working at all. Not anymore. Because of him.

"Stop it," she said. "God, just stop."

With a groan, he stood then, turned his back to her and ran a hand through his hair. Geri could almost breathe again, now that he wasn't so close. Of course, she was exhausted from the battle it had taken to push him away, and for the life of her, she couldn't stop crying. Some traitorous part of her longed to have him close again, and she had never been a foolish woman or a stupid one. She collapsed against the mattress, crying again even as she fought to hold it inside, to make it stop.

"God, Geri," Alex said.

She felt the bed give under his weight, felt him reach out and stroke her hair, her back. It wasn't long before he was lying beside her, before he'd taken her into his arms once again. She was shaking uncontrollably, and he whispered silly reassurances into her ear that he couldn't possibly believe and she was much too smart to listen to. But she was utterly exhausted. And she liked the sound of his voice—smooth and deep and almost hypnotic.

Maybe that was it. Maybe he'd hypnotized her, mesmerized her, simply made her into someone else altogether. How dared he? she thought, even as she lay there utterly defenseless in his arms, hating him the whole time. He was Alex Hathaway. This was all his fault.

How dared he be so nice to her, when it was all his fault?

Chapter 4

Alex held her for a long, long time. Until the tears stopped falling and the trembling ceased, until her body warmed to his and she was utterly relaxed against him, utterly still.

She was asleep, more trusting than any sane woman had a right to be in this day and age, and he wanted to shake her awake and tell her all about it—that she had no business trusting him, that she damned well shouldn't take off from a seedy bar with a total tranger, come home with him and then curl up in his bed fast asleep without knowing who in the hell he was or what he might do to her.

Women, he thought, even as he lay there flat on his back with her curled so trustingly against his side. They did stupid things. Women in all sorts of dire situations found him and expected him to make it all better—something he usually tried to do.

Not this time, he told himself.

It would be too dangerous for her and for him. It would be irresponsible of him to let her stay here a moment longer than necessary. Even if she was totally alone in the world and claimed to like it that way, even if she was lonely as hell and desperately needed someone and couldn't admit it, even to herself.

She didn't need *him*. Not now.

"Oh, hell," he muttered as she shifted in her sleep and one small foot insinuated itself between his ankles, bringing the entire length of her right leg into contact with his.

She didn't even stir when he jumped up out of bed, but just collapsed into the space he'd occupied and slept on. He paced the tiny room, never finding it more confining than he did right then, never hating his predicament more.

He couldn't afford to trust anyone except himself. It was the only way he was going to stay alive. Yet he wanted to trust her, to help her—ever since he'd seen the bruises, the haunted look in her eyes. She'd been desperately afraid of him when he'd turned her over and pushed her shirt out of the way, and he hadn't meant to scare her. He just had to see, to know.

Someone had hurt her—badly and repeatedly, from what she'd said.

Even now, a near-murderous rage came over him at the sight of those bruises on her soft, smooth flesh. He turned back to her now, looked at how little space she took in his bed. She was so petite, so vulnerable. It would be so easy for a man to hurt her.

How could she have let him? How could she stay with a man like that? Alex simply didn't understand. As chaotic as his childhood had been, no one had ever hit him or his sisters. He'd never felt vulnerable physically until very, very recently, and he didn't like it one bit. He hated it even more for Geri.

Alex went to the bed, knelt beside it, resting his forearms on the mattress, his chin on one of his fists. She was facing him, lying on her side, and he could see the faint bruise-

like crescents under her eyes now. How many sleepless
nights had there been for her, he wondered? How many
nights had she spent afraid? And what in the world was he
going to do with her?

He'd like nothing better than to crawl back into that bed
and spend the night with her draped all over him. He'd like
to do even more than that, if she'd let him, but he doubted
she would. He'd scared her half to death earlier, every time
he'd touched her.

Damn.

"Who are you?" he said.

He couldn't afford to ignore that key question. Why had
she come here? Why would any woman ever be so trusting
as to come here to the middle of nowhere with a total
stranger?

Sheer exhaustion? Looking at her sleeping so deeply, he
could almost accept that. That she would have gone anywhere, with anyone, to get away from whoever had done
this to her. Which made her exactly what she seemed—a
woman who'd been hurt and was in trouble, a woman who
needed him.

And if she wasn't? If everything she'd told him was a lie
and this was some offbeat plan to smoke him out? To get
someone inside this cabin, maybe inside his head, and ruin
everything he'd worked so hard to save these past few
months? Then what?

Alex shook his head and frowned. No surprises there.

He'd be dead.

About twenty minutes later, he summoned up enough
common sense to search her bag. He pawed through pretty
little lace panties that made him hard just looking at them,
more short skirts—thankfully none of them leather—and
crop tops. No bras anywhere. He was so hoping for a bra.
Not so he could paw through them, but so she could wear

one the next day and save him from having to look at her breasts pushing against another bit of cotton, swaying gently as she walked.

Damn.

Alex searched on. There were shoes—one pair of sensible shoes, three pairs of ridiculous ones—surprisingly few cosmetics, some toiletries, some very nice jewelry—chains dripping with diamonds, pearls, emeralds. She had probably cleaned out the safe before she left. He didn't want to think of the man who'd given them to her, the one who beat her.

Finally, in the bottom of the bag, he found her wallet. She had about two thousand dollars in cash, a whole slew of credit cards, a checkbook and a driver's license. According to it, her name was Regina Richardson, of Dallas, Texas. For the hell of it, Alex pulled out his cell phone and dialed Directory Assistance in Dallas, found she had an unlisted number, which proved nothing at all, but he felt marginally better knowing a woman with her name and her address existed, at least as far as the phone company was concerned.

He looked longingly at his laptop, thought of the databases he could hack his way into and what they might tell him. Nothing, he told himself. Not if she was a professional. He knew how easily information could be manipulated, planted, altered.

He could hack his way into the phone company, the state agency that issued her driver's license, her bank, her credit-card companies, and maybe if he followed the trail long enough, he'd be satisfied she was who she claimed to be, or maybe he wouldn't. If he did what he normally did— dialed through the cell phone with the modem, into a back door at one of the universities and accessed the Internet through their accounts set up for faculty and students— probably no one would ever be able to trace the calls. Probably.

It was all a risk. Every blasted thing. And in the end,

he'd probably go with his gut feeling about her—that she was simply a woman in trouble—and he would do what he could to help her. So what was the point in searching?

Alex frowned. She was a complication he definitely didn't need.

Just a little bit longer, he told himself. He'd figure out what to do, and be done with this whole mess. Maybe he would get out alive, and maybe he wouldn't. He'd accepted that now. He'd know he'd done his best.

In the meantime, he had to figure out something to do with her.

Alex fixed himself something to eat, had a warm beer— jeez, he hated warm beer—and walked around outside the cabin. The quiet closed in on him, worse than before. The absolute stillness, the loneliness. In the entire three months he'd been here, there hadn't been another human being in this cabin. Other than trips into Red Rock for groceries and cool beer, and three brief trips to Dallas, he'd been all alone.

He'd never expected it to be this hard—to be alone. As much as he worried about who Geri really was and what she was doing here, he was already dreading the moment she left and he would be alone again.

Which had him wondering exactly how she might leave, which had him eyeing the bike. Just in case, he did a little work on the engine, disabling it. They were miles from civilization, and it was already hot as hell in the daytime. He didn't relish the idea of having to hike out of here, should she decide to steal his bike and take off.

He probably shouldn't let himself go to sleep, either, even if she did seem dead to the world. He could work, he decided. He could always work.

So he did, until he was bleary-eyed and glancing longingly at his bed. It was *his* bed, after all. She was out cold. He wasn't going to do anything with her out cold like that. She'd probably be uneasy when she woke up and found him there beside her, but hell, she'd cried herself to sleep beside him in his bed. Where would she expect to find him when she woke up?

Alex took a shower—a long, cold shower. He was drying off when he heard her voice, crying out in the night, with the kind of fear that sent shivers through him.

He thought for one ghastly moment that he'd been found, that someone had gotten into the cabin, looking for him, and had found her instead. He grabbed the gun he kept in the drawer beside his computer and went charging into the room, his heart thundering, finding nothing but her whimpering in her sleep. Then he stood there, dripping wet, stark naked, scared half to death, with a gun in his hand.

"God," he muttered, his heart thundering.

He was so tired of this, and he just wanted to go home. Not the lab. Not the apartment he kept but hardly used. *Home*. He wanted to see his sisters, his nieces and nephews. They could crawl all over him and the baby could spit up on him and pull his hair and drool. They could yell and cry and watch him do silly tricks, little sleights of hand that always delighted them.

He wanted to see his father, maybe even his stepmother. He wanted to visit his sister Kelly's grave, one more time.

He wanted everything to be normal again. Or maybe for the first time. He wanted a life outside his work. For so long, there had been nothing but work, and he saw clearly now that it had been a mistake, that he missed everything else. If he got out of this mess, he was going to make some changes.

He looked down at the woman in his bed. She had to make some changes, too. And dammit all, he was going to do what he could to help her. There had to be a way. He couldn't send her back out into the world all alone.

She was still whimpering and crying a bit in her sleep, still agitated. It must have been some nightmare. He could just imagine what her nightmares were made of, and he knew what he had to do.

He sat down on the side of the bed, stowed the gun between the mattress and the box spring. Then he lay back on the bed and gathered her to him. She didn't put up any resistance. He lay on his side, holding her easily, finding she had a disturbing way of simply fitting against his body, as if they'd been made from the same mold, two halves of a whole. He didn't think anyone had ever before fit against him so well.

She curled into him, all warmth and softness, with hands that clutched at him, a face that nuzzled against the side of his neck, tears that fell against his chest. He couldn't believe she'd fought so hard earlier against the urge to cry, couldn't believe how astonished she'd been by his claim that all women cried. He didn't think any of them ever felt they had a choice in the matter, except Geri.

Alex tightened his arms around her. She was trembling, and he thought about trying to wake her up. He settled for trying to soothe her, instead. He ran his hands over her back and shoulders once again. His shirt was riding up around her waist, and somehow one of his hands ended up beneath the fabric, against her skin. How did he always find his hands on bare skin?

His body was reacting just as he knew it would, but he firmly put that out of his mind. Geri started sobbing great, gulping sobs that tore at his heart, too, and he held her closer, whispered in her ear. "Shh."

"Don't," she cried.

"Don't what?" he asked.

"Don't die."

"I'm not going to die," he said. Not if he could help it.

"Dan," she said, helplessly, hopelessly. "Don't you dare die on me."

Dan, Alex thought. Who the hell was Dan?

* * *

Alex woke slowly, shifting and sinking into the delicious warmth of the body next to his, knowing it must be a dream—one he wasn't ready to surrender just yet.

He was lying on his side, the entire front of his body pressed against the back of hers. Her head was pillowed on his arm, and his face was so close to hers. His arm was around her waist, his palm pressed against her bare stomach, his fingers splayed wide against her skin. There was a smoldering heat low in his belly. He could hear her moan. Alex nudged her hair aside and bit into her neck, feeling shivers running down her spine. He slipped one of his legs between hers, his arousal hard and swollen as he pressed his lower body against hers. At the same time, his hand slid upward, beneath her shirt, until he found her breast, took the weight of it in his hand and rubbed his thumb across her nipple.

She turned her head to his. His mouth found hers, and he kissed her urgently again and again. Soon their bodies were rocking back and forth against each other. So close, he thought. Another minute, another second, and he would slip inside her.

"Geri," he whispered.

She stiffened in his arms, and that was when he knew he wasn't dreaming at all, and no longer was she.

Looking bewildered and angry and absolutely speechless, she stared up at him. Alex groaned. She was in bed with him, pressed up against him, her body all soft and wet and willing, eager even. *For him.* She couldn't deny it.

He brought his hand to her cheek, needing to touch her, to hold her face steady so he could look into her eyes and she couldn't look away. "Geri."

She took a breath. "Please don't touch me."

He stiffened beside her, saying "Sorry," although he wasn't sorry at all.

He was furious. Five seconds ago, she'd been crawling all over him. He'd slept with her practically on top of him, draped over him as if she didn't have a bone in her entire body, all warm and soft and willing. He could have sworn she had been more than willing for this to happen. And now she looked at him like he'd attacked her and intended to finish the job.

"I don't force myself on unwilling women, no matter what the provocation," he said.

"'Provocation'?" She enunciated it so carefully. "I didn't do anything."

"Lady, you've been all over me, all night. You slept on top of me, your arms around me, your legs tangled up in mine. One minute I touch you and you practically purr, and the next you look at me like I'm some kind of maniac."

He watched as soft color flooded her cheeks when she clutched the sheet to her breasts and took in his bare chest. Her gaze dipped lower, to where the sheet pooled around his waist. He wasn't wearing a stitch, and she seemed to have just figured that out.

Something he could have sworn was shyness crept into her eyes.

It couldn't be, he told himself. A woman who pranced in red leather around seedy bars in Texas couldn't possibly be shy. Of course, he wouldn't have expected her to blush so easily, either. Neither had he expected to find the bruises on her body or to have her curl up against his back and nearly fall asleep on the bike. He hadn't expected her to let him hold her while she cried, and then sleep in his bed all night through, either.

All in all, she was one very surprising woman, and if she was lying—if somehow all of this was a lie—she was very, very good at it. It wasn't a lie, Alex told himself. Bruises didn't lie. Her fear wasn't a lie. Her shyness? He sighed. That didn't fit. No way. Maybe nothing about her did. Maybe nothing about this whole situation did, but he knew one thing—he damned well couldn't afford to lose himself in her this way.

"I started this?" she retorted.

She lifted her hand, gesturing toward him, her gaze dropping for a second to his lap. Then color flooded her cheeks once again and her gaze came back to his, guilt seemingly eating her up inside.

"Started it? Yeah," he said, then forced himself to be fair. "But believe me, I was more than willing to finish it. Damn, I still am."

Geri's breath was still coming fast and hard. "What happened? I mean... What else?"

He rolled onto his side and propped himself on his elbow so he could watch her, because he wasn't so angry now, and he liked to look at her. Because he thought the conversation was about to get very interesting.

"You were exhausted," he said. "You fell asleep, and I guess the bed isn't big enough for the two of us. Or maybe you're just a snuggler."

"'A snuggler'?"

He imagined he might have called her a hooker and gotten the same kind of sneer out of her. She couldn't stand the idea of snuggling up to him in bed? Not just that, she seemed outraged by it.

"Geri, are you trying to tell me you don't snuggle with anybody else but me?" he teased.

"No, that's not what I'm trying to tell you at all. Why do you do that, Alex? Always manage to twist things all around?"

He shrugged, thinking it was way too easy to get a rise out of her.

"So," she said cautiously. "That's all we did?"

He smiled just a little, then couldn't help but let his gaze drift lower, to that deep V-shaped opening of her shirt, which showed off the buttery soft curve of her breast so well.

"I guess we're both snugglers," he said. "We slept together in this bed, with our hands and our bodies all over each other, and woke up like this."

She looked speechless for a moment, then struggled with her words. "But, nothing else happened? I mean...last night? Exactly how far...?"

Alex decided he particularly liked the way she looked now, her hair all mussed, her face scrubbed clean of all that makeup, nothing but soft color in her cheeks and her wide brown eyes studying him as intently as he was studying her.

"I think you know exactly how far this went," he said, fighting not to smile, because the first time it had seemed to make her so nervous.

He slid his arm around her waist and hauled her up against him, managed to have one more taste of her luscious mouth before she pulled her lips from his and glared at him, pure outraged pleasure in her eyes. Her shirt was bunched up around her waist, and he didn't have a stitch on. Between them, his erection was throbbing against the satiny-soft skin of her belly.

Just like that, he was half out of his mind with wanting her, all over again.

He let his body thrust gently against hers, found it quite satisfying the way her eyes grew even wider and her breath caught in her throat.

"If I remember correctly, we were right about here," he said, allowing himself one more slow, heated kiss—one that had her closing her eyes and giving him one of those helpless little moans that came from way back in her throat. "I was maybe two seconds away from rolling you onto your back and sinking so deep inside you that with the next breath you took, you'd come apart in my arms."

She exhaled a long, shuddering breath. Alex let his hand

skim down her back and slip between her panties and those luscious curves of her bottom. He did what he'd wanted to do the night before—brushed his hand across her skin, memorizing the shape of her, teasing her with his touch and trying not to scare her too badly.

"That tiny little skirt of yours?" he whispered. "All I could think about when you were wearing that skirt was sliding my hands underneath it and doing this."

He was kneading the soft flesh now, letting his hands make big, wide circles that had him teasing at the backs of her thighs, at the heated spot between them. She was ready for him. Alex knew it.

"Is that what you want, Geri?" He closed his mouth over hers one more time, sliding his tongue inside, and thrust back and forth as he rocked his body against hers.

It was like sinking, he decided. Like being sucked into a whirlpool, spinning out of control and falling farther and faster every minute. He wasn't sure he had the strength or the will to break free.

"Part of me does," she finally admitted, with more honesty than he'd expected from her, considering the position they were in.

"Which part?" he asked wickedly.

She gave an exasperated sigh. He let himself kiss her one more time, then pulled back just enough so he could look at her and try to figure out what was going on inside her head.

She frowned at him. "Alex?"

"Hmm?"

She looked worried again. "You don't have any clothes on."

He grinned. "That's right."

"I can't do this," she said, pleading with him with nothing but the look on her face—her outrageously vulnerable face. "I'm sorry, but—"

"Okay." He sighed, somehow having known that would be her answer.

He rolled away, willing his body to relax, promising himself that he was going to have her, just once, before he sent her away. Otherwise, he'd never be able to send her away. Not now that he knew she wanted him, after all. Her body didn't lie. She wanted him. He wanted her. They were both adults. They were alone. He'd have her. And then he'd see that she was safe somewhere. He'd forget about her. Sooner or later, it had always come to that between him and a woman. He could always forget about them.

"I'm sorry about last night," she said. "If I led you to believe I wanted this..."

"Oh, baby. Don't even go there."

"What?" she said, irritated again.

"Don't even try to tell me you don't want me." He put his fingertip to her lips. "Even you're not that good a liar, Geri. Granted, you're good. I'm afraid you're very good. You could probably tell me the moon was made of green cheese and I'd buy it, but you'd never, ever convince me that you don't want me."

She looked as if she were about to spit fire, and he laughed.

"Maybe you know it's not smart," he conceded. "That you don't know me, and I don't know you. That you damned well shouldn't trust me, and believe me, I don't trust you, either. But I still want you, and lady, you want me, too. Bad."

Alex waited, thinking that if nothing else, he was enjoying this little time they had together more than he'd enjoyed himself in months. He hadn't laughed like this in ages. Maybe he'd forgotten how. She always managed to surprise him, always kept him guessing. And he loved teasing her. At the moment, she looked like she was ready to hit him.

Not that she could hurt him; he outweighed her by seventy-five pounds, at least.

"Go ahead," he invited. "Take your best shot."

"Don't tempt me," she warned.

He just grinned, and he had her off-balance enough that he figured this was his best chance to ask about the nightmare. She might actually tell him the truth right now. "Geri?"

"Hmm?"

"Who's Dan?"

She paled. "What?"

"You heard what I said. Dan."

"I..." She swore. "I was dreaming about him, too?"

"Baby, you were dreaming about me. You were having a nightmare about him."

"Don't do that!" she cried.

"Do what?"

"Call me baby. I'm nobody's baby. Certainly not yours. I'm a grown woman, and I'm perfectly capable of taking care of myself—"

"You stay with a man who beats you, Geri," he said softly. And suddenly, the conversation wasn't any fun anymore.

He backed away from her, stretched out flat on the bed and put his hands behind his head, trying to look more relaxed than he felt. God, she had him tied up in knots.

"I'm not staying with him," she said finally.

"Good. Who's Dan?"

"None of your business," she replied.

"Fine," Alex lied. "Did he die? Or did all your begging and pleading make a difference?"

"What?"

"You were crying in your sleep," he said. "You were begging him not to die, and I was just wondering if it worked, if he made it."

She paled, then seemed to stop breathing altogether. He saw a brief hint of fear, which reminded him of her bruises, reminded him a man had put them there, that there must be a part of her that had been taught to fear any man, that he was a louse for teasing her in a sexual way, if she honestly was afraid of him. He should have remembered that—even half-asleep and naked and more turned-on than he'd ever been in his life.

"Geri, I'm not going to hurt you," he said. "Being here with me might not be the best thing for you. It might not be the safest thing. But I am not going to hurt you, and I'm not going to force you into doing anything you don't want to do. I swear. If you don't believe anything else I say, believe that."

She just sat there, gazing at him. More than once, she opened her mouth to say something, then shut it again. Finally she said, "I'm just no good at this, okay?"

"'This'?"

She gestured toward him, toward the bed. "Men. I'm no good with men. I've never been that comfortable in situations like this. I never will be. If I'm overreacting to this situation—"

"'Situation'? I'm naked. You're practically naked, and we're in bed together. A few minutes ago, we were crawling all over each other, and now we've decided we're not going to do that, even though we both want to. It's not the kind of situation that inspires calm, rational discussion," he conceded. "But go ahead, please. Try to explain."

She frowned. He tried not to watch the rise and fall of her breasts beneath his shirt. He'd burn that shirt, he decided. He'd never be able to wear it again without thinking of her and her breasts encased in that material and the way she looked, sitting here all tousled and sleepy in his bed.

"I'm sure you'll be able to control yourself just fine,"

she said. "Believe me, I know I'm not the kind of woman who moves men to uncontrollable fits of lust—"

"Geri?"

"Hmm?"

"You'd be wrong about that."

She glared at him.

"The fits-of-uncontrollable-lust part?" he clarified. "You'd be wrong. I'm barely holding it together over here."

"Do you always make jokes about everything?" she asked.

"If I can. I'm a fairly happy guy. But I'm not joking about this. If you want to come over here, I'd be happy to show you exactly how you make me feel. If you don't want to do that, one of us should probably get the hell out of this bed."

He'd left her speechless. He could see the wheels turning in her brain. She was running through all sorts of conclusions, seemingly discarding them all.

"Can it be that hard for you to believe I want you?" he asked, amazed.

"I don't know." She sighed.

He rolled his eyes, wondering what in the world he'd done to deserve her. She was the most frustrating, confusing woman he'd ever known, and she'd shown up in his life at exactly the worst time, and he simply couldn't let himself trust her. Not if he had half a brain inside his thick skull. He couldn't.

Hell, he thought. If she was staying here, and she was already making him this crazy, he might as well keep going.

"Who's Dan?" he asked for the third damned time.

"A man," she replied.

"God," he muttered. "You really know how to shoot off that smart mouth of yours, don't you?"

She was still glaring at him. He didn't think any woman

had ever looked at him with such loathing while she was in his bed.

"I'll make you a deal," she said finally. "You tell me exactly what happened last night. Exactly what I said and what we did. And I'll tell you about Dan."

"Me first?"

She nodded.

"So you can get your story straight? Figure out what you have to tell me and what you can leave out? What you can lie about?"

Alex grinned. She wanted to hit him so badly. He knew it. "Want to go a few rounds, Geri? Right here? Who knows what that might lead to?"

She raised her hand and nearly smacked him across the face before he could react. Damn, she was fast. He'd barely caught her hand before it connected solidly with his face, and they practically arm wrestled right there on the bed for a minute. She was awkward about the whole thing, frustrated and holding back, he sensed, but dying to hurt him, and all he was trying to do was keep her from doing that, without hurting or scaring her. As tussles went, it was quite interesting. But the sheet was getting lost in the heat of the battle, and one glance from her at what she was about to uncover, and she was done. She quit fighting him and backed away to her corner of the bed.

"You're tough," he said admiringly.

"Tougher than you know. I've been battling with one man or another for most of my life."

"I'll keep that in mind," he said, enjoying just watching the agitated way she was breathing. He really had to get her to put on a lot more clothes, if he was going to keep his wits about him.

"You're an incredibly frustrating person," she complained.

"And you think you're not?" he retorted.

"I think you're enjoying yourself."

His mouth twitched, verging on a smile. She'd probably hit him again. "It so happens I am. I didn't realize how bored I'd been until you showed up."

"Oh, great," she said. "I'm better than being bored?"

"Much, much better," he said.

"Oh, Alex, what am I going to do with you?"

"What do you want to do with me?" he invited.

"Forget," she said. "Dammit, I just want to forget everything with you. Everything that's important. Everything that makes sense. Everything that's right."

He sensed it was the most honest thing she'd ever said to him, sensed that he was getting somewhere with her, finally.

He reached for her, with nothing but absolute honest need, and brought her mouth down to his. The kiss was hard and deep and the most truthful thing he'd shown her, and so was her reaction.

She just melted—right into him. They were plastered together, kneeling there on the bed, as he devoured her with his mouth and his hands, knowing that any minute she was going to stop him, and already regretting it.

When it finally ended—when they were struggling for breath and looking at each other in a mixture of awe and absolute bewilderment—he told her, "Me, too, babe. That's exactly what you do to me. You make me want to forget everything but this, even if I know it would be one colossal mistake."

Chapter 5

Her face took on that painfully vulnerable look, the one that made him feel like a louse because he'd probably put it there, because he'd pushed too hard when she was obviously at her wit's end.

"Is it so bad? That I feel the same way?" he asked. "That we both know this isn't the smartest thing we could do, but we want to do it anyway?"

"It might be easier if one of us didn't," she countered.

"Sorry." He grinned. "I want to."

"Do you always do what you want, Alex?"

"As often as I can manage it. Don't you?"

"No," she said.

"Why not?"

"Because I can't."

"Why not?"

"It doesn't work that way, Alex."

"Sure it does. You're a grown woman. You can do anything you want. You can make your life into anything you want it to be."

He saw fragility again. *Damn.*

"Geri?" He reached for her.

She backed away. "I'm trying to change, okay? I know something has to change, and I'm trying."

"All right."

"I can't do it all at once."

"Okay," he said. There were certainly things he'd like to change right now that he simply couldn't.

She sighed. "I'm sorry. I can't just hop into bed with you and—"

"Geri, you *are* in bed with me."

She hit him again, with a pillow this time. "You're incorrigible," she complained.

"It's one of my best qualities."

She rolled her eyes, and he couldn't quite believe he was sitting here naked in his bed, laughing with this woman, but damn, it felt good.

"Let me help you," he said, all serious again. "Tell me what I can do."

"Oh, Alex..." She sobered just as quickly. "Everything is so messed up. My whole life is a mess, and most of the time I'm scared to even try to change it. I don't even want to think about how messed up it is."

"Everybody messes up from time to time. It doesn't mean things will always be that way."

"I know."

"Will you tell me about Dan?"

She stared at him. "You almost sound jealous."

"Maybe I am," he said, straight-faced. *Damn,* he was.

"That's crazy. You don't even know me."

He shrugged. "I know enough to know I want you and that I'm jealous. Why don't you put me out of my misery and tell me something."

"Dan's just a man I used to know."

"The one in Virginia?"

"Yes."

"He's more than a man you used to know, Geri."

"Okay, we're close," she admitted.

"Lovers?"

"No. Friends. As close a friend as anyone. As close as I let anyone get."

Alex nodded, liking the sound of this a little better. They weren't lovers. Good. He wanted very much to be Geri's lover.

"He had an...accident. A bad one. What did I say about him—when I was dreaming?"

"That you didn't want him to die. Tell me about it, Geri. Did he die?"

"No," she whispered. "That's why you came back to bed with me?"

"Well, I can't say I wasn't looking for an excuse." Alex just couldn't leave the subject alone. He knew from the intensity of her reaction that it wasn't the first time she'd had that particular nightmare. "How long ago did it happen, Geri?"

She shrugged her shoulder. "A year or so ago."

"What else?" he asked. "There's something else, isn't there? Why is this so important to you? Not just because you were there or because you were his friend. What else?"

"I can't tell you," she said.

Alex swore. She'd turned pale and cold, and her eyes were huge and rounded, with a haunted look to them that just about broke his heart.

"Come on, Geri. We're two absolute strangers who'd never seen each other twenty-four hours ago, and before another twenty-four hours is up, you'll be gone. We'll probably never see each other again. So why don't you just tell me. Tell me everything, and let me try to help you."

"I can't," she replied. "Honestly, I wish I could. You

just don't know, Alex, how much I wish I could, how amazing it is that I even want to. But I can't.''

"Okay," he said.

"What did you mean when you said I'd be gone by tomorrow?"

"You can't stay here," he said. "It isn't safe."

"Why not?"

"I can't tell you." He summoned up a smile. "I didn't mean that the way it sounded. I'm not trying to get back at you for keeping things from me. I just can't tell you. You've got your secrets. I'm going to have to have mine."

"Oh," she said, rubbing at her forehead as if it hurt.

He could help her with that. He could rub out all the tension from her head and her shoulders. But then he'd have his hands all over her again, which would definitely lead to trouble. Which meant he had to get out of this bed.

"Hungry?" he asked.

"Yes."

"I'll see what I can find in the kitchen."

"Thanks," she said. "If you don't mind, I think I'll have another shower to wake me up and clear my head."

"Make yourself at home." Alex touched a finger to the bandages on her chest. "How does this feel? Do I get to play doctor again?"

"I don't think so, Alex. I don't think I could handle it if you did."

"Me neither," he admitted. At least not without making love to her this time. Then he threw back the covers and climbed out of the bed.

Geri watched with her mouth hanging open while he strolled out of the room as if he didn't have a care in the world. He honestly didn't have a stitch on. She'd known he had a wonderful body, because they'd been all over each other in the past eight hours or so. But to see him like this...

He moved with an easy grace, muscles stretching and

flexing in a veritable symphony. She found herself fascinated by the sight of all that bare skin, the wide shoulders,
narrow waist, and those glorious thighs.

Geri groaned, then rolled over and buried her head in the
pillow, which was a mistake. She'd landed on the spot in
the bed that still held the warmth of his body, the clean
smell of him. She couldn't remember ever noticing the scent
of a man's skin, or being tempted to bury her face, close
her eyes and pretend it was him and not a soft cotton sheet
she had her nose pressed against.

This whole scene had taken on an air of unreality. She
felt like Alice, who'd fallen down the rabbit hole and found
herself in a completely other world. She was in a man's
bed, scarcely clothed, unarmed, and had been totally unconcerned for most of the past twelve hours about her mission. They had calmly discussed the fact that he wanted to
have sex with her, even though he knew it wasn't smart but
knew she wanted the same thing. She'd told him a little
about Dan, about being lonely and needing to rearrange her
whole life, and he'd been sympathetic, understanding. She'd
cried all over him, and he'd held her in his arms, very nearly
made love to her.

Everything he'd said to her—about his sisters, about his
mother dying young—indicated that he was Alex Hathaway. Everything about the way he treated her, the way he
touched her, told her he wasn't. Either he was the best liar
she'd ever met, or there was something very wrong with
the information she'd been given about him.

Geri thought about it. His fingerprints were on the
weapon used to shoot and kill Doc. She'd been guarding
his lab that night, when Dan nearly died and she was shot,
as well. There was no mistake about that. She hadn't seen
him shoot Doc. She hadn't checked the fingerprints on the
gun herself. She hadn't seen him slink off. But that's where
she and Dan had been—guarding Alex.

So how did she make it fit together? How could she connect what she'd been told about Dr. Alexander Hathaway—genius, traitor, murderer—and what she'd seen with her own two eyes, heard with her own ears, from Alex—the kind, funny, sexy man?

This was no rabbit hole, no other world. This was the Texas panhandle, and she was an agent on a mission. She'd fallen asleep here in his arms when she was supposed to be searching this cabin. She should have been gone by now, should have reported everything she'd found out about him to her superiors and left it to them to decide what to do next. And whether they sent her right back here to bring him in, or to kill him?

Geri prayed the day would never come when she received that order. After all, she'd slept wrapped in his arms all night long, had very nearly had sex with him this morning. Worst of all, her traitorous body wanted him, wanted all the pleasure he had to offer, wanted oblivion in his arms.

Was it merely about power, she wondered? Was he one of those men who liked to toy with women, like a cat with a mouse? Was he getting her to relax in his presence and throw her off-balance just enough that when he moved in for the kill, it would be that much easier?

Was that possible? Could Alex, the seemingly open, honest, funny, caring man, be that devious? That good? Was he waging some kind of psychological war with her? If he was, he was winning, she thought grimly.

Feeling older than her years and totally inadequate for the job she'd been given, Geri tried to clear her head, to think like an agent, at least for a few minutes. There was nothing left to do but play this out. She hadn't accomplished anything yet, except catching Alex's attention and getting into his cabin. But that was a start.

Relax, she instructed herself. Think. Play it out.

Looking down at her predicament, half-clothed, rumpled,

tired, still aching for him, she added one more curt demand
to herself.

Stay the hell out of his bed.

Showered, her hair still wet, her face bare, she dressed in
a T-shirt and a pair of cutoffs. The shorts were too short,
and she still didn't have a bra, but all in all, it was a welcome change after the outfit she'd donned yesterday.

She'd given herself a thorough dressing-down while she
showered, imagined the water and the creamy soap erasing
the feel of his hands on her body, taking away any desire
she had to feel those hands on her again. She remembered
visiting Doc's grave, remembered Dan in the wheelchair,
herself on the firing range her first day back after the accident, when nothing was working the way it once had. She
remembered being scared and hurt and doubting everything
she'd ever believed about herself, everything she'd ever
wanted. And she remembered it was all his fault—all of it.

How hard could it be to hate him for that?

When she opened the bathroom door, the smell coming
from the kitchen reminded her that she'd slept through dinner the night before, that nerves had kept her from risking
lunch that day. So it had been more than twenty-four hours
since her last meal.

Tucked into a corner of the main room, Alex stood in
front of the tiny propane stove stirring something in a pot.

"This is like camping out," Geri said.

He turned and gazed at her, taking in every aspect of her
appearance before he looked back at the stove.

"No electrical lines out here," he explained. "I have a
small generator for lights and hot water. But it's easier to
cook with propane. I'm afraid there's no refrigerator, either.
So we're stuck with whatever comes in a can or a box."

Interesting. The man had a chemical formula worth mil-
lions, and he chose to live this way? Why? Because he

hadn't perfected it yet? That was the theory. Something wasn't right with Alex's formula, and he was holed up here, working out the bugs. As soon as he was done, he'd cut his deal and take off for some corner of the world, live a life of luxury and decadence, a conscienceless existence where he would ignore the havoc he caused.

Could he do that? Geri wondered. Could he be that conscienceless man?

"It's really not that bad," Alex said.

Damn, she'd lost it again. "What?"

"The food. You were frowning. I wanted to reassure you that breakfast from a can, lunch from a can, even dinner from a can—it's not that bad."

"Oh. I was thinking about something else, that's all. And I'm hungry enough that I don't care where the food came from."

"Help yourself to a can of some liquid from the cabinet." He nodded to his right. "And grab something for me, too."

Geri found canned soda, individual serving bottles of fruit juice, bottled water and canned beer. "You drink warm beer?"

He pulled two bowls from the cabinet to his left and dished out the stew. "When I'm desperate enough and I don't want to put up with the ambience at my neighborhood bar."

Geri sat down at the tiny table, opened a can of juice for Alex and one for herself. He put a bowl of stew in front of her, then sat down himself.

"What were you doing there, Geri?"

"What?" She schooled her features not to show anything.

"At the bar."

"I was thirsty," she insisted, biting into her stew.

"Come on," Alex said. "Dressed like that? Walking

alone into some seedy bar? You had to know you were asking for trouble.''

She decided anger was her best tactic. "So a woman who dresses like that and chooses to walk into a bar in the evening gets whatever she deserves? Is that how you think it works? That I deserved it?''

"That's not what I said.''

She let herself remember the fear when she'd been down on the floor and the huge, angry man standing over her had a broken whiskey bottle in his hand—fear that she would carelessly let one more situation rush dangerously out of control because she just wasn't herself. She was suddenly so angry. And she decided to use every bit of that anger, as she'd been trained to do. Manipulation, when called for, had once been as natural to her as breathing, after all.

"You know,'' she said, her voice weak and trembling, "the last time I heard that particular reasoning—that I deserved what I was getting? It was when I got those bruises you found on my body last night.''

"Geri—''

"Don't you dare tell me I deserved it.''

She expected an apology, expected him to ask nicely for her forgiveness, maybe for him to take her in his arms. Instead, he sat with his arms folded across his chest and stared. Geri fought the urge to panic. He was brilliant, she knew, but he was still a man, and he'd obviously relished his role as her reluctant protector the day before. Still, something was wrong. Something in the way he looked at her. *Don't make me think you care, Alex,* she silently begged. *Don't.*

"I never said you deserved any of that,'' he said tightly. "There was nothing you could have done to justify their behavior. How they choose to respond is their responsibility. But still you were hurt because you put yourself in an incredibly precarious situation. That's what I meant. Why would you be so callous about your own safety? Anything could have happened. And you had to know that, when you walked into the bar. So I can't quite figure out why you did it. Why you'd take so few precautions with your own safety."

She hadn't chosen to do that, of course. She'd known Alex was there.

"And another thing—if you were trying to get away from some man, why would you do it dressed like that? Every man who saw you would have remembered you. And that car. It's memorable. Why call so much attention to yourself when you're trying to disappear?"

"I was trying to call attention to myself," she said, refusing to let him get her all flustered. That was a rookie mistake, and she was no rookie.

"Really?"

"It's not the first time I've left him, Alex. And I learned a few things in the times before. He has a lot of money, and he'll come after me. I knew he'd be watching the airport, so I didn't even try that. I knew I had to leave a trail for him to follow—a false trail. So I took his flashy BMW and put on an outfit guaranteed to stop traffic and I laid the trail for him. I stopped three times between here and Dallas, made sure lots of people saw me. And I was going to leave the car somewhere for him to find, then change everything I could about myself—my hair, my clothes, even the color of my eyes—then head off in another direction and hope that this time I would manage to get away."

Geri recited the whole story without looking at him. She let her nerves shine through, because the woman she was pretending to be would be very nervous, and she hoped Alex would fall for her act. When she let herself glance at his face, she wasn't sure he had.

"You don't believe me?" she demanded with as much indignation as she could muster.

"I didn't say that."

"You didn't have to say it," she blurted out, angry now. She would do whatever it took, be whatever kind of woman he responded to if it meant getting the job done.

What she hadn't expected was to feel guilty for that. She deceived people practically every day of her life. It had been so bad lately, she wasn't sure she was capable of feeling any genuine emotion at all. It had gotten to the point where she merely soaked up experiences and emotions that might prove useful to her someday, to be put on display at the proper time. That was what her life had become until one mission had gone desperately wrong. Until he had come along and messed it all up.

The guilt and fear and uncertainty had been the first real emotions she'd felt in years, and that frightened her. It had her wondering what her life had become, and what would be left for her if she couldn't do her job. Nothing, she realized. Absolutely nothing.

Alex was right. Sometimes you waited too late to try to change things, and you were simply alone. Maybe it was already too late for her.

"I'm sorry," she said, backing off, letting him see her very real struggle for control. "I'm not good at trusting people."

Alex slid his hand across the table and took one of her hands in his. "Why?" he asked gently.

Spewing out an awful combination of truth and lies, she said, "It's not easy to let someone get close. I used to want that. I remember wanting that more than anything, but..."

It was scary. She'd been disappointed so many times, mostly by her father. She'd grown up seeing him totally alone, dependent on no one, strong and brave, distant and cold, and it had seemed natural to try to emulate him. It had seemed to be the way of the world to her.

She was still surprised to find that it wasn't; that there

were people who talked about their problems openly, who cried and yelled and rejoiced and loved, who lived life to the fullest. People who had friends and loved ones and relatives they saw voluntarily, even eagerly, instead of only when tradition or appearances demanded it. It was all so different from the way she'd been raised.

"Geri?" he said. "Sometimes you've got to take a risk. You've got to reach out to people. You can't think life is going to stand still around you, that once you finally come to your senses and work up your courage the people you need will be standing right there waiting for you to make things right—to need them, to want them, to love them. I know about these things. I've seen a lot of people come and go in my life."

"You waited too long with someone?"

He nodded.

"Your mother?"

"No. I was too little to screw up that relationship. Now, given some time…" He managed a wry smile. "It was one of my sisters. Very nearly two of them, actually. My oldest sister and I didn't talk for years. I was mad at her for years, thinking…well, thinking a lot of stuff that just wasn't true and being too stubborn and too hurt to ask. I could very easily have lost her forever."

Geri knew. His oldest sister had practically raised him and his two sisters after their mother had died, even though she'd been only a teenager herself. Alex had been in grade school when their father had remarried, and soon after, his oldest sister had left for college and seldom come back. Apparently there had been a great deal of tension between her and her new stepmother, but Alex… Geri could easily see him feeling abandoned for the second time in his life.

"What happened?" she asked, because she wasn't supposed to know that much about him.

"She was like a mother to me, and then she had to go

away. I blamed her for leaving—maybe the same way I blamed my mother for dying. Did you ever do that? Blame your mother for dying?''

"The whole time I was growing up," Geri admitted. Maybe she still did.

Alex shrugged. "It's hard not to when you want something you can't have. Especially when you're a kid. Anyway, I wasn't very nice to my oldest sister for a while, and I tried with my stepmother, but things weren't great there, either, and I probably held back a lot more than I should have with everybody in my life after that."

He sighed. "Then I really lost a sister."

"What do you mean?" Geri asked sadly, knowingly.

"She died," Alex said.

"And you weren't...close?"

"Not as close as we should have been. You stand by and watch people leave you all the time, and eventually you come to rely on yourself more and more. You tell yourself you don't need anyone, right?"

"I suppose."

He made a face at her. "Come on, Geri. You know. This is you, too. We're a lot alike."

"Maybe," she said.

"Anyway, I waited too long for me and my other sister. If I want to see her now, I'm looking at her photograph or standing by her grave. Or visiting her boys. She has great boys. But it's not the same as having her. Nothing will ever be the same as having her."

"I'm sorry, Alex."

"Do you understand what I'm trying to tell you? Take the risk, Geri. Let somebody in. It's scary, but so's finding yourself all alone. These last few months..." He broke off, looking surprised and wary for a moment, then shaking his head. "Hey, this was supposed to be about you, wasn't it?"

"Maybe."

"Don't be scared, Geri."

"I'll try not to," she promised. "I've just made some bad choices...."

"The man who hurt you," he said.

She nodded, thinking of a job that was at the same time killing her and yet had been her entire life.

"Surely there was someone who would have helped you, Geri. Someone to turn to."

"I don't know. Maybe," she said honestly.

If she'd reached out to someone earlier, if she'd known how... And then she remembered the act, the game. How could she keep forgetting the game?

"I couldn't let anyone in, Alex. I was ashamed. I didn't want anyone to know." Closing her eyes, she said calculatingly, "I never let anyone see the bruises."

Alex swore softly, and she knew she had him. She'd done exactly what she had to do. And still managed to tell him more about herself than anyone else had heard in years. There were bruises deep inside her—not unlike the discolorations on her ribs—and no one had ever seen them. Until Alex.

Geri heard the scrape of wood on wood, then realized he'd slid his chair across the floor until he was sitting sideways, next to her. One of his arms slipped around her shoulders, and he pulled her to him until her head was tucked against his chest.

"You don't have to say any more." He stroked her hair, dropped a kiss on the top of her head. "I believe you, okay? You don't have to talk about it."

"I'm sorry," she said again, because she was. With him, she honestly was.

"It's all right," he said, then smiled. "You know, this has gotten way too maudlin. Can we forget all about this? Just for the rest of today?"

"What do you mean?"

"I mean I've been alone for a long time now, and I didn't know how much I missed being around someone until you came along. I want one day with you. Just as friends. Can you give me that, Geri? One day?"

"I don't know."

"We can just be two people getting to know each other."

"I'm not sure that's a good idea."

"Probably not, but it's what I want," he said.

"I can't go to bed with you, Alex."

"I don't recall asking. Not recently, anyway." He grinned. "Not that I won't before the day's over... But for right now, just talk to me. Come outside and walk around with me. Take a ride on the bike with me. We'll go look around, just the two of us. We'll talk. I'll make you forget about being so serious all the time, make you laugh. You know I can."

"We can't run away from everything. I wish we could, but—"

"We can for a day," he insisted.

Geri sighed, wanting it desperately, wanting to forget that everything he'd told her fit what she'd been told about Alex Hathaway's family, yet he wasn't anything like what she'd expected. There had to be some explanation, something to help her make sense of him. One way or another, they were going to spend the day together. As long as she didn't tell him anything more about herself, as long as she didn't let him kiss her, as long as she stayed out of his bed, she'd be fine.

And tonight?

Tonight would take care of itself, and then she'd leave. She'd forget his wickedly sexy smile, his gentle touch, his kind concern—everything. She'd walk away without a second thought, without a twinge of conscience.

"Is it that hard?" Alex asked. "To give me one day?"

"Yes," she admitted. "You're a dangerous man, Alex."

He nodded, grinning. "You've got that right."

She swore, wondering if he somehow knew that she'd like nothing better than to have one day with Alex the man, simply as Geri the woman—two people they should never be. They were enemies, after all, in the middle of an undeclared war.

"It's so odd," she said. "Like you're reading my mind." In telling her just what she wanted to hear, offering her something she couldn't have.

"I wish I was. Then I'd know all your secrets." He sobered. "But let's forget about yours and mine. Just for today."

"What happens then?" she asked.

"Then you have to go," he told her. "I'll help you find someplace safe. I promise."

"Why would you do that for me? I mean, it's not your problem."

He looked surprised. "I like you, Geri. Why wouldn't I want to help you? And what kind of world do you live in if you're so surprised by someone wanting to help you?"

"It's…" *Damn.* "You wouldn't like it, Alex. Not at all. I don't even like it myself."

"Give me today," he said again, mesmerizing her until she wanted the same thing he did.

One day, she thought. She could think of it as a test. Surely she could resist him for one day.

Chapter 6

They finished breakfast, and she helped him clean up, which proved interesting in the tiny space.

They kept bumping into each other, laughing about it as the heat flared between them. He didn't try to touch her, to kiss her, but he made it clear that he still wanted her. He flirted shamelessly, but made light of it, and she didn't feel nearly as pressured or as nervous about what he did as she did by the way he made her feel.

She was starting to wonder if he'd drugged her somehow, if he wasn't a desperately potent drug himself—his smile, the sound of his voice, the sight of his hands doing something as mundane as drying a dish. He was a brilliant chemist, after all, and there were all sorts of experiments these days involving the science of attraction, about hormones and scents and such.

Alex would know all about those. Maybe he'd found a way to use them to get whatever he wanted from women. Maybe it wasn't her fault she felt this way. Maybe there was nothing she could do to fight it; maybe she should just give in.

"You're worrying again," he complained, as he settled the helmet on her head.

She was, because old habits truly did die hard. For years, she'd lived to work, like a robot—a well-trained, precise, obedient soldier. In her entire life, she'd never done anything truly reckless with a man. It seemed there'd never been a time with no worries, no responsibilities, no guilt, no desperate longing to prove something to herself and her father. And she was so weary of it all.

Inside her was a traitorous woman who liked the idea of being the one in the sexy outfit racing through the deserted Texas plains with an equally sexy man, letting herself get utterly lost in both the man and the nothingness surrounding them. She could be the woman she'd invented for him, and he could be... He could be anyone except who she feared he was.

"Make me stop worrying," she challenged, liking the idea more and more all the time. "Please. Just for today."

A truly dangerous glint came into his eyes, and he laughed. "You'd better watch out. I told you I want you. You already know how good it's going to be between us."

"Do I?"

"Oh, yeah. I have no doubt."

"You're being a bit presumptuous, aren't you? You sound like you know it's going to happen."

"I do. I've already made up my mind, and I think you have, too. Before you leave here, we're going to be together."

"You're outrageous," she said.

"Why? What's outrageous about wanting to make love to you? You're gorgeous—"

"No, I'm not."

"Fishing?" he asked.

"No."

"Geri, you nearly gave me a heart attack in that leather miniskirt."

"It was the outfit."

"I could look at a little leather skirt all day and not get all hot and bothered. Believe me, it was you in it."

"Alex, you don't have to do this."

"Do what?"

"Say these things about me."

"Why wouldn't I? They're true. I find you incredibly attractive."

"You're just lonely," she said. "And I'm here."

"No way. I could have a woman hanging on each arm and I'd still look at you and think you were attractive. I'd still want to drag you off to my bed."

"Gee, thanks."

"My pleasure, I'm sure. No thanks necessary."

"You're incorrigible, Alex," she complained. "Do you ever take anything seriously?"

"Not today. Come on. Get on the bike."

She did, taking off with him on his motorcycle with no idea where they were going or what he might do to her when they got there. And just like the last time, she didn't care in the least. She just wished he would never stop.

They rode for hours, seeing nothing but the barren, colorless, mostly flat plains, dotted infrequently with oil derricks and windmills. No people. No roads. No cars. No houses. Nothing but her and Alex and the bike.

He stopped around midday and they hiked up a majestic butte, to a point where they could see for miles in every direction. He spread a blanket on the ground, and they lay on their backs in the hot spring sunshine, and they played a silly game of Twenty Questions, steering clear of any weighty issues. She knew his favorite color was yellow, that he loved basketball and thought major-league baseball was the most boring sport ever invented. She told him her main weaknesses were sad movies, very expensive chocolate and Ireland—she thought Ireland was the most beautiful place on earth. He told her a bit more about his sisters—silly little things—and she told him funny stories about the different places she'd lived and things she'd seen.

She didn't want the day ever to end, but all good things, she knew, did. Alex climbed back on the bike, and she settled herself against him once again. The engine rumbled and the bike vibrated, her body sinking into his. She'd never known riding a bike could be so intimate, so erotic.

They rode for a long, long time. She tried to be good, to be smart, but it was beyond her at the moment. She had to hang on to him; she had no choice if she wanted to stay on the bike. And she tried to keep it from being personal, but he just wouldn't leave her alone. He took her palm and spread it flat against his abdomen, tugged on her arm to bring her more fully against him. His stomach was flat. His skin when he tugged up his shirt and pushed her hand inside was hot to the touch.

She thought about letting that hand roam at will, thought about exploring every inch of him while they rode. No one would ever know, she realized. Just him and her. It sounded so wicked. Geri had never done anything wicked in her life. How had she gotten to be almost thirty and so cautious, so careful, so ignorant of sexual need that she'd never even been wicked?

Unlike Alex. Alex was the embodiment of "wicked."

She turned her head sideways and laid it against his broad back, daring to snuggle a bit closer. Her thighs were spread wide to either side of his denim-clad hips. Tentatively, she laid her hand against the pocket of his jeans and rubbed her palm along the length of his thigh.

She felt him stiffen at her touch, then laugh.

"Didn't think you had it in you, Geri," he said.

She took her hand away.

He put it right back. "Go ahead. Explore all you want."

Could it be that easy? she wondered. Yes. With him, it would be, if she could silence every bit of common sense in her head.

She spread her fingers wide over one pocket at the back of his jeans, rubbing in slow circles, taking in the back of his thigh—the long, broad muscle there. Then her hand slid up the front of his thigh, so firm, so hard. *Oh.*

She wanted to touch him intimately, to stroke him. It was shocking, really, how much she wanted to do that. And she wondered what he'd do if she did. Probably stop the bike, pull her off and throw her onto the ground and take her, right there. The image set her heart to thundering.

"Go ahead," Alex said. "I dare you."

"You would," she retorted.

"You're just touching me. What's wrong with that?"

"Alex—"

He put his hand over hers and pulled hers upward. It slid over denim, worn smooth and soft. She felt a satisfying little hitch in his breath, felt her body seem to shoot to life, awareness like a palpable thing between them. She felt feverish and achy and so very needy, wondering how it was possible to feel so very much, so many different things, all at once. And to feel them so urgently, so completely. To need him this much.

His hand pushed hers to a spot near the juncture of his thighs where tension had pulled the fabric tight over a hard, rounded bulge. She couldn't help but explore, tracing its length, its fullness, feeling it shift and grow beneath her hand.

The bike shot forward, and he was trembling, she realized. She loved the idea that she could make him tremble with need. She shifted restlessly against his back, trying to get closer. It was impossible. She was already plastered against him, but still she wanted more. So she kept doing what she was doing, finding it exciting beyond belief, simply touching him. She felt powerful and wanton and wicked, and she liked it. Damn, he made her like it all, want it all, need it all, so very much.

She shuddered, heat pooling between her thighs, desire raging out of control. She wanted to kiss him, too. She looked up, searching for skin, saw the back of his neck. He'd drawn his hair into a ponytail again, and she pressed her lips to the sun-browned skin at the nape of his neck. It was hot, tasted slightly of sweat, but mostly of man. Then she put her lips against his ear and said, "This is crazy, Alex. Crazy."

"Uh-hmm," he said, sounding totally unconcerned.

She closed her eyes, relaxed against him once again. She absolutely loved touching him.

It might have been seconds or minutes later when the bike rumbled to a stop. He put his feet down to brace them and pulled her around until she was sitting on the seat in front of him, practically on his lap, with his arms tightly around her, his wicked mouth coming down to hers, taking it in a kiss positively steamy and dripping with sexual innuendo. His tongue thrust into her mouth, again and again, until she was absolutely limp with need for him, beyond caring about anything, it seemed.

And when he finally lifted his head, she saw that they'd made it back to the cabin, and he was ready to finish what they'd started.

"Don't get scared on me," he said. "I'm not going to pounce on you the second I have you inside the door, tempting as that may be."

"Oh, Alex," she said hopelessly.

"Come on," he said. "Let's get out of the sun, at least."

She let him lead her inside. He grabbed a drink of water, offered her one as well, and they gulped it down. She couldn't help but look over that long, lean body she'd touched so intimately. He was still breathing hard, still looking impossibly strong and tall, still obviously aroused.

He caught her staring, a sinful smile on his face. "I think I need a shower," he said. "A cold one. And you need to think, Geri. Do me a favor. Before you lay a hand on me again, decide just how far you want this to go."

She glanced up at him, guiltily. "I don't do this, Alex."

"Do what?"

"Have sex with people I barely know."

"Neither do I," he claimed.

"I don't believe that."

"It's true."

She made a sound of disgust.

"What? You think I make a habit of picking up women in that bar and riding off into the night with them, hoping I'll find their hands all over me before we're through?"

"I think you've been with a lot of women."

"I don't know," he said. "I didn't exactly keep a list. How many's a lot?"

"Forget it. I don't want to know."

"No. Wait a minute. I'll tell you. I need to tell you. I haven't had a lot of luck with women when it comes to long-term relationships. They tend to come and go. I tend to come and go. I'll admit it. I don't know if it's me or if I just haven't found anyone who's made me want to stay. It just always seems to fizzle out and die."

Geri nodded. She knew that.

"But I don't lie to them," he claimed. "I'm up-front about it. I've not been looking to make a commitment to anyone, beyond being faithful to her for as long as we're together. And I'm sure as hell not in a position to offer you anything except today. *Tonight*. That's it, Geri. After that, you've got to go. I'll help you find a place. But you've got to go."

"What do you mean, you'll help me?"

"You need a place to hide out. From the man who did that to you." He touched a hand to the bruise on the inside of her upper arm.

"Yes," she said, though she'd forgotten all about that woman, all about anything but him and her and taking off on the bike and never coming back, never even slowing down.

"I can help you."

"I don't know if I can let you do that, Alex," she lied. God, she hated the lies. "He's dangerous."

He winked at her, looking totally unconcerned. "I live for danger."

Did he? Was this some kind of game for him? Could he be enjoying it? There was a time when she had—when there was nothing like that rush of adrenaline that came from doing something incredibly dangerous, and doing it well.

Not anymore.

"God, you look so sad," he said. "I don't want you to be sad anymore, Geri. Or scared."

"It matters to you?" she asked.

He nodded, and she wanted to believe him. All along, she'd wanted to believe him.

"So," he said. "You don't have anyplace to go? No relatives? No friends?"

She shook her head. "Not anymore."

"Dan?" he asked.

"No."

"I know somebody who'll help you. Somebody I trust. I won't lie to you. It's not without risks—"

"Risks?"

"Because of me," he claimed. "I'm in the middle of something, something bad. Otherwise, I wouldn't let you go. Not after one night."

"Really?" she asked, like some needy little woman, desperate for reassurance. She hated the whole idea of needing or wanting anyone this much. Especially him, when she knew better.

Stupid, pointless tears stung her eyes, and she had that sensation once again of literally drowning in emotion, in the moment. Everything was so intense, so vivid, so real. It was as if all her life, she'd been in some sort of cocoon, somehow removed from everything, isolated, standing back from life in an effort to protect herself, and now it had just dissolved. She had no protection at all.

"Oh, baby," he said, reaching for her. "Don't cry."

"I'm not a baby," she protested, though she did let him take her in his arms. "I'm a grown woman, and I don't need any man to protect me."

"So sue me," he murmured, kissing her. "I want to protect you."

"Dammit," she said.

He laughed. "Do you always fight so hard against the things you want? Against the things that feel good? Things that would be good?"

"I don't know, Alex. Nothing ever felt this good," she confessed miserably. "Or this bad. This wrong."

"Why? Why is it so wrong?"

And there was nothing else she could tell him, nothing but more lies, and she was sick of those. So she just let him hold her, comfort her, let her feel safe and secure, which was crazy. How could she feel so secure in his arms, knowing who he was, what he was? But maybe that was the answer. Maybe she knew, and that was why it felt right to be with him. Maybe it was all some terrible mistake—the explosives and his escape and what had happened to Doc. Maybe he hadn't done it. Maybe he simply wasn't the man she'd thought.

God, she wanted to believe that. More than she'd ever wanted anything in her life, she wanted him to be the man she'd come to know, to want. She wanted him to be funny and tender and kind and oh, so sexy.

He was, she thought. He'd shown her nothing but that, the entire, intense twenty-four hours or so they'd spent together. All he'd shown her was tenderness, kindness, and the kind of desire that was driving her mad.

"I do want you, Alex," she said.

He rolled his eyes theatrically. "Wow. There's a surprise."

She laughed too, then.

He sobered instantly, touching his fingers to her chin. "You know something?"

"What?"

"That's the first time I've heard you laugh. I've been waiting for that, wanting to make it happen. Almost as much as I want you back in my bed."

She paused, touched. Nobody had ever worked to make her laugh before, worked to do nothing but please her and tempt her so outrageously. No one had ever treated her like she was special.

"I can't quite believe this is real. That you're real," she said.

He took her hand and pushed it against his chest, over his heart. It was pounding. "I'm very, very real. And I'm hot and sweaty and aching. I'm about half a second from throwing you over my shoulder, taking you into the other room and putting you down on the bed. Are you ready for that?"

He waited, must have seen the doubts in her eyes.

"Didn't think so," he said easily, shaking his head. "I'm going to get in the shower, Geri."

He peeled off his shirt right then and there, wiping at the sweat on his forehead with it, then balling it up in his hand. Then he stood still, all gleaming skin and muscle.

"Think about it," he said. "Make up your mind."

He turned around and headed for the bathroom. She stood there in the middle of his tiny cabin, wishing with all her heart that she could leave her entire messed-up life behind and be with him, be the kind of woman who could just stay with him and explore this potent attraction between them.

It would be totally irresponsible, and she'd never been irresponsible before. It was one in a long list of things she wanted to do for the very first time—with him.

"It's all your fault, Alex," she whispered, amazed at the strength of her feelings for him, her longing.

His bed was right in the next room. All she had to do was go and climb into it, be there waiting for him when he got out of the shower. He would take care of the rest. Guide her. Teach her. Take her.

It would be so good. She knew it.

To hell with guilt and duty and caution. She was so very tempted.

She waited there, her heart pounding, her body one constant, aching need. She was a woman, after all. Didn't all women find something like this at least once in their lives? A man who made no sense, a relationship that didn't, either? Someone they simply couldn't resist? Someone they knew would likely hurt them, but took them to the point where they simply didn't care anymore?

She didn't want to care. She just wanted him.

"Alex?" she said, looking up and finding him standing there dripping wet in nothing but a towel wrapped precariously around his trim hips.

"Hmm?" he replied, arching a brow.

"I do want you," she said bravely.

He smiled sinfully. "Tell me something I don't already know, Geri."

"You awful man!" she said, as he caught her close.

"I am. I admit it."

"I was trying to tell you I've made up my mind. About...us."

She blushed, and he smiled at her. "Good."

Her hands caught at the towel at his back. "You're going to lose this," she warned.

"Any minute," he said. "If I'm lucky."

She leaned forward, kissing his shoulder—wet, clean, fresh-smelling skin. "I can't believe I'm doing this."

"It'll be good between us, Geri. You know that."

She nodded, hoping she wouldn't disappoint him, feeling nervous and excited, almost giddy, now that she'd given in. She wanted him, and she was going to have him. She felt wonderfully free just admitting it to herself and to him.

"I want a shower, too," she said, needing a minute to catch her breath.

"Hurry," he told her.

She did, her body already tingling with an awareness that was almost painful now. It was going to be perfect. She could hardly wait another second. She climbed out of the shower and donned a pair of lacy panties and another of his shirts. This time, he would take it off her.

When she came back into the room, he had pulled out a laptop computer and was busy tapping away, concentrating on the screen. Feeling uneasy, as if stark-raving reality had just intruded into her perfect little fantasy world, she walked over to him. He slid an arm around her waist, just as he hit the send button on a message she hadn't had time to read.

"What was that?" she asked.

"I needed to get a message to my brother-in-law."

"Oh?" she said cautiously. If he was Alex Hathaway, he had a brother-in-law.

"I told you I was going to help you get away. I've got to say this one more time. I want to be absolutely clear, Geri. All I can give you is tonight. Right now. Tomorrow, you've got to go. It just isn't safe for you to be here with me. It wouldn't be fair of me to let you stay.''

"Okay," she said, not wanting to hear any of this and helpless to stop it.

"There are people after me. Dangerous people. I don't want you caught in the middle of it."

"Why are they after you?"

"Because they want something I have, and I can't let them have it."

"Why not?" she persisted.

"Because I can't. It wouldn't be right."

"Right?"

He nodded. "I'm sorry. The more I tell you, the more dangerous it is for you."

"You make it sound crazy, Alex. It sounds crazy."

"It is," he said grimly, taking her hand in his. "It's not too late for you to change your mind. About us. If you want, I can get you out of here tonight. We can leave right now."

She hesitated. "I don't…I don't know what I want. Except for all of this to go away. All of it."

"Believe me, babe, if I could wish it all away, I would. But I can't. I'm doing the best I can, here. This is all I have to offer you. You can stay with me tonight. I want to make love to you, about a dozen different ways. And you can leave tomorrow. Or you can go tonight. Either way, Mitch will be waiting."

He held on to her hand so patiently and waited for her to tell him what she'd decided. She sorted through the words, knowing there was something there she didn't like, something she absolutely hated, something that had her trembling with fear, with rage.

"'Mitch'?" she questioned.

He nodded. "My brother-in-law. He's a cop in Chicago. He's going to help you."

Geri froze. It was like stepping off a ledge on a fifty-story building and finding nothing but air beneath her feet, like suffocating in the midst of all that air, unable to save herself, unable to take it in.

She had so wanted to believe that somehow, he wasn't the man she'd thought. She'd been lying to herself so well. Almost as well as she'd been lying to everyone else, all through the years.

"You can trust me," Alex said, so convincingly.

If she'd had to deliver that same line, she couldn't have done it with nearly the sincerity he displayed. She'd never be able to paint such a convincing portrait of a woman so desperate, so needy for a man, as he'd seemed to be for her.

"Geri?" he prompted, worried.

"I'm fine," she lied, badly, she thought.

"You don't have to be afraid," he said. "You can trust Mitch, too. I wouldn't send you to him unless I was absolutely sure of that."

Geri nodded. It was all she could do.

Mitch. It couldn't be a coincidence.

Alexander Hathaway had a brother-in-law who was a Chicago cop, and his name was Mitch.

story building and finding nothing but air beneath her feet. Life suffocating in the night of all that air, unable to even breath, unable to ease it all.

She had so much to believe that somehow, he was a no-man she'd thought, she'd been lying to herself so well, almost as well as she'd been lying to everyone, she, all through the years.

You can trust me. A cry's such so convincingly.

She'd also understood that same that she couldn't have been down upon the silently be displayed, she'd never be able to regain some convincing portrait of a woman so draped and so needy, for a man, as she'd succumbed to be.

"I had," he wanted...

"In fact," she said, softly, she thought...

You don't have to be, but..." he said... "You can feel..."

Honey, I wouldn't want you to find it out later, I won't—

Chapter 7

She knew what she had to do. While he was busy shutting down his computer, she went back into the bathroom for a second to get something from her bag, then told him she needed a drink and offered to get him one, too.

Warm beer would do just as well as anything. She was a little uneasy about mixing the drug with alcohol, but it was just a sedative. No reason for her to feel guilty about anything.

After all, she knew who he was now. There could be no doubt. No more fooling herself. No more succumbing to this mind-numbing sexual heat he generated so expertly and aimed right at her. It had to be an act, she realized. A carefully practiced art of deception. If she'd known sex could be so potent a weapon, she would have made it a part of her arsenal years ago.

She popped open the tops of two beers, tipped a tiny capsule—packaged to look like an antihistamine—into one of them, then took a drink from the other and grimaced.

"You're right," she said, hearing Alex coming up behind her. "Warm beer is miserable."

"Mmm." His hands landed on either side of her waist. He leaned over and nuzzled her neck.

She shivered, stiffened, hating him, hating herself. Him for making her trust him and letting him see just a bit beneath the facade she presented to the world. For making her want him. And herself, for believing him.

"Nervous?" he asked.

"A little."

"We'll go slow," he said.

God, he was so good at this. Geri closed her eyes, telling herself one more time to play it out. There was nothing else she could do.

She turned around, dislodging herself from his hold, and handed him the beer. Somehow, she managed to look up at him and to smile. He took a long, deep drink from the bottle. She watched the rippling action of his throat as the liquid slid down, and she felt better. It wouldn't be long now.

She should probably lead him to the bed. She didn't want him to fall down when the drug kicked in. If he wasn't that far under, it would startle him. He might realize what she'd done and make trouble before the drug put him out completely. If he was already lying down, he'd just find himself feeling incredibly sleepy and soon, he'd be gone.

She could do her job and get the hell out of here. In time, she'd put him totally out of her mind, eradicate the touch of his hands and his mouth, the false kindness and concern. She could do that. She'd forgotten so many things over the years. Things she'd done. Things she'd been ordered to do. Sounds and sights and smells that might have haunted another person incessantly. Geri could push them all away, bury them so deep they'd never surface again, and one day soon, she'd do the same with the shooting and with him.

She looked up to find Alex eyeing her suspiciously. "You're worrying," he said.

"A little." She took a breath, letting the nerves show. They worked for her now.

This felt like the worst of betrayals to her—what he'd done to her. Any other time, she would have said he was simply doing what he had to do, as she always did herself—that it was about duty, orders, the way of the world in which she'd chosen to live. But it didn't feel like that with him. He'd made it personal, and she felt betrayed, felt a burning kind of anger that threatened to choke her.

She wanted to scream at him, to let him see that he'd hurt her, to demand some kind of explanation—which was so stupid. He wouldn't care how she felt or what he'd made her feel. It was stupid of her to think that he would, and she couldn't figure out when she'd turned into such a stupid woman.

Looking up at him, striving for a distance from the whole situation, she asked, "Could we just go into the bedroom?"

He arched a brow. "You sound like you're facing a firing squad, Geri. I swear, I'm much better than that."

She forced a half smile, took another drink of the beer, and he did, too. She needed to get at least half of it in him.

"It's been a long time," she said, "since I was with someone new."

He was still suspicious, and she felt like a mouse, with Alex, the big, hungry cat, toying with her. She wondered when he was going to make his move, wondered exactly what he wanted from her and why he'd let her stay here so long. Maybe he just wanted to bed her, to see if he could. Maybe it was some kind of game to him. Maybe he enjoyed it—the power, the danger. Maybe he got off on it. Maybe he was even more devious than she'd imagined.

"Geri?"

She took another drink. "I'll be fine. Really. I want to do this."

"You look like you'd rather have a tooth pulled, babe."

She laughed, the sound forced and strained. She took him by the hand and tugged him toward the bedroom. "Come on."

He came, somewhat reluctantly, and she watched as he took one more drink from his beer before setting it on the nightstand. That should do it. Ten minutes, tops, and she could relax. He'd be dead to the world.

Surely she could put him off for ten minutes, could put up with the feel of those big, hot hands of his on her body and his mouth on hers for ten lousy minutes. She could do anything. It was her job, and until recently, she'd done it very well.

Geri sat down on the side of the bed and looked up at him warily, as he stood there in nothing but a towel. He really was a beautiful man—amazingly, deceptively beautiful—and he managed to look so open, so honest, seeming to take such absolute delight in life itself. She'd thought she was such a chameleon, so talented at putting on whole different personas. But this man was brilliant at it, a true master of the game.

He reached for the hem of her shirt and, when she didn't make a sound of protest, slowly drew it over her head, a lazy smile spreading across his lips, a languid heat coming into his eyes. Geri fought the urge to fold her arms across her chest. She could feel his hungry gaze on her breasts. They seemed to swell and tighten from nothing more than the look on his face.

He extended a hand to touch her, then stopped abruptly as his thumb brushed across the scar tissue high on her right shoulder, just below the collarbone, where the bullet had driven into her skin. It was a full two inches from the worst of the scrapes and scratches she'd gotten in the fight at the bar, and he'd never completely undressed her that first night. Still, he seemed surprised he'd missed this.

"Dammit, Geri," he said, as if it hurt him, as well. "What did he do to you?"

He? It might as well have been Alex who'd pulled the trigger.

Now it was Alex who leaned down, settling his warm mouth over the scar, kissing her there.

Geri couldn't help it. She pushed him away. "Don't," she said. "Not now. I don't want to think about that now."

"Okay," he said softly, gently. "We won't. Not now."

She held herself absolutely still as he resumed his teasing, hypnotic touch, stroking her arm with the back of his hand, then her collarbone, her neck, her jaw, all the while watching her so intently. What did he think he was going to see? she wondered. She'd shown him more than she'd ever shown anyone. Shown him vulnerability and loneliness and doubts. He'd acted as if he cared, damn him.

He touched her breast then, and she closed her eyes, trying to analyze the touch with the detachment necessary for her to get through this. How could it possibly feel good to her? To have him do nothing but stroke her breast that way? Even if the touch was slow and soft, deceptively tender, it was still *his* hand, *his* fingertips. And she knew what he was now. What he'd done.

Her mind couldn't possibly welcome his touch, but somehow, her body did.

Maybe she was just lonely, she thought. Maybe it had been so long since anyone had touched her or kissed her, she could be with the devil himself and like it.

He took his thumb and ran it back and forth across her nipple, encircled it, teasing her, until she could hardly breathe. His hands were hot and gentle and so very patient. Her skin was on fire, wanting those hands everywhere, wanting him. Alex, the liar. The thief. The traitor.

She felt him shift in front of her, had maybe half a second of warning, of hot breath against her breast, before his hand and his fingertips were replaced by his mouth and his tongue.

She gasped, unable to help herself, and he steadied her with his hands, holding her easily and gently. The touch of his mouth was electrifying, running through her like a current. She felt the physical sensations so vividly. And just as vividly, she felt the emotional firestorm of wanting him, hating him, hating herself, hating all the lies.

"Alex?" she said, tears seeping out of the corners of her eyes and running down her cheeks.

"Hmm?" he murmured, without lifting his head from her breast.

He was laving her with his tongue. She didn't think it was possible to be this aroused from one simple caress. If she made it out of here alive, she was going to have to explore this neglected side of her life. She'd find some other man, some skillful, patient lover, to teach her all about this. Surely it would be even better with someone she didn't despise, as she ought to despise him.

She cried for the man he'd pretended to be, the one she wanted to run away with on the back of the bike and never stop. The one who wasn't Alexander Hathaway, traitor, murderer, but Alex the smiling, laughing man. She was crying for someone he could never be, for something they would never have together.

He'd finished tormenting her breast, was working his way up the side of her neck, burying his head in the sensitive knot of nerves there at the base. He brought her fully into his embrace, and she realized he'd lost his towel somewhere along the way, that he was naked, and she might as well be. She felt the muscles of his thighs shifting against hers. Her naked breasts were buried against his chest. His mouth came up to hers, his hands to either side of her face, and that was when he found the tears.

He pulled backed instantly, capturing her face in his hands. "What is it? What's wrong?"

She tried to calculate how many minutes had gone by, how much more of this she had to endure, but she'd lost track of time and she lied to him once more. "I'm thinking too much."

"About what?" he asked, painting a very credible picture of a patient, considerate man.

"Everything," she said. "I can't help it."

"We'll stop," he offered, his breathing heavy and laden. But he gestured toward the bed and said, "We'll just lie here. I'll hold you, and you can tell me about all these things you can't stop thinking about."

She tilted her head to the side and studied his face—his beautiful, lying face. No wonder he'd gotten away with all that he had so far, she thought. He was so good at it—at lying, at convincing people he was something he was not.

"Come on," he said. "Lie back."

She did, and he drew the thin sheet over her, then climbed into the bed beside her, pulling her into his arms. Her head rested on his shoulder, his arms were around her, and she tried not to think of the intimate way they were still touching, bare skin to gloriously bare skin. He rolled her on top of him, into an even more intimate position. Her legs were tangled with his, and she could feel his arousal, so big and so hard, between them. But he didn't try to push himself upon her. Instead, he merely rubbed at the tension in her back and shoulders.

It was useless, she wanted to tell him. There was no way she could relax at this moment, and the last thing she wanted was fake kindness, false concern.

She still wanted to scream at him, to demand answers, to make him account for all he'd done and all he still planned to do. To make him sorry. Was it possible for someone like him to be sorry for anything he'd done? Sorry about anyone he'd hurt? He'd probably laugh at her if she so much as asked, laugh at her for believing in him and his little games. He had no conscience, she reminded herself. No feelings. He obviously used his body as easily as he used his mind—anything to get what he wanted, what he needed.

She hated it. All of it. When this assignment was over, she was done. She was getting out, salvaging what she could of her life and moving on. She'd start over. She'd forget.

Alex and his magic hands, his lying eyes, his false concern.

"I hate this," she said, never intending to speak the words aloud.

He shifted again, until she was lying on her back, and he was leaning over her, staring with hard, glittering eyes. "What's going on here, Geri? If you don't want to be here with me, all you have to do is say so. I told you I won't force myself on you."

"I know," she said. "I'm sorry. I can't do this."

"You won't let yourself," he insisted. "Your body says one thing, but that head of yours is determined to say something else entirely. Why is that?"

"I don't know," she lied.

He shook his head, then blinked, as if to clear his vision. "Damn, I'm tired," he said, a slight slur to the words. "And I don't think I'll ever understand you. No matter how hard I try."

He looked down at her, breathing hard, fighting the sedative. Geri pushed him onto his back, and again he pulled her along with him, his hands playing lazily on her spine, still stroking, still gentle. She felt all the muscles in his body slowly relax, saw nothing but a brief flicker of alarm in his eyes. And then he was gone, utterly still, sinking into unconsciousness.

She waited for one full minute, counting off the seconds in her head. She'd made so many mistakes already, she couldn't afford any others.

Without letting herself so much as look at him, without letting herself think, she climbed out of the bed, pulled on her shirt and checked Alex's bottle of beer. It was more than half gone. She calculated she had about six hours before she had to worry about him coming to.

Determined to see this through without any more screw-ups, she went to the other room, to his computer, and booted it up. She searched methodically, if hurriedly, through his hard drive and all the CD-ROMs in the case by the computer, finding games. All sorts of computer games. It was a virtual video-game heaven, about blowing things up, shooting things, playing spy.

She frowned at the irony of that. Alex always seemed to be playing. He never seemed to take anything seriously.

She didn't find anything that looked remotely like work, like any kind of research, any chemical formula. There were no hidden files that she could detect. She clicked on the communications software. She tried to find the e-mail he'd supposedly sent to his brother-in-law, but couldn't even access that. It was password protected, and though there was equipment that could have figured out his password, she hadn't brought any with her. Her superiors had felt it was too great a risk to take at this point.

They could have come charging in here with guns drawn, ready to take him in, but they didn't just want him; they wanted the formula. Geri didn't think there was any way he'd have cut a deal to sell it yet or that he'd delivered it. So if it was here, she would find it. If not, they'd begin less subtle tactics—probably tomorrow, as soon as she was out of here. She would take a great deal of satisfaction from seeing him brought down.

Geri continued to fight her way through his computer for

nearly four hours and found nothing. She'd been warned he was very, very good at what he did, and that computers were his hobby. But she was good, too, and this was still the most frustrating computer she'd ever had the misfortune to tangle with.

It was nearly three o'clock in the morning before she gave up, knowing her time was running out. She went to work over the cabin, methodically going through everything—every drawer, every corner, even the bedroom while he slept. He had about five thousand dollars in cash, a gun and several extra clips of ammunition—nothing else that seemed at all significant. Close to four o'clock, she went outside to check the bike, again finding nothing. He'd disabled it yesterday. She'd noticed him putting it back together before they went on their little ride. He hadn't bothered to disable it afterward. She didn't want to think about what had been on his mind then.

Standing outside in the pleasantly cool night, she wrapped her arms around her waist and stared up at the stars, a brilliant blaze of light. She was exhausted and angry and felt like an absolute failure. There was nothing here, no clue as to where he might have stashed that formula. Unless it was on his computer, hidden somewhere. Maybe he had part of it—the part he was still working on. But he wouldn't keep the whole thing here. It was too valuable. It left him too vulnerable, as well, if someone could come here, grab him and get the complete formula. So where would he hide it?

They hadn't found anything he owned—no house, no boat, no safe deposit box, no rented storage unit—nothing. They'd been watching his entire family ever since he'd disappeared, and he hadn't sent them anything. They'd been watching his friends. Nothing. So where was it?

Disgusted, Geri turned to go back inside when she had an odd sense that something wasn't right. Instincts, honed over the years, led her to turn around slowly, her eyes scanning the area as far as she could see. She caught a glimpse of something out of the corner of her eye, something far-off and indistinguishable at this distance. But something. Something moving, she realized, crouching down instinctively behind the bike.

What the hell was it? There was nothing out here. No sound. No people. No cars. Nothing close to the cabin at all.

Geri waited, unmoving, for five full minutes before she saw something moving again. *Someone* coming toward the cabin.

Her heart started pounding, adrenaline rushing in. Someone was coming for them? For Alex? She stayed where she was for a minute, staring, needing to be sure.

This couldn't be anyone Geri worked with. The mission parameters had been absolutely clear. The plan was for her to be in and out in twenty-four hours, but they'd given her forty-eight, just in case, before anyone would make a move on the cabin. Forty-eight hours with an absolute communications blackout. They weren't taking any chances on this one. No one would make a move to help her, to get her out, either, until forty-eight hours had passed. Whoever this was, he wasn't from Division One.

"Damn," Geri muttered.

There were only about a half-dozen other terrorist groups after what Alex had. Just her luck, one of them had finally found him.

She took one more look into the dark night, crept around the cabin to search from all angles. There were two of them, she decided—moving cautiously, slowly. She didn't think they'd detected her presence outside.

Slipping back inside, she thought about simply trying to pick them off as they moved close. But all she had was a .45, and they were sure to have something much more deadly, with greater range. She'd checked earlier—Alex didn't have a silencer—so she couldn't count on the element of surprise. She could wait for them to slip into the cabin and try to take them out, one by one, but it was risky. She'd rather pick her time and her place to confront them, not leave everything up to them.

And loathsome as the thought of protecting Alex Hathaway was, she had to keep him alive, at least until she figured out what he'd done with the formula. Geri swore at the irony of it—protecting Alex—when she'd toyed with the idea of coming here and killing him outright.

She went back to the bedroom, saw him lying there on the bed, unconscious, helpless. She thought about taking the laptop and the gun and leaving him here to face them alone. She might be able to slip away undetected, and there had to be something in that computer to tell them where he'd hidden the formula.

Do it, she thought. Leave him here, as vulnerable as a baby. Let them kill him, torture him, tear him limb from limb. No one would ever be able to pin his death on her. All she had to do was leave him this way. It was tantamount to signing his death warrant. Disgusted, Geri found that she couldn't. She didn't even want to think of the reasons why.

Cursing even more viciously than before, she looked at the clock. A little more than five hours had passed since she'd slipped him the tranquillizer. Somehow, she had to wake him up, fast. She'd have to deal with whatever happened next. He was likely to be furious, once he could think clearly, and she had to get him to cooperate, to trust her—that was a laugh—at least long enough for them to get out of here.

Geri went to the bed and shook him firmly by the shoulders. Bleary-eyed, he looked at her, his pupils slowly focusing on her.

"Alex, get up," she said firmly, shaking him some more.

"What?" His speech was slurred, and his hand reached for his head, as if he weren't quite sure it was still attached to his body.

"Listen to me," she said. "Someone's outside. They're heading this way, and we've got to get out of here. Do you understand what I'm telling you?"

"What?" He was still out of it.

She slapped him hard across the face, finding it moderately satisfying. He blinked twice, then seemed a bit more alert.

"Alex, I mean it. We don't have much time. They'll be here soon. They'll kill us, if we don't get out of here. Now get up."

He propped himself up on his elbows, swung his legs over the side of the bed, and she pulled him up the rest of the way. The sheet fell to his waist, and she realized he was still naked, and she was wearing nothing but a shirt and panties. One more thing they had to take care of quickly.

"Where are your clothes?" she asked. Then she remembered. She'd searched the entire cabin, after all. She found him a pair of pants and a shirt, some socks and his shoes, and threw them at him. "Get dressed."

He was wavering back and forth as he sat there staring at her.

It was hopeless, she decided, itching to check the progress of the men making their way toward the cabin. She hurried into her own clothes and shoes, collected his gun and ammunition, then grabbed the keys to the motorcycle. If they managed to eliminate the two men closing in on them, they'd need a way to get out of here quickly, in case the two had backup. That done, Geri checked the windows. There they were. Both of them. Still coming closer, but still moving slowly.

She went to grab her own bag from the bathroom, wanting the sophisticated tracking device inside it, and when she turned back around, Alex was standing in the doorway, leaning weakly against the frame, a gun in his none-too-steady hand, pointed directly at her.

Where the hell had he gotten that gun? She still had his tucked into the waistband of her shorts.

"Who are you?" he demanded.

Her chin came up. Of all the times to argue, this was not it. "Does it matter right now? There are some men on their way here. Right now. Look outside if you don't believe me."

"Believe you?" He laughed. "That's rich."

"Okay, so neither one of us is a model of virtue. It doesn't matter right now, Alex. We're going to die, and soon, if we don't find a way out of here."

"You drugged me," he said, like he still couldn't believe it.

"Yes, I did," she admitted. "Could we argue about this later?"

"Give me my other gun," he ordered.

Geri hesitated, knowing she could likely draw her weapon and beat him to the trigger. Much as she'd longed to shoot him earlier, she couldn't do it now. It would tip off the men outside, and she needed all the advantage she could get.

"The gun, Geri."

"Alex, you don't want me to do that."

"I don't?" He laughed for a second before his jaw clenched hard with resolve and his finger squeezed back a fraction on the trigger. "Give it to me."

Geri did. He'd just about convinced her he'd shoot her.

"Who do you work for?" he asked.

"The United States of America. Forgive me, I don't have my ID on me."

"The good old U.S. of A. got me into this damned mess," he complained.

"You got yourself into this, you bastard," she hissed, hating him, absolutely hating him, and finding out too late that she had a burning desire to live a little longer at least. She wanted the satisfaction of seeing him punished.

They probably would have gone another round or two, but there was a sound from outside the cabin—a tiny, nearly imperceptible sound—from the front porch, she guessed. *Damn.*

"I told you. We can't afford to fight with each other right now, Alex. Later, I promise you, I'd love to have it out with you. But not now."

He hesitated, still holding his gun on her.

"Somebody's going to come creeping through the front door any minute now. Somebody else is probably standing outside that window behind your head. If you want to die, just keep doing what you're doing. If you don't, give the gun back to me."

Chapter 8

Alex couldn't think. It was as if a thick, blanketing fog had invaded his own head, and he had to think his way through it. He shook his head in a vain attempt to clear it and stared down at the woman who'd so absolutely betrayed him. He could still hardly believe it.

She'd drugged him. That was why he couldn't think. Because she'd drugged him. She'd lied to him and used him and now she was probably going to kill him.

"Give me the gun, Alex," she whispered.

"Why the hell would I give you a weapon?"

"Because I'm not the one on the edge of a drug-induced haze right now, and I'm a damned good shot. From all I've read about you, you're a lousy shot stone-cold sober."

He swore, because it was true. All of it.

"Alex," she said. "If I wanted you dead, you would be. Believe me, I've had plenty of chances."

He swore viciously. In this entire mess, no one's betrayal had hurt the way hers did. He'd fallen asleep holding her in his arms, making love to her, and woken up to the knowledge that everything she'd said to him had been a lie.

Alex thought he heard something else from outside—a muffled curse, perhaps. He'd strung a crude booby trap around the cabin, thinking that if anyone tried to sneak up on him at night, he might at least hear about it first. Evidently it was working. And they had to be close.

He looked up and saw two blurry images of Geri floating toward each other, blinked to clear his vision, to no avail. "What the hell did you give me?"

She named a substance he recognized.

He swore again. "How much?"

"Maybe four CCs. Alex, give me the damned gun."

He handed her one, because he couldn't even calculate the effect of four CCs of that drug on someone of his body weight and had no idea how long it had been in his system. Because he couldn't even see straight, and as she'd so sweetly pointed out, if she wanted to kill him, she'd had all night to do it.

It happened fast after that. They barely picked up the sound of footsteps on the porch, the door creaking open. Geri shoved him behind her, aimed and fired. The intruder's gun fired as he went down, the bullet zipping past her right ear and Alex's. Alex swore. She didn't even blink, just kept her gun trained on the fallen man, cool as could be.

Evidently he'd hooked up with a real pro.

Geri made her way over to the intruder, checked for a pulse, then pocketed her own weapon in favor of his, a wicked-looking little submachine gun. She cleaned the body of spare ammunition, as well, her face a carefully blank mask when she turned around.

He didn't even know her, he realized. He had no idea who she was. He started to say something, but she held up a hand to stop him and motioned toward the door. They waited for what seemed like forever, crouched in the corner behind cover that was dubious at best. She didn't even seem to breathe, her gaze never wavering, her patience finally rewarded.

The door inched open once again, a gunman clad entirely in black slipped inside, and she nailed him, too. He collapsed onto the floor, and Alex watched as she quickly disarmed the man, then searched both bodies thoroughly.

She tossed Alex a wallet she'd taken from one man. He flipped it open to what seemed to be a government-issued ID. "'Border Patrol'?"

She shrugged. "They're fake, but they might come in handy before the night's over. You might pass for that one in a pinch. We don't exactly have a lot of resources to work with, here. We'll have to take what we can get."

"'We'?" he asked.

She nodded. "Want to stay alive until morning?"

"That's one of the best invitations I've had in days," he quipped.

"We can't fight them and fight each other," she said.

"'Them'? You just killed them."

"Two of them. We don't know how many more there might be. We need to get out of here, Dr. Hathaway. Do you want to fight with me or do you want to make a run for it?"

He glanced down at the dead bodies on the floor, at the submachine gun in her hand, at the blank face of a woman he'd held and kissed and nearly made love to in what seemed another lifetime.

"God, this has got to be nightmare," he said. But the effects of the drug were receding, and there was no mistaking the sight of two dead bodies in his cabin or the look on her face.

"Your choice," she said. "Stay or go? Live or die?"

He arched a brow. "And *you're* not going to kill me?"

"Don't tempt me."

She hated him, he realized. This sweet, lost, vulnerable

woman was one of the best liars he'd ever seen, and she hated him. Or she hated who she thought he was, hated what she'd been told about him. He wondered who she really worked for and where she was going to take him. Months on the run, and he'd never thought somebody like her would be the one to bring him down.

Of course, it was his own damned fault. He'd fallen for her act—every little whimper, every tear, every shudder, every bruise.

"God, you're good at this," he said.

Her head came up, hatred flaring in her eyes.

Alex shrugged as easily as he could manage. "Hey, it was a compliment."

She brought the nose of the gun to the center of his chest, murder in her eyes. "Don't."

"All right." Alex dared to smile. "I've made up my mind. I'll live for the moment. Let's get the hell out of here."

They took a quick look outside at her insistence, but didn't see anything. He glanced at the time and saw that they had an hour or so before dawn. She checked over the dead men lying on the floor once more, slowly, and pulled something out of one of their pockets that had her staring.

"What's that?" he asked.

"Probably nothing," she said.

But she was absolutely still, all color gone from her face. It was the first crack in her composure he'd seen. Maybe the lady was human after all.

"We need to go," she said, all starch and polish once again. "Get dressed."

He did so hurriedly, and they threw some things into her leather bag—clothes, guns, ammunition, his laptop, his cash and hers, some food, some bottled water. She looked at him questioningly.

"Believe me," he said, "I've thought a lot about how I'd

clear out of here if I had to. We're going cross-country, where there are no roads. Unless you have a better plan?''

"I just want out. Now."

"Give me a second," he said, going to the propane tank. She followed him. "What are you doing?"

"I told you, I've thought a lot about leaving. The bike makes a lot of noise. We'll just call this a diversion. Plus we've got bodies in here. There won't be much left of them when this thing blows. Let whoever's out there wonder if the explosion got us. Maybe that'll slow 'em down long enough for us to get away."

He opened a valve, and gas started to hiss from the tank. Geri swore and looked at him suspiciously.

"Hey," he said. "You're great with a gun? I'm fabulous with explosives. Let's go."

They jumped on the bike. She didn't want to let him drive, but he assured her the gunfire and all the blood had cleared his head like nothing else could have. He might have added one more thing—the betrayal. *Hers.* But the damned cabin was about to blow. The way he felt about her would keep.

He gunned the engine. Twenty seconds later, the sky exploded like it was the Fourth of July and the cabin blew up in a thousand pieces. They looked over their shoulders, watching as best they could for a few moments, then settled in for the long haul over the flat, colorless, deserted land, her traitorous little body once again plastered against his.

Nothing like a motorcycle ride, Alex thought.

For all the drama of its beginning, the ride was relatively uneventful. They headed north, skirting around Lubbock and Amarillo, then crossing into New Mexico. It had been a long, hot, exhausting flight. There were several times when they thought they were being followed, but so far, no one had come too close.

Finally, around dusk, thinking they'd made good their escape, they agreed to stop for the night. They found a tired-looking motel near Tucumcari, New Mexico, the kind of place that took cash and didn't ask for credit cards or ID. They picked up some fast food before they checked in, then faced each other across the room, two tired, hot, hungry, bloodthirsty combatants.

"What do you say we save the fight for after dinner and after we've had a chance to clean up?" Alex suggested.

Geri, her face still that carefully sculpted mask, eyed him warily.

"I'm starving," he said. "I'm tired. I'd kill for a cold shower. You can sit outside the bathroom door with your machine gun, if it makes you feel better."

"You think this is funny?" she retorted, glaring at him.

"No, and I'm too tired to fight with you. If you want to shoot me, do it now. Otherwise, I'm taking a shower."

He grabbed the duffel bag.

She stopped him. "Not the computer."

"Fine. Keep it," he said easily, confident that she hadn't found what she was looking for in it. If she had, he wouldn't still be alive.

Alex grabbed a change of clothes and went into the bathroom. He stripped and climbed under the weak spray of icy-cold water. He put a hand on either side of the shower fixture and leaned into the water, face first, needing to clear his head. He didn't know if it was the mind-numbing ride or the residual effects of the drug, but he still couldn't seem to think straight. Maybe it was his life, he decided. His life was too bizarre to contemplate at this point.

And Geri... *God,* Geri.

He hadn't let anyone near him in months, hadn't trusted anyone, hadn't dropped his guard in the least. Until her.

Alex took a deep breath, shaking his head. He couldn't think about her. It made him too angry—at his own stupidity, at her duplicity. And if he was too angry, he couldn't think about how he was going to get out of this. And he had to get out of this.

Alex picked up the soap and washed, then shut off the shower and reached for a towel. He dressed quickly, hesitating for only a moment in a twinge of conscience he couldn't afford, one he fought off as he remembered everything. He didn't really know her, after all. He might have thought he did, might have thought she cared, but he'd been dead wrong. *Nearly dead wrong,* he amended. He still might die if he wasn't very careful and very lucky.

In his tenuous position, people were either with him or against him. There was no in-between, seldom room for mistakes. He'd already made too damned many with her. Alex pushed aside any stray feelings of guilt he might have and took a minute to do what he had to do. She wouldn't hesitate, he reminded himself. She wouldn't have her conscience nagging her.

He was toweling his hair dry when he stepped out of the bathroom a moment later. He found her standing by the door, checking out one of the wicked-looking weapons she'd taken from the intruders at the cabin.

"It's all yours," he said, nodding toward the bathroom.

She hesitated.

He forced a smile across his face, a teasing manner that was hard to come by, and whistled. "You know you want to, Geri. Wash off the grime. Clear your head. We can have a truce for another five minutes, can't we?"

"A truce? Like two kids playing some game? That's all it is to you, isn't it? A game."

He shrugged. "I like games. But I have to say, this one hasn't been much fun lately. I'm getting tired of it."

"You could always turn yourself in," she suggested. "You and your little bomb recipe."

He cursed, already tired of the whole conversation. "I'm hungry, Geri. I'm tired. I'm going to eat."

He sat down on one of the beds, gulped down two burgers, some cold fries and a cola, remembering too late her penchant for drugging people. Oh, well. As she'd so sweetly pointed out, if she'd wanted him dead, he'd be dead by now.

He polished off his meal and looked up into the face of his enemy. She fought off a yawn, her eyelids drooping. If she'd gone to the trouble of drugging him last night, she must have spent the whole time searching his computer and the cabin. She wouldn't have gotten any sleep at all. She'd have to collapse sooner or later. Sleep was one of those things the human body could do without for only so long. He could have waited, his conscience pointed out, rather than have left that little surprise for her in the bathroom.

Thinking of that, he had to get her into the bathroom. "Go ahead," he said. "Hop in the shower. I'll be good."

"I'm not turning my back on you for a minute."

"I could come in with you, if that would make you more comfortable," he offered.

She blanched.

"It's not like you've got anything I haven't already seen," he said. "Not a lot I haven't touched, either. So what's the problem?"

"I despise you," she declared.

"Maybe you do, but your body has some ideas of its own where I'm concerned."

Alex grinned, because it was the first time all day she'd looked human. He'd found a weak spot. God knew, she probably didn't have many of those. He bit back his own fury at the entire situation—especially at her—and took one menacing step toward her. She raised the barrel of the weapon, dead center to his chest.

"You can't shoot me," he said. "You haven't found what you were looking for, and if I'm dead, you won't ever find it."

"We'll find it," she boasted.

He laughed. "Think about it, Geri. I'm a genius. I've had months to plan for the likelihood that someone would find me and take me in. You think I'm not ready for this? You think I haven't done all I possibly can to save my own neck? You've got to have me. Otherwise, you'll never have those explosives."

"How do you live with yourself?" she asked.

He was in no mood for this, and he let loose, lashing right back at her. "How do you live with yourself? How do you pull that trigger and watch somebody fall? Strip the body of anything of value and then take off? Even if they are scum, how do you do that?"

She paled a bit, but her chin came up, and she pointed the gun at him again. "Years of practice. What about you?"

"Me?" He shook his head back and forth. Was it so easy for everyone to believe he was evil? Selfish? Money hungry? That he was a killer? Was it so damned easy for *her* to believe? That was the worst part of all. That she believed it so easily.

"I haven't killed anybody," he said.

She scoffed at that.

"I haven't," Alex repeated, going with the anger. It was much safer than anything else he might feel at the moment. "Believe me, with you, I'm tempted, too. But so far, I've managed to resist."

"The guard," she said. "Remember? The night you disappeared? Surely you remember the guard. You had to step over his body to get out. You left him lying there bleeding to death when you took off."

"I didn't kill that guard."

She sounded outraged, purely outraged. "We found the gun, Doctor. The one you shot him with. Your prints were all over it."

He folded his arms across his chest. "So you really are with the government?"

"I really am."

"Forgive me if that doesn't exactly reassure me."

"I don't give a damn how that makes you feel, but that man you killed? He had a name. Doc. And he happened to be a friend of mine."

"Really?" he retorted, telling himself not to believe anything she said.

"Yes," she said, murder in her eyes.

Alex reminded himself that it was indeed a dangerous, deadly game; that he didn't know her; that he shouldn't care and still found himself trying to explain. "Look, I'm sorry about what happened to your friend. But I didn't kill him. He was already dead when I took off."

"Fingerprints," she said. "Yours were on the weapon. The ballistics report said the bullet that killed him came from your gun."

"And I suppose you believe everything a ballistics report says? Everything a fingerprint expert says? Everything whatever agency you work for tells you? Do you still believe all that, Geri?"

"More than anything a crook like you tells me."

"I guess I can't blame you for that," he said. "I used to think like that, too. I just don't anymore."

"So you're telling me what? That somebody double-crossed you? That this is all some misunderstanding, and you haven't done anything wrong?"

"Would you believe me if I did?"

"No."

"Then I'll save my breath," he said. "You want a shower?"

"Do you want me to get in the shower? You want me to turn my back on you? Do you think I'm that stupid?"

"I thought it might help that sour little temper of yours," he replied, needling her. After all, he had an agenda here. He couldn't forget that.

PLAY...

"ROLL A DOUBLE!"

NO RISK, NO OBLIGATION TO BUY...NOW OR EVER!

GUARANTEED

PLAY "ROLL A DOUBLE"
AND YOU GET FREE GIFTS!
HERE'S HOW TO PLAY:

1. Peel off label from front cover. Place it in space provided at right. With a coin, carefully scratch off the silver dice. Then check the claim chart to see what we have for you – TWO FREE BOOKS and a mystery gift – ALL YOURS! ALL FREE!

2. Send back this card and you'll receive brand-new Silhouette Intimate Moments® novels. These books have a cover price of $4.25 each in the U.S. and $4.75 each in Canada, but they are yours to keep absolutely free.

3. There's no catch. You're under no obligation to buy anything. We charge nothing – ZERO – for your first shipment. And you don't have to make any minimum number of purchases – not even one!

4. The fact is, thousands of readers enjoy receiving books by mail from the Silhouette Reader Service™. They like the convenience of home delivery...they like getting the best new novels BEFORE they're available in stores...and they love our discount prices!

5. We hope that after receiving your free books you'll want to remain a subscriber. But the choice is yours – to continue or cancel any time at all! So why not take us up on our invitation, with no risk of any kind. You'll be glad you did!

The Silhouette Reader Service™ — Here's how it works:

Accepting your 2 free books and mystery gift places you under no obligation to buy anything. You may keep the books and gift and return the shipping statement marked "cancel." If you do not cancel, about a month later we'll send you 6 additional novels and bill you just $3.57 each in the U.S., or $3.96 each in Canada, plus 25¢ delivery per book and applicable taxes if any.* That's the complete price and — compared to the cover price of $4.25 in the U.S. and $4.75 in Canada — it's quite a bargain! You may cancel at any time, but if you choose to continue, every month we'll send you 6 more books, which you may either purchase at the discount price or return to us and cancel your subscription.

*Terms and prices subject to change without notice. Sales tax applicable in N.Y. Canadian residents will be charged applicable provincial taxes and GST.

If offer card is missing write to: Silhouette Reader Service, 3010 Walden Ave., P.O. Box 1867, Buffalo NY 14240-1867

BUSINESS REPLY MAIL

FIRST-CLASS MAIL   PERMIT NO. 717   BUFFALO, NY

POSTAGE WILL BE PAID BY ADDRESSEE

SILHOUETTE READER SERVICE
3010 WALDEN AVE
PO BOX 1867
BUFFALO NY 14240-9952

NO POSTAGE
NECESSARY
IF MAILED
IN THE
UNITED STATES

"I could kill you," she said. "I really could."

Alex shook his head, itching for a fight. She hated him, and he'd make it work for him. "You can't do that," he said. "You have orders. I'll bet you're somebody who's followed the rules your whole life. Was Daddy really a general? Was any of that true?"

She said something vile.

He grinned back. Quite pleased with himself, he decided he'd never seen a woman this mad. He was ready to press his advantage when her attention shifted from him to the door.

"What?" he asked. He hadn't heard a thing.

She brushed past him, intent on getting to the door, or so he thought. The next second he felt something close around his wrist, heard a click of metal.

Alex looked down and found himself handcuffed to a metal bar on the wall—the one the TV was bolted to. *Well, hell.*

Geri slipped away from him with a smile and said, "You know, I think I will have that shower now."

She was still fuming when she got into the shower, although the water was cold enough that she nearly screamed in outrage. He was the most arrogant, insufferable man she'd ever met. The lying, scheming snake had her close to committing out-and-out murder. No, she thought, justifiable homicide. He deserved it.

She quickly washed off the worst of the grime of the road, soaped her hair, fatigue dogging her. She was tired, and she couldn't trust those handcuffs she'd taken from the alleged Border Patrol agent. Which meant she had to go back out there and face him. Had to decide what to do.

She should have stopped somewhere today and called in, had someone come haul Alex away. She could have been back in D.C. by now, debriefed and having the satisfaction of knowing he was behind bars, that he would be there for a long, long time. But something had stopped her. Something about those two men who'd broken into the cabin. Something she'd found on one of the two she'd killed.

Geri shut off the shower, quickly toweled off and dressed in a pair of shorts and one of Alex's shirts. She couldn't take those little, bitty tops a minute longer. A no-nonsense T-shirt was infinitely preferable to that, even if the shirt did belong to him.

She opened the bathroom door, finding him sitting on the waist-high dresser beside the TV. He smiled and waved, obligingly holding up his hand to show that he was still cuffed, right there where she'd left him.

Satisfied he wasn't going anywhere at the moment, Geri closed the door again and pulled from her pocket the tracking device she'd taken from one of the bodies at the cabin. It looked like a beeper, like something thousands of other people wore strapped to their belts or inside a shirt pocket. But it was actually a very sophisticated piece of communications equipment.

She'd disabled it earlier; she knew exactly how, because she often carried one of these herself. The gadget masters at Division One had designed it two years ago, and it functioned as a pager, a communications unit and a very sophisticated tracking device.

And as far as she knew, the only people who'd ever used them were Division One agents.

So how had this one come to be on one of the bodies at the cabin? How had it been set to hone in on the coordinates of the tiny tracking device she carried in her bag? Why would those men be tracking *her?*

She didn't pretend to know that she was acquainted with everyone who worked inside the top-secret agency known as Division One. But they didn't go around killing each other, and those two men who had slipped into the cabin earlier had been more than willing to kill her. She knew it. She'd seen the look on their faces in that instant before she'd pulled the trigger.

No one she worked for would have sent them in without a warning to her. If the mission plan was being thrown out and agents were coming in, she would have been warned. Her comm unit would have alerted her.

It hadn't, and they'd come charging in, willing and able to kill her.

That didn't make any sense. Unless someone had decided her life was expendable. That things had gotten so completely out of control, the man in the next room had to be taken at any cost, including her life. She didn't pretend to believe that people's lives weren't sacrificed along the way, but she had a little trouble swallowing the fact that she'd almost lost hers. That after all she'd been through, all she'd done for her country, she'd be discarded like this.

Something was wrong, she decided. And until she was satisfied that she knew exactly what it was, she and the mad scientist in the next room weren't going anywhere.

She was stuck with him.

He waited as innocent as a lamb while she came out of the bathroom and sat down on the edge of the bed, eyeing him warily.

"We're going to have to come to an agreement," she said.

"Mmm." He nodded. "Where'd you get the cuffs?"

"From our friends with the Border Patrol."

Alex just smiled, as if he didn't have a care in the world. She was starting to wonder if he did, if there could be some mental imbalance that let him live a guilt-free, worry-free existence.

"Hey," he said. "What's that? You almost smiled. What were you thinking?"

"I was wondering about your mental state, actually. Are you on any medication, Doctor?"

"Just an occasional antihistamine," he quipped.

She glared at him.

"That's where it was, right? You had some in your bag. In those little foil medical packets labeled Antihistamine."

Geri didn't acknowledge that in any way.

"That was good," he said admiringly. "I never suspected a thing."

Geri's mouth twitched. She couldn't help it.

"What?" he asked. "Tell me. I could use a laugh."

"I was thinking that handcuffs probably aren't sufficient," she admitted. "A gag might be in order."

Alex laughed, long and loud, not one of those short, cynical bursts from before. He really didn't give a damn about anything, she decided. Not if he could laugh like that in a predicament like this.

"Geri?" he said.

"Hmm?"

"I didn't shoot your friend. And until three and a half months ago, the only gun I'd ever held in my hand came from a man who took me target practicing and gave me my first lesson in handguns. Know where we were?"

"Don't know, and I don't care."

He named an air-force base near D.C., where he'd been held for a month or so before being taken to the safe house inside a seemingly deserted warehouse she and Dan had been guarding the night he'd disappeared.

"It was a .45," Alex said. "Would have had my prints all over it."

"Really?"

He nodded. "What was your friend shot with?"

"A .45," she replied. "Which anyone who's read the newspapers would know."

"Know who put that gun into my hands? Who decided I needed to know something about defending myself, just in case something happened?"

"No," she said, offhandedly. "Who?"

"A military guy. Or maybe FBI. I can't be sure. He wasn't too specific. Said the name of the agency he worked for wouldn't mean anything to me, anyway, even if he said it. But I know what he looked like."

"I guess you want to tell me, right? You think it's going to mean something to me?"

He shrugged. "A guy can hope, can't he?"

Losing her patience with him once again, she said, "Go ahead. Tell me. What did he look like?"

Alex wasn't smiling anymore. He looked deadly serious as he replied, "Mid-forties, five-eleven, one-eighty, short brown hair, military cut, green eyes, wire-frame glasses—the little oval-shaped ones. He said I could call him Marty."

Geri's expression carefully gave nothing away. She even managed a shrug. "Could be any of thousands of guys in the military."

"I didn't keep that .45," Alex declared. "I've never been comfortable around guns, and I've seen the stats. Somebody with a gun in their home is more likely to be shot with it themselves than to ever use it successfully to defend themselves. I decided I didn't want it. But I did fire that weapon that day, and I'm sure my fingerprints are on it. I didn't fire it at your friend. I didn't kill him."

"And…what? I'm supposed to believe you?"

He shrugged. "I thought you might. Geri?"

"Hmm?"

"The man who gave me the gun, the one who left with it that day? After my shooting lesson, we collected my computer and the rest of my things and we got into his car. He drove me to that safe house and told me not to worry about a thing, because his own people were going to take care of me, and everything was going to be just fine. Lucky for me, I didn't take his word for that."

Chapter 9

"You're trying to tell me that the man whose agency was given the job of keeping you alive double-crossed you and set you up for the murder of one of his own agents?"

He shrugged—that maddening, careless shrug. "Well, if you were me, what would you think? Somebody turns up dead outside my lab, from a bullet fired from a gun with my fingerprints on it? And the only gun I'd touched in my life before that happened to be one of the same caliber, given to me earlier by the same man? And all hell just happened to break loose in my lab on his people's watch? What would a reasonable person assume, Geri?"

"You're not a reasonable person," she complained.

"Are you? What would you say happened?"

"I'd say you're a liar. A damned good one."

"So why haven't you taken me in? To whoever you work for?"

Geri turned her head and swore, absolutely hating the way his mind worked.

"Are you an agent, Geri? Do you work for him?"

She said nothing. There was nothing to say. He was terribly clever, and she didn't believe him. Not for a second.

"What's the matter?" Alex continued. "Don't you trust him? Is that why you haven't taken me in? Because you're just not sure anymore that you can trust him?"

"I've worked with that man for four years," she said.

Alex shrugged. "People change. They can fool you. Look at you. You did a bang-up job of making me believe you were some scared, needy little woman trying to get away from a man who beat her."

"'Needy'?" she fumed. *"Needy?"*

He nodded.

"I hate you," she said.

"Yeah, I noticed. So who is this guy? My buddy, Marty. I've been digging into every computer database I can find, trying to figure it out. He wasn't in uniform, and nobody saluted him, but he was military. Or ex-military. He had the haircut. The body stance. People were throwing a lot of 'sirs' at him—military brass and everybody. So I know he's somebody fairly high up in the power structure."

"That's what you've been doing the past few months? Trying to figure out who he is?"

"Among other things. Staying alive has taken up a good bit of my time, lately. I've found I really would like to stay alive. There's a lot I haven't done yet, a lot of things I don't want to miss out on," he said. "So, my guy, Marty—he's not army, air force, marine or navy. I haven't been able to dig as far as I'd like into the CIA or the FBI, so far, but I haven't found him there, either. So who is he? Who am I up against?"

"Not military. Not CIA or FBI. Nobody you've ever heard of."

"You could tell me, but you'd have to kill me, right?"

"I told you. Don't tempt me," she said.

Alex grinned. "Okay. Fine. About the dead guys at the cabin—what did you find on them? What shook you up so bad and made you decide not to take me in today?"

"What?" Geri blinked, hating him even more. He saw too damned much.

"I thought maybe the fact that you'd killed them was bothering you, but now that I think about it, you handled that just fine. It was while you were searching them that you got upset. Did you recognize them? Or did you find something on them? Something that just didn't add up?"

Geri thought about strangling him. She got up to do it, but suddenly didn't think she had the strength. Her head felt so heavy. So did her limbs. She couldn't even think straight anymore.

"Hey, babe," he said. "You might want to sit back down."

"What?" she asked, the words sounding strange to her own ears, all the strength going out of her legs. She sat.

Alex was smiling at her—a new smile, almost apologetic—and her head started spinning as a deep, seductive lethargy invaded her veins, and she knew exactly what was wrong.

He'd drugged her.

Damn him. Somehow, he'd drugged her.

She had nightmares about him, the most horrible nightmares. About that night at the lab. About a dark alley, crawling down it on her knees and her one good arm, about blood and tears and wretched pleas.

Sometimes he was the devil himself, put on this planet just to irritate her, to torment her, and sometimes he was the man from the cabin, the one who'd taken such tender care of her, who'd made such a fool of her. And always, she hated him. She kept telling him over and over again that she hated him. She thought sometimes he said he knew it, that he understood, that maybe he hated himself a bit, as well. It didn't make her feel better. In fact, she felt horrible. She fought him off—fought again the efficient but tender hands that tried to soothe her, the cool cloth on her forehead, the water he let her sip from time to time. But he just wouldn't go away.

It could have been hours later, it could have been days. Geri had no way of knowing when she finally opened her eyes and found herself lying on a bed in the motel room. She felt like she was looking at the whole scene through a curious fog—the bed, the TV tuned to what looked like a music-video channel, the beat going all the way through her, making her head hurt.

Alex—*damn, Alex*—was leaning against the headboard of the other bed, his feet stretched out in front of him, his computer on his lap. He was studying the screen intently. Working, she thought at first. She'd found him working. Then she heard the sound effects over the music. Exploding things, gunfire, a voice that sounded like an alien's taunting him. He was playing a damned game. He'd drugged her to play some stupid game?

Fury had her rushing when she shouldn't have. She went to sit up, maybe to tackle him, the rat, but she still wasn't clear of the effects of the drug, and her body wasn't cooperating. Her head really wasn't cooperating, and her hands...

Her hands didn't go anywhere, and there was this damned racket—metal banging on metal. She turned her head. It hurt, but she did it, and saw that he'd gotten out of the handcuffs and used them on her.

He'd drugged her and chained her to the bed.

"I'm going to kill you," she groaned.

But he kept playing the damned game. It was a full three seconds before he looked up from the computer screen and said, "I had a feeling you might wake up wanting to."

"So you cuffed me to the bed!"

"Hey, you brought the handcuffs into this, and you weren't exactly eaten up with remorse about sending me off into never-never land last night," he said. "Remember, I haven't done anything to you that you haven't done to me first."

She jerked hard against the cuffs, sending them biting into the base of her hands and making the worst racket she'd ever heard. She'd sooner shoot herself than have to listen to that noise ricocheting through her aching head again.

"I swear to God," she said. "When I take you in, I am going to torment you. Torture you—"

"The government's into torture these days?" he quipped.

"*I* am," she promised.

He still had the nerve to smile. "Who do you work for, Geri? This has been fun and all, but I really do have to take care of some things—serious things—and I need to know if you and I are going to help each other or if I'm going to leave you here and take care of this on my own."

She laughed—one of the sickly cynical laughs he favored from time to time. He'd corrupted her brain to the point where he had her doing it, too. "You want to know if I'm going to be useful to you somehow? Or if you should get up and walk out and leave me here like this?"

"That's right."

"And there's nothing I could say to you that would make a difference? Nothing you'd believe?"

"Maybe. What do you say we play Twenty Questions again? We'll take turns. I get one, then you get one. No more jokes. We answer. And then we'll decide what to do."

"Have you lost your mind?" she retorted. "You could tell me the sky's blue and that the sun rises in the east, and I wouldn't believe you. I wouldn't believe anything you said."

"Oh, I think you already do. In fact, if I'd known you'd listen to me enough to have the conversation we did before the drug kicked in, I wouldn't have done that to you."

"Yeah, right."

He put his computer aside and came to sit by her. "It's true."

Geri wanted to crawl away, as far as she could get, but she wouldn't let him see that. Her pride wouldn't let her.

"I am sorry for that." He touched a hand to the side of her face. His thumb gently lifted her brow, and he looked into her eyes, then reached for her wrist.

"Don't touch me," she said, thinking to hell with not showing him anything.

"Fine." He threw up his hands in mock surrender. "How's your throat?"

She grimaced. Her throat was raw. He produced a cup with a straw, which she eyed warily.

"What?" he said. "I'm going to let you wake up, only to knock you out again. Why would I do that?"

"Why do you do anything?" she complained. "You're totally unpredictable."

"Is that your first question?"

"No. I'm not playing your damned game."

"Come on. Twenty Questions, and I'll either let you go or leave myself. Either way, you'll be rid of me. It should be worth it to you—putting up with a little conversation with me just for the chance to be rid of me."

"You are insane," she said.

"No, just determined. I'm surprised you didn't find that out about me. They must have given you all sorts of background reports about me. In fact, that's where I'd like to start. First question—what was it in my background that led you to believe I would do something like turn the formula for these explosives over to anybody who happened to have the money to pay for them?"

"What?" she demanded.

"It's a fair question. Do you think I'm evil? Do I seem that crazy to you, Geri?" He laughed cynically. "I have to live in this world, after all. My family lives here. I have nieces, nephews. I still have *two* sisters. You know that, right?''

"I know all about you, Alex. Born in a suburb of Chicago, the youngest of four children. Your mother died when you were two. Your oldest sister helped raise you for a time. Your father remarried years later, giving you a stepmother with whom you've sometimes gotten along, sometimes not. Your oldest sister is a photographer who's traveled around the world, estranged from the family for a long time. Your middle sister married young, to the policeman you mentioned—''

"The one who was going to help you," he reminded her.

Geri ignored him. "That sister died several years ago—''

"Kelly." His mouth stretched into a grim line. "She had a name. Kelly. It didn't mean anything to you? When I told you about her? When I told you how much I regretted the fact that we weren't closer in the time she was alive?''

Geri paused, watching him. If she believed anything about him, she would swear that still hurt him; that, if nothing else, he cared about his family. Shaking her head, telling herself it didn't matter, Geri went on.

"Kelly died several years ago, shortly after giving birth to twin boys, whom your brother-in-law, Mitch, and your oldest sister, Leanne, are now raising together. They married, actually, which didn't sit well with you or the rest of your family. The youngest sister, Amy, is an accountant. You've spent most of your life in one school or another. You keep to yourself, work all the time, like to ski—water and snow— climb mountains, run, go white-water rafting, when you let yourself outside. There wasn't any special woman in your life at the time you disappeared. Never has been one that lasted long, just an endless parade of women in and out of your life.''

"You got that right," he said.

Geri frowned. "You present a picture of a fine, upstanding

citizen. Working for a government contractor, dating infrequently, spending time with those four nieces and nephews of yours. I think I've seen some family snapshots.'' She smiled with as much sarcasm as she could muster. "Quite touching, really.''

"Was it?''

"Mmm. I wanted to throw up every time I saw you with those kids.''

"Looking happy, you mean? Content? Looking like I love being around them? Because I do. I love them very much,'' he said. "Think about it, Geri. My family's very important to me. We haven't always been as close as we should be, but we've gotten better at it over the years. My sisters... I know what it's like to lose one. I don't ever want to go through something like that again. And my nieces and nephews... They have to live in this world, just like you and I do. It's crazy enough, as is. Why would I do something like this to them? Why would I turn over some fabulous recipe for a bomb to a terrorist? Why would I let that kind of evil loose in the world in which they live?''

"I wouldn't presume to understand why you do anything,'' she said.

"Geri.'' He frowned, shook his head. "You're not playing the game. Come on. What can it hurt to play the game? The way things are now, you've got nothing but time, and this won't take long. Just think about my question for a minute. Why would I do this?''

"Money,'' she suggested. "People will do almost anything for money.''

He frowned. "Oh, that's weak. But we're just getting started. I'll let you slide for now. Just think about it, okay? Think about why I did this awful thing.''

She frowned. In truth, he hadn't seemed the type who needed a moneyed life-style. Oh, he didn't make a fortune doing what he did, although the company for which he worked certainly profited handsomely from his work. But he seemed to find it easy to live within his more-than-modest means. When he played, he played hard. But he didn't have extravagant tastes. In fact, he had a hefty savings account—probably because he spent nearly all his time in the lab.

But maybe he was tired of that. Alex's inventions were owned by his employer. If there was a patent involved, a juicy government contract, the company raked in the fortune, and he might get a small percentage through a profit-sharing incentive program, but that had to get old after a while.

Greed and discontent had a way of growing inside a person, a way of eating people alive—of blinding them to reason, to their conscience, to the consequences of their actions. It had happened to thousands of people over the years. It could easily have happened to him.

"Your turn," Alex said. "Go ahead. Ask me anything."

She groaned.

"Indulge me, Geri. I'm crazy, remember? Crazy people should be indulged from time to time."

"Okay. How did you drug me?" She was honestly dying to know. She hadn't taken a drink of anything, hadn't eaten anything he'd had access to. And they'd left the cabin so quickly, she didn't think he'd had time to grab any but the most basic of provisions. Plus, she hadn't found anything resembling a drug when she searched the cabin.

"Good question," he said appreciatively. "I am a chemist by trade, remember, and I told you—I've had a lot of time to think about someone finding me, about diversionary tactics."

"Play the game, Alex," she countered. "Answer the question."

He named a drug combination she recognized.

"But I didn't swallow anything. You didn't inject me with anything."

"You can inhale it and get the same effect, if you use it

in the right concentrations, in an enclosed space. It's trickier, of course. The calculations are a bit complicated. But it can be done. I poured some of it on the bathroom wall, pulled the shower curtain closed and then all I had to do was get you into the shower.''

She felt dizzy just thinking about it. "You could have killed me," she protested.

"I have a Ph.D. in chemistry." He had the nerve to sound insulted. "I'll admit, I was a little uneasy about being chained to the furniture and thinking you might collapse in there with all that vapor."

"You could have killed me," she repeated.

"Geri, I don't go around hurting women," he said softly. "I've never killed a person in my life, and I'm not about to start with you. There was a time when I honestly liked you."

"You're insane," she said. "If you think I believe that, you—"

"My question," he interrupted. "You're doing great, by the way. I'm glad to see you getting into the game."

She muttered an oath, told him exactly what he could do with his game.

Alex ignored her and went right on. "That man I described to you? Marty? Is he your boss?"

"Yes," she said, thinking, what was the harm?

It didn't really tell him anything. He didn't know whom she worked for. He probably didn't believe anything she said, just as she'd vowed not to believe him, which should have made this an exercise in futility. Still, the idea of being able to ask him a question and getting an answer—even a false one—was tempting. And it was her turn. She thought about all she wanted to know.

"Come on, Geri," he coaxed. "Play the game."

Exasperated, she asked, "Why are you doing this?"

"'This'?"

"Running. Living in that shack. Kept away from everyone

you know, everything you own. You're on top of the FBI's Ten Most Wanted list. You have been for months. Do you know what that means? If anyone catches you? And they will catch you, Alex. It's only a matter of time. What do you think you're accomplishing?''

He looked her right in the eye. "Someone's out to steal this godforsaken thing I invented, and I'm not going to let that happen.''

"Steal it?" she repeated.

She'd heard those accusations before—that security wasn't what it should have been in his lab, that he'd claimed there had been a series of mysterious break-ins; that he'd insisted on being moved repeatedly. Even once he'd been put under protective custody by the government, until that night he'd ended up with Division One and finally gotten away. That was the theory—that he'd needed to be in a situation where he could get away, that he kept complaining of these mysterious break-ins until he was in a place where he could disappear.

"So you're saying this is some kind of humanitarian gesture?'' Geri asked. "That you're out to save the world? Not blow it up?''

"Nobody's going to blow it up with something I invented,'' he declared. "Not if I have anything to say about it.''

Geri gaped at him. He was trying to tell her he was one of the good guys? The corners of her mouth twitched. "You're kidding.''

"No, I'm not,'' he said sharply, as if her inference greatly offended him. "My question. Where did you get the bruises?''

She grimaced. "Mexico. Trying to find you.''

"I haven't been in Mexico,'' he told her.

"So I discovered.''

He arched a brow. "And got beaten up for your troubles?''

"Things got a little out of hand. My question. How did you get out of the lab that night?"

"I walked out," he replied.

"Come on. Make up something more elaborate than that."

"I'm not making up anything. I walked out. Somebody broke in—"

"People can't break in there. You saw the security setup."

"Somebody was in there, where nobody was supposed to be, and I knew what they'd come for. I wasn't about to let them have it. And forgive me, but I'd lost all faith in my own government to safeguard my work. So I took off."

"How?"

"A little chemical surprise. Basically, the same thing I used on you, only something that takes effect much more quickly. I knew someone would be coming for me sooner or later, and I made sure I was ready. I grabbed my laptop, some cash, and I was gone."

"You never saw this mysterious person who came after you?"

"I was tempted, believe me. But I didn't know how many of them there were or what kind of trouble I was going to have getting out. I thought I needed to get out, that I could make my explanations later. I didn't think the people protecting my work were the ones out to steal it until later— until my fingerprints were found on the weapon that supposedly killed the guard."

"Doc," she said. "His name was Doc. You're sticking with that story? That Doc was already dead before any of this happened?"

"When I got to the door, it was open. He was slumped over in the doorway. I checked. He was already dead. The guards who were supposed to be outside were gone, and I took off."

Geri frowned, finding it totally implausible. "Nobody could get into that lab."

"Somebody who knew the setup could. Somebody responsible for guarding me there could," he argued. "Think about it, Geri. That's all I'm asking you to do. Think."

"It won't change my mind," she said.

"My question," he countered. "Why do you keep doing this?"

"'This'?"

"This job. You hate it."

"It's all I've ever done," she said.

"You've always hated it?"

"No. I haven't always hated it. I just... For the longest time, it was all I ever imagined doing."

"Your father really is a general, isn't he?"

She stiffened, wishing she'd never told him anything about herself. "My question."

Geri thought about it, thought about the fact that her head hurt, and her arms ached, and that this whole thing was pointless anyway. "Never mind," she said. "I'm tired of this. I don't want to play, Alex."

"Oh, babe. Giving up already?"

"All right." She swore. He had to be the most exasperating man she'd ever met, and she had thought of one more question. "Did you have some kind of plastic surgery? On your face? There's something different about you. You look different somehow from all the photos we have of you."

He grimaced. "I feel like I've aged ten years in the past few months, but no, I didn't have plastic surgery on my face. I did get my nose broken seven or eight weeks ago, and my own face has seemed odd to me ever since."

Geri nodded, satisfied on that point.

"My question," he said. "Your father really is a general?"

"Yes."

"And you wanted to impress him?"

"What if I did?"

"That's not an answer."

"Oh, hell," she muttered. "Yes, there was a time in my life when I wanted very much to impress him."

"Give it up, babe," he advised. "It's eating you alive."

She laughed pitifully. "What does that have to do with anything?"

"It has to do with you, and part of this is about me and you. I told you, I like you, Geri. Sometimes, I really like you. When I'm not furious with you. When you're not telling me you hate me and that you'd like to see me dead. Which leads me to my next question. Why do you hate me so much?"

"You're a traitor," she said. "And a murderer."

"No, I'm not."

"Alex, this is pointless. Don't you see that? We're never going to agree, and I'm not going to help you. If you're going to shoot me, please go ahead. It doesn't sound so bad to me anymore. If you're going to leave, then leave. Much as I hate the idea of seeing you again, I'll get out of this mess and hunt you down. So it really doesn't matter what you do, but God, I wish you'd just go ahead and do it."

He ignored her and went on with his game. Holding up the communications unit she'd found on the body of one of the men at the cabin, he asked, "What's this, Geri?"

She swore, thoroughly exasperated. "Is it possible to irritate someone to death? Because if it is, you're dangerously close."

"You didn't have this when I hauled you back to the cabin with me, and it isn't mine. So unless you stole it somewhere along the way yesterday, you found it on one of the bodies at the cabin. I'd say this is what has you so worried."

Geri glared at him.

"I'm not that good with electronics, but this... This is a cool toy. Or at least, I'll bet it was before somebody pulled all these wires loose. That would be you?"

"Yes, Alex. That was me."

"Why'd you take it?"

"I like toys," she replied. "You said it—'It's a cool toy.'"

"Why'd you disable it?"

"Alex—"

"Come on. This is petty stuff. We have so many bigger issues to argue about. Let's dispense with the small ones, okay? They knew where you were, didn't they?"

"I don't know," she insisted.

"They were tracking you with this. Think about it. Your organization is tracking me down, and someone behind the scenes—your boss, maybe?—is watching and waiting, and when someone from your group finally finds me, what does he do? He uses your own equipment against you. He gives it to his people and punches in the frequency of some little tracker he put on you—something you probably didn't even know you were carrying—to send somebody to take you out and probably to blame me for it. Meanwhile, his people get me and the formula for the explosives." Alex sighed. "That's evil."

She shook her head, grimacing because it still hurt. "That's…"

"Possible," he argued. "Admit it. It's possible. And it means we've got to figure out how they're tracking you, so we can stop them and get the hell out of here before the next set of goons finds us."

"Why would I believe you?" she demanded. "Why would I believe anything you say? You're a liar. You're one of the best I've ever met, Alex."

"Me?"

He spat out the word. Gone was the easygoing, boyishly charming man. If she thought this meant nothing to him, she was mistaken. She'd finally found an exposed nerve and stepped all over it.

"Yes," she said, baiting him. She was tired of being the only one on edge, here. "What about that stupid game we were playing at the cabin?"

"I wasn't playing at anything," he said.

"Oh, hell. Everything's a game with you. Nothing's real. Nothing matters."

"You mean when I touched you?" he asked, his eyes glittering dangerously. "When I kissed you? When you had your hands all over me on the bike?"

Her face burned at the memory. "It was a game, Alex. We were just playing a game."

"Really? It's just something you do? Part of the job at times? Using your body or whatever it takes to get the job done?"

"Whatever it takes," she lied.

"You know, that's the part of this that's really made me mad."

"Your ego can't take the fact that I'm not really attracted to you? That there's a woman on earth who can resist you?"

"This is not about my ego," he said. "And I'm not ready to concede the notion that you're not attracted to me."

"Then I must be a better liar than I thought."

"*I* didn't lie to *you*, Geri."

She scoffed at that. "All that false concern—"

"I was concerned about you."

"The kindness? The tenderness?"

"I make it a point to be very nice to women, especially to women I'm interested in," he said.

She laughed. "Thank goodness you're not interested in me anymore. I don't think I could take any more of your particular brand of charm."

"I gave you the impression I was uninterested?" he asked.

She gaped at him. "We're ready to kill each other, to put ourselves out of the misery of being together."

"Oh, babe. It's not that I'm uninterested. Not necessarily.

I haven't really thought about it. You see, I'm just too mad at you right now to think about anything else."

"It was all an act, Alex. Don't even try to pretend it wasn't."

"You know, it does makes me wonder.... You were so surprised I was nice to you. Why wouldn't I be, Geri? What's the matter? Men aren't usually nice to you? They don't know how to treat you?"

"It's none of your business what my relationships with men are like."

"I don't think you've had a lot," he said.

"Oh, please. Spare me your analysis of my love life."

"I think you're starved for a little kindness, a little gentleness. A sweet, soft touch."

She frowned. It was the last thing she wanted or needed.

"I think all of that back at the cabin—the man-to-woman part? I think all of that was real," he said. "I think that's why you're so mad. I know it's why I am."

Geri shoved the personal part of it away to deal with later, if she ever could. If not she would bury it, as she buried everything else. She would stick to business, as best she could, to the implausibility of what he was telling her.

"Let me get this straight. You're wanted by every law-enforcement agency in this country. For murder. And treason. You've got some supersecret formula for explosives that's worth a billion dollars, conservatively, on the black market. Two people tried to kill us yesterday, and we're intent on doing bodily harm to each other, and the thing you're mad about is this silly, annoying relationship between the two of us?"

"'Silly'?" he questioned.

"Yes."

"'Annoying'?"

"We're driving each other crazy, Alex."

"We were great together."

"Until we started telling the truth about who we are and what we were doing in that cabin."

"It wasn't all a lie," he insisted.

"What wasn't? What wasn't a lie?"

His face softened. He leaned closer, and she scooted over as much as her bindings would allow.

"Nervous?"

"No," she lied.

He looked her over from head to toe—appreciatively, if she could read the gleam in his eyes. He reached for her, his big, warm hand coming up against her belly, pushing up the fabric of the shirt she was wearing, skin landing on warm, quivering skin. She jerked hard with her arms, the cuffs holding her firm, and she was in trouble—she knew it.

"This part," he said with a wolfish grin. "This wasn't a lie."

Chapter 10

He sat down on the bed beside her because he wanted to. Because he had her handcuffed to the damned bed, and he'd been arguing with her to no avail for ten minutes, all the while seeing her stretched out on the mattress glaring at him and swearing that she hated him.

He was getting really tired of hearing that she hated him and thinking she'd played him for a fool. He didn't quite believe it, either—especially not when he touched her. And if he couldn't talk her into admitting she doubted at least a little bit that he was some lying, murdering traitor, he was going to make her admit she was wrong about one thing— about what happened when he touched her.

He reached for her again, letting his hand skim across the surface of her skin. He felt her suck in a breath, saw her eyelids come down and her mouth stretch into a taut line. It was the most satisfying exchange they'd ever had, he decided. And one of the most honest. The lady wasn't immune to him, after all.

"Don't do that," she said.

"Why not?"

"Because I don't want you to."

"Oh, I think you do."

"And I think you're delusional," she retorted.

He laughed. "The mad scientist? Finally gone over the edge? I don't think so, Geri. Although if anyone could take me to the breaking point, it would be you."

"Thank you," she said. "I'll take comfort in that."

"And double your efforts, I'll bet."

He pushed up her shirt, until it was bunched under her breasts, and stared at her midsection. It was trim, slightly tanned, the skin stretching over her bruised ribs, then dipping down over her belly. He whistled appreciatively.

"What are you doing?" she asked.

"Looking at you. I like looking at you."

"Alex, if you think anything's going to happen between us while I'm handcuffed to this bed, you really are delusional."

He just smiled. "I guess we'll see, won't we?" Then, with the tips of two fingers, he started tracing circles on her belly. The skin and muscles danced and contracted subtly beneath the play of his fingers. He found it infinitely satisfying.

"Stop that," she said.

"Why? It doesn't mean anything to you anyway, right? You didn't really like it when I held you, when I kissed you, when you had your hands all over me? It was nothing. Right, Geri?"

"It was a job. You were a target. Still are. Nothing else."

"Really?" He let his hand move lower, tracing that delicate ribbon of skin just above her panties. "So think of this as another part of the job."

He leaned down and kissed her, tracing her belly button with his tongue. The handcuffs rattled against the metal

headboard as she jerked her arms down as far as she could
and cursed him.

"Ticklish?" he asked.

"Furious."

"I just want the truth about this one simple thing," he
said, finding that he very much liked the taste of her skin.
He teased at it with his tongue, and she wriggled beneath
him, breathing hard now.

"You wouldn't know the truth if it jumped up and bit
you, you—"

He *bit* her, lightly, bit her bottom rib on her right side.
It quieted her more effectively than anything he'd ever said
to her, and he found himself nearly intoxicated by the taste
of sweet, silky skin.

Alex had told himself he could do this and not lose track
of his objective, and not lose himself in her. He'd told himself he was too furious to make this anything other than
what it was—a war waged with long, slow, openmouthed
kisses and silky expanses of skin. But maybe he was wrong
about that. Or maybe he underestimated just how badly she
got to him, on every level imaginable.

Target, hell, he thought.

He couldn't figure out how he could want her so much
and be so damned mad at her, but he did and he was. He
couldn't understand why he was so convinced the soft, vulnerable, lost-looking woman in his bed at the cabin had
been the real her, but he believed it. He wanted the Geri he
knew back again, and he was willing to play dirty to get
her.

He nudged the shirt higher, with his nose. She tried to
jerk her arms down again, getting nowhere, again.

"Lady, you may just be the death of me yet," he muttered, taking great satisfaction in every little hitch in her
breath, every restless wriggle of her hips and jerk of her
hands against the bindings.

"When I get out of this, I promise you—"

He set his mouth upon her breast, finding her nipple easily as the fabric of her shirt bunched against it. Her entire body seemed to heave upward and then sink back into the mattress at the touch. He fought the urge to stretch out beside her, place his entire body in line with hers, fought the urge to settle himself on top of her and sink into all that waiting softness.

"You are killing me," he admitted, burying his face against the side of her neck.

Giving up the fight, he settled himself on top of her. Their legs scissored together, thigh to soft, silky thigh, heat to answering heat. They were both gasping for air, and Geri was muttering a string of disjointed curses, but her tone— hot and sexy and yielding—ruined whatever sentiment she was trying to express.

He laughed, then silenced her with a kiss. Her mouth opened greedily beneath his, taking him deep inside, sucking him down into that vortex of pleasure he'd never found with anyone but her. He could admit it now. She'd become an obsession with him. Everything else just fell away—the sense of danger, the fear, the outrage—as soon as he touched her.

"It would be so good," he said raggedly, pulling his mouth from hers and staring down into her deeply troubled eyes.

"You're dreaming," she said.

He lay heavily on her, his body pressed intimately to hers, with nothing but a few scraps of cloth keeping him from being way up inside her. "Yeah," he admitted. "Maybe I am."

"It isn't me," she said. "None of this is me. You couldn't touch the real me, no matter how far you take this."

"Liar," he accused, liking that desperate tone of her voice.

"You're supposed to be so smart, Alex. Don't you understand? I can be a dozen different women. A hundred. If that's what it takes to get the job done, and none of them is me. Nothing that touches them gets to me."

"I did," he said, putting his hand on the side of her face, running his thumb across her bottom lip. "Feel that, Geri. That's me. Touching you."

His hand fell to the sweet peak of her breast. "And that? Don't even try to tell me you don't feel that. Don't tell me your body is like some weapon you can use at will. That you can open yourself up like this and be so sweet and so soft for any man who comes along. Don't try to tell me it has nothing to do with me—with who I am and how you feel about me."

"It doesn't!" she cried.

He settled himself more fully on top of her, shifted his hips, thrusting smoothly against her, finding a heat like none he'd ever known, a feeling that was almost more than he could bear. It would be so easy to have her.

"I need you, Geri," he admitted. "You think that's easy for me to say? You think I like it? I hate it. I hate opening myself up one more time to anyone. I've always had trouble trusting women, and I hate the idea even more right now. I hate being in this situation and not knowing how to get out. I hate needing you—not just like this, but because you could help me, if you'd believe in me just a little bit. I hate it."

"Then we're even, because—"

He smothered her words by kissing her again—long, hard, drugging kisses that left her limp in his arms and begging him with her eyes.

"I hate the way you just swept into my life and turned it upside down," he said. "The way you made me forget that I had to do this by myself, that I had to be alone. I'm damned sick and tired of being all alone. And I really hate thinking I could have been so wrong about you, about us.''

"What do you want from me, Alex?'' she asked raggedly.

Everything, he thought. Every damned thing.

With a groan, he pulled himself off her, because he simply couldn't stand being this close to her anymore without having her. Lying on his back on the mattress beside her, he shook his head, wanting her and thinking it was going to be a cold day in hell before he had her, before they had anything together.

So what did he want? What could he hope to get?

"Tell me you want me,'' he said. "Give me this, at least. Tell me this part of it was real.''

"Sorry to break it to you, but I'm not going to let myself be attracted to some homicidal scientist gone mad.''

"I am not a madman,'' he said. "I'm not a killer, and I'm not a traitor. I'm just a man—one who liked having you in his bed. And I can't accept that none of that was real.''

"I can't help what you believe. Or the lies you choose to tell yourself,'' she said.

"And I can't quite keep my hands off you. Or my mouth,'' he said, still painfully aroused. "You want to go for round two in this little bondage extravaganza of ours?''

"Only if you're the one who's shackled to the bed this time,'' she replied.

"Hey, let's do it,'' he said. "I'm easy.''

"No.'' She glared at him. "There's nothing about you that's easy or simple.''

They lay there staring at each other for a long moment, his gaze taking in her swollen lips, the rapid rise and fall of her chest. He was more than ready for round two of this little war between them. He could keep her just like this, he thought, cuffed to the bed, so she couldn't get away. He could keep pushing until she couldn't lie to him or to herself anymore, and before he was through, he'd find her warm and wet and willing. He knew it.

"Alex—don't look at me that way," she begged. "What are you trying to prove, here? What do you want?"

"You, dammit. I want you. The woman from the cabin. Without all the lies."

"You want me to admit that I want you, too? Would that be enough?"

"No, but it would be a damned good start."

"Okay, I want you. I hate myself for it. I think it's got to be one of the stupidest things I've ever done, that my body has turned traitor on me, and every bit of common sense and training I ever had has deserted me. But I want you. Satisfied, now?"

"Gee, when you put it like that..." he said sarcastically. "You want me, and I'm your worst nightmare?"

"I don't know what else I can give you, Alex. Not now."

He waited, lying by her side on the bed. She was still breathing hard and she wouldn't look at him. "I never lied to you," he said. "There's a lot I never told you. But that man you got to know at the cabin, that was me. As real as it gets. And I think deep down you know that."

"Alex—"

"Think about this. About me. *Us.* Think with your heart instead of that hard head of yours, Geri. I think, in your heart, you know I'm not a murderer. Or a traitor. I don't think you could feel the way you do in my arms and believe that about me. I don't think you're the kind of woman who's that good at separating what's going on with your body from what's going on in your head. I don't think you're nearly as cold-blooded as you'd have me think."

"Alex—"

"You know something isn't right about this. You know it."

"That doesn't mean—"

"Think about that communications unit. That's got to tell you something, Geri."

"I don't know what," she said.

"If that piece doesn't fit, you know there are going to be others. There's got to be something you could do to check out what I've told you. Something to make you believe me. I told you what happened. Exactly what happened."

"I don't—" She broke off, thinking. "Okay. I'll talk about it, dammit. Just don't touch me, okay?"

"If you insist."

"I insist." She sighed heavily. "I didn't see anything in any reports about traces of drugs found in the safe house. We had units on the scene in twelve minutes flat. There was nobody else in that lab. There were no fingerprints."

"Except your own people's?"

"Yes."

"Twelve minutes is more than enough time for what I used to wear off and for whoever was there to clear out. I needed it to act fast, remember? You sacrifice the time it remains in somebody's system when you need to knock them out quickly."

"Alex, really—"

"Ask somebody. There's got to be somebody you trust. Ask them if they found traces of that tranquillizer in the lab that night."

"But the reports—"

"Would you put that in a written report coming out of your own agency if you could help it? If it explained how I got out? If it was a little piece that didn't fit? Say you wanted everybody to think I offed the guard and walked out of there on my own?"

Geri took another minute. He was making progress. He could feel it. Finally, someone was going to believe him. He wasn't going to be in this all alone anymore.

"You thought of something else, didn't you? Something that didn't fit."

She shook her head, looking overwhelmed and sad and still mad as hell at him. "The timing—"

"What about it?"

"Just…something. Something off in the timing."

"Tell me," he said urgently. "Dammit, just tell me."

"You tell me," she retorted. "Tell me who helped you get out of there."

"Nobody helped me do anything."

"I mean it, Alex. There's a part of me that wants to listen—a foolish part, I'm sure—but I want to hear what you have to say. And if you want me to have any hope of trusting you, you have to tell me the truth now."

"Nobody helped me. Why do you think somebody did?"

"God, I knew it was hopeless. I knew it was foolish to even think about trusting you."

"Why do you think somebody helped me? And what does that have to do with the timing of the shooting? Tell me, dammit. Just tell me."

Furious, she asked, "How many people were guarding you that night, Alex?"

"I don't know. Why?"

"How many!"

"Three, I think. I'm not sure. I had a lot of different people guarding me, a lot of different setups. Why?"

"Three," she said. "One inside that building, two outside. What happened to the guards outside?"

"I don't know. They just weren't there. Why? Why is this so important to you?"

"Did you ever even wonder where they went? Or what happened to them?"

"Frankly, I was a little too worried about staying alive at that point. And I've been having trouble accepting the fact that I'm wanted for murder, that I've been branded a traitor, and that there is no one I can turn to for help!'' he yelled.

She glared at him. He had this oddly surreal premonition of doom. There'd always been something potently irrational about her reaction to him. Not sexually. Emotionally. The anger. The hatred.

He didn't want to know, Alex decided. But, damn, he really had to know. He swore softly and whispered, ''Why?''

Looking stricken and emotionally spent, she said, ''Because I was one of them. The bullet wound on my shoulder? That's my little souvenir of my time spent trying to save your sorry ass.''

Alex backed up a step and stared down at her. She was breathing rapidly, her chest rising and falling. He felt dizzy and sick inside, and he knew. *Ah, damn.* Now he knew one more undeniable piece of the complex puzzle that was her.

''This is why you hate me,'' he said.

She shook her head and looked away.

''You do.'' He finally believed it. ''You hate me.''

''Not so much for me,'' she told him. ''I've been shot before, worse than this. But Dan... Dan is my partner. *Was* my partner. He took a bullet that shattered one of his vertebrae. The last time I saw him, he was in a wheelchair, and I'm not sure if he's ever going to get out, and that— *that*—is just one of the reasons I despise you, and I wish you'd just leave me alone and let me despise you, Alex. It's about the only thing that's kept me going the past few months, and if I lose that, I don't know what would be left of me.''

A few minutes later Geri lay back on the bed, cursing herself, trying to not even breathe while he leaned over her, working on the lock on the handcuffs. She didn't have the key, hadn't planned on having to worry about getting the cuffs open. She'd planned to leave him in this room, chained to the wall, and wait outside until somebody came to pick him up.

She didn't want to be anywhere near him now, but he was trying to pick the lock on the handcuffs—again—to set her free this time.

They hadn't said a word since Geri's emotional outburst a moment ago, and she couldn't even look at him. She didn't want to think about the way she'd lost control, about all she'd told him, all she'd shown him. Her reaction to him was, as it always had been, purely emotional, and edgy and out of control—nothing like that of the cool, impersonal professional she was supposed to be. And she hated him for that, too. One more thing to add to the list of reasons.

She heard a click. He worked over her hands for another minute, and the cuffs came loose. Carefully, she lowered her arms, which were stiff and sore from even the brief time they'd been held above her head.

He looked like he was thinking of rubbing some of the soreness out of them, but she shot him a killing glance.

"Sorry," he said softly, watching her with an expression she didn't care to decipher. "We need to get out of here."

"I know."

"Leave everything behind? Except the laptop?"

She nodded. Someone was tracking her, she believed, and she had no idea how. Bugs could be infinitesimal these days. She could be carrying it on nearly anything—her clothes, her shoes—and not even know it.

"We'll need clothes," she said, finally managing to think. "Shoes. Wallets. Some kind of bag. Toothbrushes. Toothpaste. The whole bit. We don't take anything out of this room that we had with us in the cabin."

He nodded, keeping his distance. "Does your head still hurt?"

"Yes," she admitted.

"It shouldn't last much longer," he said, almost regretfully. "An hour, max."

"I'll live," she said.

Alex frowned. "Geri, I—"

"Don't," she interrupted wearily, thinking he was going to apologize about every damned thing, thinking he might be sincere. "Just don't."

He nodded, not saying another word.

They moved quickly from there. Buying what they considered the essentials from an all-night convenience store nearby, outfitting themselves for colder weather, grabbing some burgers and coffee, changing at the motel. Alex bundled up everything they'd brought with them and threw it under the tarp covering a fancy speedboat being towed by a half-ton pickup parked in the parking lot, thinking that maybe it would buy them a little time.

They were ready to get on the road when Geri spied a pay phone by the side of the road. "I need to make a phone call," she said. "It's probably not the smartest thing to do, but we're leaving anyway."

"Do whatever you have to do," Alex said.

She ought to be calling Tanner, too. Checking in. All hell would be breaking loose now that she'd gone so long without calling in and the cabin had blown up with two bodies in it. She was risking her career, she realized. And for what? A gut feeling? A dangerously stupid attraction to an infuriatingly smug, handsome, self-assured genius accused of murder? She'd never been stupid until she met him.

Geri looked down at the comm unit in her hand. She'd taken the time to study it now. It was definitely one of Division One's, which meant she had to accept the possibility that someone at her office had betrayed her. She remembered the look on the faces of the intruders at the cabin. They'd had no intention of letting her leave there alive. Geri was a long way from believing that her boss, Martin Tanner, was involved in a plot to frame Alex Hathaway and steal his nifty little explosives. Tanner was a man who'd devoted his life to serving his country, and she couldn't see him suddenly betraying her or the organization or his country this way, even if Alex had described Tanner to a T earlier.

No, Geri wasn't ready to believe that Tanner was a traitor, but...could she afford to rule it out altogether? Thinking of the comm unit, Geri didn't see how she could. Still, she needed to know what was going on at headquarters. Instinct told her something had broken loose on the case, something that would help her. She needed to know.

Of course by calling someone now, she'd likely be putting her life into that person's hands. So she needed someone she trusted implicitly.

Geri picked up the phone and dialed a hospital in Virginia. The switchboard operator told her Dan Reese was no longer a patient there.

"Where else would he be?" Alex looked concerned. "If he was hurt that badly... You don't think he..."

"No," she said. "It was touch and go for a while after the shooting, but he's been off the critical list for months. He was in a rehab hospital the last time I talked to him."

Alex looked grim. "He meant a lot to you. I'm sorry."

Geri ignored that. She didn't want sympathy from Alex. She didn't care if he was sorry. She didn't want to think he was human.

She tried Dan's apartment and got nothing. She'd never heard him talk about anyone special in his life, except right after the shooting.... Jamie Douglass, she thought. Another agent, one caught up in this whole mess, as well. Could something be going on between Dan and Jamie? Jamie had investigated the shooting at the warehouse. She'd written the official report of the agency's findings on how and why it had happened, and had come to all the wrong conclusions,

Geri thought. And she and Jamie had fought about it—about what had actually happened and who was at fault. But Geri had thought that was her own guilt talking. She certainly hadn't entertained any suspicions about her boss having betrayed them all.

"What's it going to be, Geri?" Alex asked.

She thought about it. She'd missed the time she was supposed to check in with headquarters by more than twelve hours. They would know what had happened at the cabin by now. They would have found the bodies. She would be putting Jamie in an awkward position by contacting her and asking her to stay quiet about their conversation. But Geri had to know.

She picked up the phone and dialed. A groggy male voice said, "Hello."

"Dan?" she said.

"Yes. Geri?"

"Yes."

She could hear a sleepy female murmur something, could hear Dan telling her not to worry, to go back to sleep, heard him speaking in a warm, sexy tone she'd never have believed could come from him.

Geri smiled. Her partner was a dynamic-looking man, and he could be charming, when he worked hard at it. Most of the time, he didn't. She'd never heard him like this. She would have sworn he'd never talk to a woman in quite that way. Interesting, she thought. Dan and Jamie.

Dan cleared his throat. "I know you didn't call just to chat, not at this hour," he said. "And how did you know I was here?"

"Just a hunch," she replied.

He swore. "I'm that transparent."

"A hunch. Really. I need to know something. From Jamie. About the night of the shooting." She looked right at

Alex as she said, "Ask her if anyone found any traces of a tranquillizer called LH-7 in the lab."

"Almonds," Alex told her. "It would have smelled like almonds."

Geri relayed the message.

"What's going on?" Dan asked.

"Would you believe I'm just wondering?"

"No."

"Ask Jamie."

He did, then came back to the phone. "She doesn't remember anything like that. But she wasn't on the scene until more than twenty-four hours later. Tanner was the first one on the scene that night. He was coordinating things from there for the first twelve hours or so. Why? What did you find out?"

She thought about Tanner—a guy who spent his life behind a desk—coordinating action on the scene. She didn't think he'd done that since he'd become a section leader. Of course, Division One had never lost an agent in the field, either, and this had happened about fifteen minutes from Division One headquarters. It wasn't so unusual, Tanner being in charge of the scene, when she thought about it that way.

"Geri?" Dan prompted.

"I'm not sure what's going on," she said.

"Where are you?"

"I shouldn't say. Not on an unsecured line."

"I don't like the sound of this. Who's with you? Who's covering your back?"

"Nobody."

"I don't like that at all. And we need to talk. Some things have happened you should know about. Things about the shooting."

"Oh," she said, more curious than ever. "Look, I can't stay here. I've been here too long already, and somebody's tailing me. Let me call you somewhere. Twelve hours," she said. "Remember where we used to call that kid who worked on the Brazilian ambassador's staff? The one helping us with—"

"Yeah. I'll be there. Watch your back."

"You, too," she said, then turned to Alex. "Let's go."

They climbed back onto the bike. It was pitch-black and they'd traveled far enough to the north the day before so it was cold now, and she was once again hanging on to the back of a man she alternately despised and desired. She couldn't figure out if she was stupid or just tired or naive, and until she knew, she was stuck with him. She couldn't let him out of her sight.

Chapter 11

They rode for what was left of the night, heading north into Colorado, along the edge of the mountains. Shortly after sunrise, they stopped for breakfast at a small café near Greeley, then got a room at a motel there. They'd said little to each other all this time. Geri was exhausted. She'd been drowsy for what seemed like hours. Somehow it had seemed the easiest thing in the world for her to curl up against Alex Hathaway on the bike and find herself utterly relaxed, strangely content.

In the room, she ran for the shower, mainly to warm up, then climbed into one of the double beds, expecting to fall asleep quickly, easily. Alex took a shower as well, staying in there a long time. She was still awake when he walked back into the room. He checked the lock on the door, took note of the gun she'd left on the nightstand between the two beds. They'd parked the bike inside the room, to hide it from sight. He went to the window and looked outside.

"See anything?" she asked.

"No."

"We've done all we can for now," Geri said. "Let's just get some sleep. This afternoon, we'll see what Dan has to say, and we'll take it from there."

Alex nodded, looking serious, somber. She didn't recall ever seeing him this way. Everything seemed to have changed between them. There hadn't been a single teasing word from him—nothing designed to throw her off-balance, to irritate her, to bait her.

It was as if some undeclared truce existed between them, and they'd never negotiated the terms. But she felt she understood them fairly easily. They were going to coexist as peacefully as possible on this journey toward the truth, extending to each other enough trust that there would be no more little hostilities like tranquillizers or handcuffs, no more guns pointed at each other. She wasn't worried he would disappear the next time she turned her back, and she didn't think he worried that she was going to take him in— at least not yet.

She didn't want to think about whether anything he'd told her was true or about what had happened between them at the cabin. It was too fresh, too raw, too hurtful.

Alex came to stand beside her bed. He stuck his hands into the pockets of his jeans and rocked back on his heels, still studying her intently. Finally he spoke. "Will you tell me about that night? When you got shot?"

She rolled over onto her back and covered her head with her hands. "Alex, I don't think I've slept an entire night through since the shooting, and I swear, I've never been this tired. I can't go over it right now. Even if there might be details that didn't fit, I don't think I could spot them tonight."

He stayed where he was, just looking at her. "I wasn't asking you to go over the details so we could try to spot some inconsistency. I wanted to know about you. It haunts you, Geri. Even now. You have nightmares about it, three and a half months later. God, I hate that.''

"I'm fine," she said, which was a bald-faced lie, one she felt entitled to. She chose to ignore any emotion she thought she heard in his voice, anything in his words.

"I hate what it's done to you," he told her. "What it did to your friend. There's nothing anyone can do to help him walk again?"

"I'm not sure. I don't know if he knows himself at this point. He's a very private person, and I haven't asked. But his career as an agent's over, and I can't imagine how he's going to handle that. I'm grateful that he's still alive, but he's even more devoted to his job than I am, and for him to lose that…"

"You found him with another woman last night, didn't you?"

She nodded.

"You okay with that?"

"We didn't have *that* kind of relationship, Alex."

"Still," he said, "just because you didn't have that kind of relationship doesn't mean you never wanted to have that with him."

Geri sighed, wondering why they were talking about this, why he cared. But she told him, because she was tired and he had a way of finding out what he wanted, of not giving up until he did.

"I thought for a while that something might happen between me and Dan. We're alike, in a lot of ways. Maybe too much so. But nothing ever did happen. I admire him. I trust him. I think he's a wonderful man. But that's it."

"Okay."

"Get some sleep, Alex. We'll need to be alert later, in case anything happens."

"You trust me enough to fall asleep and believe I'll still be here when you wake up?"

"I'm too tired to do anything else," she said, and then knew she couldn't leave it at that. Things had changed between them. "We're in this together now, right? You and me. To the end. No matter what."

"You mean that?"

"I want the truth, Alex." She thought about Doc, about Dan, about how screwed up her whole life was as a result of that one, disastrous night. "No, I don't just want it. I have to have it."

"So do I," he said. "What are they going to do to you for not bringing me in yesterday?"

She almost smiled. "Worried about me?"

"Is that so hard to believe?"

"They could do anything they wanted to with me for disobeying an order. But it will probably depend on how this whole thing shakes out. On whether my boss is guilty. On whether you're innocent."

"I'm innocent," he said, then added, "I'm sorry I drugged you."

Geri laughed. It just bubbled out of her. She was helpless to stop it.

"What's so funny?"

"I don't think any man's ever drugged me and then apologized for it."

He shrugged. "So, I'll be the first."

"No one's ever chained me to his bed before, either," she told him. "I've been handcuffed. Tied up. Gagged. You name it. But never handcuffed to a bed and assaulted quite like that."

"You want me to apologize for that, too?" he asked, with none of that teasing tone she knew so well. "I will."

As blindingly honest as she could be, she said, "I don't know what I want from you, Alex."

He nodded, accepting. "Okay."

Inside her was a reckless little voice that said, *Trust him.*

Take him. Anything he has to give. Give him anything he wants in return. Geri fought it. It seemed she'd been fighting her whole life, and she wasn't sure if she'd accomplished anything by it.

Her father alternately tolerated her and ignored her, likely still lamented the fact that she'd been born a female instead of a male. Her mother had died so long ago, Geri didn't even remember her, and there'd never been a man in her life who'd ever gotten really close to her. A physical relationship, she could handle. An emotional commitment was another thing altogether. She told herself she didn't need that, that she was fine without it. She'd never been the kind of woman who wanted to spill her guts to a man and have him tell her all his secrets in return.

And now she did. She wanted a half-crazy, supposedly homicidal genius who was being hunted down by the FBI, the CIA and every covert spy agency in the U.S. and probably by all of its enemies, but as long as she stayed mad at him, she'd probably be okay. Trouble was, now that she'd told him about that night—just a little about it—it was hard to stay angry at him. It was hard not to tell him everything. Her part in it. Her mistakes. Her regrets. Especially when it was so easy to see that he had so many regrets himself.

He was getting to her, she realized. Despite logic and caution and all evidence to the contrary, he was getting to her.

"Damn," she muttered.

"What?" Alex asked.

"Why are you doing this?" she demanded, giving in to the need to dig herself just a little bit deeper into the kind of trouble that followed him.

He was still standing by her bed, his hands shoved deeply into his pockets, gazing down at her. "Doing what?"

"Running like this. It's dangerous, Alex. Do you even realize how dangerous it is?"

"I know a whole lot of people would eagerly kill me for what I possess."

"So why do it? Why not turn yourself in? Tell your story?"

"Turn myself in to who?" he asked. "Believe me, if there was somebody I thought I could trust, I would. But the last person the government turned me over to is trying to frame me for murder right now. The damned FBI's convinced I did it. So if you were me, and you even wanted to turn yourself in, where would you go? The first thing they'll do, if I'm lucky, is haul me off to jail. Who's going to listen to me from a jail cell?"

"I don't know, but you can't keep running forever."

"I realize that."

"You must have some kind of a plan."

"I do."

"Want to tell me about it?"

"Going to believe me if I do?" he asked softly.

"I don't know. But if someone other than an agent of the U.S. government finds you and the formula for those explosives, they'll kill you when they're through with you."

"I know," he said bluntly.

"Then I don't understand. What do you hope to accomplish by running?"

"Think about it, Geri. I made something that can kill people," he said. "Can you imagine how that feels? Somebody wants to take something I made and use it to terrorize innocent people. Can you imagine the chaos that would result if people were suddenly afraid to fly? If planes were exploding in midair? Do you remember how crazy people were after that plane exploded over Long Island and everybody was convinced, at first, that it was a missile? That someone had come that close to U.S. soil and committed an act of sheer terrorism?"

"Yes. I remember."

"I never set out to make the perfect bomb or a terrorist's dream weapon," he said. "I was working on a security system when I found this. Can you understand how much I hate that I found this?"

"I—" Geri hesitated. "No. I guess I didn't think of that."

"I wish I'd never told anyone what I found, that I'd just destroyed the whole thing the minute I realized what I had," he said. "But it's too late for that. People found out. People went crazy. I swear there were people in the military practically drooling over this, and I didn't want to give it to them. It's one of the reasons they started to distrust me. I didn't want them or anyone else to have it, and they knew it."

"Better them than the other people who are after it," she said.

"But what are they going to do with it, Geri? What's anyone going to do with it? It's the next generation of plastic explosives. People are going to use it to blow things up, and I will not let something I've made with my own two hands be used to kill people."

Geri lay there watching him. She was more than surprised. Stunned, actually. He was adamant about this. Passionate. Weary and troubled and angry at himself, too, it seemed.

"What can you hope to do now?"

"I'll do whatever it takes to stop that," he claimed. "How can I not? I created this mess. I have a responsibility to stop it."

"How?" she asked.

"I'm working on it," he said, his gaze narrowing on her. "And you sound like you believe me. Do you, Geri? Do you believe me now?"

"I want to," she admitted.

He nodded. "That's a start. I want you to know something. I absolutely hate the fact that you've been dragged into this mess. I hate that you've been hurt. That your friend died and that your other friend's life is all messed up because all of you were trying to protect me. I hate that.''

Geri lay there, turning her face away from his. She believed him about this, she realized. That he hated that she and Dan had been hurt, and that Doc was dead. Who could say about the rest of it? But this she believed.

"Will you tell me about that night?" he asked. "Please?"

"I don't talk about it. I had to, for a while. There were reports, investigations and things, and I had to talk about it. Now I just want to forget."

"Geri, I don't think you *can* forget."

"Maybe not," she admitted. "It's changed everything. Made everything different. I'm different now. I'm a mess."

"And you got through this by hating me," he said softly.

She started to tell him then, to explain. It wasn't just him. It was her. "Alex—"

"Shh," he said, sitting down beside her, his hand on her shoulder. "It's all right, babe. Hate me, if it helps. Do whatever you have to do. I won't ask again. And I'm sorry. If I could change it, I would. If there was anything I could do differently..."

"Sounds so easy, doesn't it? You know how it turned out now. You know what was really happening all the time. If you had a split second of insight like that beforehand, it all would have been different."

"Yeah," he said, sighing, his hand running softly across her back. "It would have."

She closed her eyes, and there it was again. His touch— consoling her, soothing her. She'd never known a man's hands could be so gentle, could bring comfort and an irrational feeling of being safe, could chase away that awful sense of loneliness. She wanted to turn toward his touch, to invite it. She wanted so many things from him.

"I'm tired, Alex," she admitted. "So tired of all this."

"Okay. We won't talk about it anymore right now." He kept on rubbing his hand along her back, soothing. "Go to sleep, babe."

Geri had the nightmare again. She jerked awake, sitting up in the bed, her heart thundering, a choked-off cry on her lips. She had only a second to realize that someone was outside before the door swung open.

Geri grabbed the gun from the nightstand and had it in her hand, had her finger on the hair trigger, when a man came charging through the door.

There was a second when she thought she was still dreaming, still back in that other ghastly night, and she'd gotten a second chance to make things right. She wanted that so much—a second chance. All she had to do was pull the trigger. But something was wrong about this.

It wasn't night. It was the middle of the day. Near-blinding sunlight assaulted her eyes, flooding the room from the open doorway. The man was backlit so that she couldn't quite see his face.

She saw another face instead. A teenager's. How could she fire at him? He was just a kid.

"Oh," she gasped, thinking, *Second chances.* Nobody got second chances, did they?

She waited, the roaring in her ears finally receding, and she heard Alex's voice, amazingly calm.

"Geri? It's me. Look. Look at my face. It's me." He smiled—some funny, scared little smile—and tried to make light of it. "I know you hate me. I know you're dying for a chance to kill me. But…do you think we could talk about this some more? Before you pull the trigger?"

Trembling so badly that she was afraid she might shoot

him by accident before she could lower the gun, Geri just sat there, fighting to breathe, to clear her head. Ever so slowly, she turned the gun away, clicked the safety back on.

"Sorry," she said, her voice breaking on the word.

"'Sorry'?" Alex laughed then. He could laugh at anything.

"You startled me."

He closed the door behind him, shrugged out of his jacket and came to stand beside her bed. "You were screaming," he said. "I thought somebody had found us, that they were hurting you."

"Oh," she said, embarrassed now. It had been *that* bad? She'd been that out of control?

"*Oh,*" he repeated.

She changed the subject. "Where have you been?"

"I went to grab some food from the restaurant across the road. And coffee. I thought you might like some coffee when I woke you up."

"Oh," she said again, the power of speech seemingly deserting her. He was being kind and concerned, she realized with a sinking feeling. Alex, kind and concerned, was even more treacherous than Alex, baiting her, needling her. She tried changing the subject. "What time is it?"

"About that time. If we're going to make the phone call on time, we need to get moving."

"Okay. I'll get up."

"Are you? Okay, I mean?"

She nodded.

"You almost shot me," he said, more calmly than she would have been under the circumstances.

"I know," she admitted.

"You were looking at me like you couldn't even see me."

"I couldn't. I just heard a noise and woke up, right before

you came charging in here, and the sun's so bright. It threw your face into the shadows.''

Alex nodded slowly. ''You looked like you weren't even here. Where were you, Geri?''

She glanced up at him helplessly, reaction setting in, hot and heavy. Realizing that she had nearly shot him, that she'd looked up at him and had seen someone else's face entirely. She was trembling. God, she hated it when she started trembling like this. She wouldn't be able to aim worth a damn like this—wouldn't be able to think, either. The nightmare always did this to her. Except the last time, she realized. The last time she'd had it, she'd been with Alex, had ended up sleeping in his arms.

He had beautiful arms, sleek and deceptively strong, exquisitely gentle. Looking up at him now, she knew that all it would take was one word from her, and she could be in those arms once again. She could forget the nightmare altogether. Could she forget who she was, too? Who he was? Would it be so bad? Just for a little while?

''Geri?'' he said, reaching for her.

She scrambled away, off the other side of the bed, not caring that she was making a fool of herself or that she was standing there with her legs bare and nothing but his long shirt covering the rest of her.

''I'm going to jump in the shower,'' she said, because she had to have a few minutes to pull herself together.

He nodded. She expected some teasing comment, some wry smile. But he'd hardly said anything like that since she'd told him about the shooting. He'd been surprisingly serious, and she could swear he knew exactly where she went when the nightmare came.

She missed the old Alex, she realized. The teasing. The sparring. The challenge—and she wished he didn't know so very much about her. She'd rather have him angry than sorry, sensed that she'd been safer when she hadn't trusted him at all than she was now. Wanting to trust him, to help him, made her vulnerable. It made her want him even more, and she already wanted him so much. Even when she'd been spouting off dire threats about wanting to kill him, about hating him, she'd still wanted him.

Alex, she thought, her heart aching, her body stirring to life.

"What?" he asked. "What's wrong now?"

She shook her head, the words tumbling out. "I was just thinking that everything was so much simpler when I could hate you."

Heat flared in his eyes. Hope, too. She thought he was going to come charging across the bed to her, that he'd grab her and wouldn't ever let go, and maybe that wouldn't be such a bad thing. But he must have seen the panic in her eyes. Because he backed up one more step and gave her a wry smile.

"I could work on being annoying again," he said. "If that would help."

She smiled, thoroughly aware of the expression unfurling across her face, and that it was ridiculous to be smiling, given the situation they were in. But there it was. A genuine smile.

"You don't do that very often," he said, and she remembered how happy he'd been to make her laugh the other night.

No one had ever worried about making her laugh. No one seemed to notice how seldom she smiled.

Suddenly she wasn't so very tired. She didn't feel so old, so worn down, so devoid of hope. Life seemed infinitely better, more interesting, more promising, just because he was here and because he made her feel. Even when it was anger and frustration and something very close to hate, he made her feel more than she had in years. Her deadened senses came alive around him, and she found that was so much better than being numb. Scarier, but better.

Before, she had wanted so much to be numb again. That was the last thing she wanted now. She was actually looking forward to what was left of the day—a day spent on the run with a man wanted for murder. It was crazy—truly, unspeakably crazy—but she didn't mind that part anymore, either.

Alex came to her. He cupped her chin with his hand. Her whole body seemed to tremble anew at his touch.

"You're a dangerous man," she said.

He nodded. "Know something else?"

"What?"

"I'd do anything for you." He kissed her, softly, his lips hardly lingering at all. "Anything I can. Anything you need. I don't want to see you hurt again."

Oh, she thought, taking it like a blow, the full impact of his considerable charms coming to bear in the soft, sweet promise.

He was concerned about her, and she sensed that he wanted to protect her, which was silly. She was a highly trained special agent. Even with her head all messed up, mistakes piling around her, she could hold her own with almost anyone. He, on the other hand, was just a man. Very smart, highly skilled, but he spent his life cooking up things in his lab. Although there didn't appear to be a single geek gene in his altogether-impressive body, he was still a man who worked with his brain, not his body.

And *he* wanted to take care of *her?*

So this was sentiment, some odd, inconsequential bit of fluff, she told herself—all to no avail. Inside she was melting, and not just from the considerable sexual heat he generated.

"What is it?" he asked. "I've never seen you so reticent

about telling me anything as you've been today. Go ahead. Let me have it."

"Nothing," she insisted. "I was just thinking."

"About what?"

Oh, he'd hate it. She knew he would, and she wasn't above needling him a little, just to change this oddly explosive atmosphere between them.

"I was thinking of what you said. About your wanting to keep me safe. It was sweet, Alex."

"'Sweet'?" He said it like a dirty word, gave her an odd look, like she'd said the world was flat or something equally ridiculous. "You're insulting me again, right? I'm just too dense to figure it out anymore?"

"No. I'm not trying to insult you at all."

Exasperated, he said, "Geri, there's nothing remotely *sweet* about my feelings for you."

And just as deftly, he'd put the ball right back in her court. He liked her. Maybe it was more than that. A lot more. And he wasn't going to let her ignore it. Petty little half insults weren't going to dissuade him.

Coward that she was, she said, "I need to get in the shower. I need some help waking up." She waited until she was inside the bathroom, behind the locked door before she said, "Alex? The other night? When I told you I could be all those different women so easily?"

"Yes."

"Somewhere along the way, I've kind of forgotten how to be myself," she confessed. "Especially around a man."

The doorknob rattled. Clearly, he wanted in. "I never imagined you were such a coward, Geri," he taunted.

"Now you know," she whispered. She'd told him more about herself than she'd told anyone in years.

Chapter 12

The news was bad. Alex knew by the look on her face when she was on the phone with her partner, a man she cried over in her sleep.

They'd checked out of the motel, ridden for an hour to put more miles between them and anyone who might be tracking them, before she made her call. She stayed on the phone longer than she said she would, ignoring the additional precaution of keeping the conversation brief, no matter how unlikely it was that anyone was tracing the call. She listened, saying little in return, except to ask about the chemical traces and to request that he get a photo of their boss ready to fax to her. Then she asked about her own status with the agency.

She called it "the agency."

The CIA? Alex wondered. Or something...worse? Something even more dangerous? He knew it was dangerous, but just how dangerous was only now starting to sink in. He still hadn't gotten the full story about the shooting. Alex eared she had a very good reason to hate him. He wondered f she always would, wondered why that tore at him so.

She finally hung up the phone. They hopped on the bike, earing off through the back roads, until they stopped in ome other little town near the Wyoming border for food nd another night in a dingy motel.

Inside the room, Geri turned the heat up full blast. She hrugged out of her jacket and shoes and wrapped herself n a big thermal blanket from the bed, then sat, cross-legged, n the middle of it with her back propped against the head-oard. Alex stretched out along the foot of the bed, watch-ng her. When she'd gotten off the phone earlier, she'd sim-ly told him to drive, and he'd done it. The fear in her eyes ad been enough to keep him from asking any questions. ut that was hours ago, and now he had to know.

"So," he said, "we're talking disaster here? Or just a najor setback?"

She sighed. "Alex, that night... Nobody helped you get way?"

"No," he replied.

"Nobody knew what you were doing?"

"I wasn't doing anything. I was just expecting trouble. Not the kind I got—not somebody on the inside coming fter me. But I knew I had to be ready. Why?"

"Do you know a man named Rob Jansen? He's FBI, a omputer expert."

"No," he said impatiently. "Why?"

"He was picked up late last night. Apparently a group inked to certain terrorist activities in the Middle East paid im a great deal of money to help get you out of the coun-ry. He had a fake passport and a plane ticket waiting for im. He was picked up ready to leave the country."

"Which means what? Everybody still thinks I'm a trai-or? A murderer? Did he tell your people that?"

"He didn't say much of anything. He was only in custody

for a few hours in the middle of last night. There were
people searching his apartment overnight, piecing together
a case, and when they went back to interrogate him first
thing this morning, he was dead in his cell.''

''Dead?'' Alex hissed.

''I'm afraid so.''

He laughed. What else could he do. ''That's convenient.
He never got a chance to talk? To tell what he knows?''

''No.''

''Did your boss happen to pay Jansen a visit in his cell
last night?''

''I don't know,'' she said. ''We—the agency—didn't exactly have Jansen. It, uh... The military got involved somehow. I couldn't take the time to ask about everything. But
some special-ops people and some of the agency's people
picked him up, and he was in a holding cell at the Marine
Corps training center at Quantico, Virginia, when he died.''

''Died?'' Alex repeated. This was just getting worse. ''Or
when he was killed before he could say anything?''

''I don't know. Nobody knows. They just found him this
morning. He had asthma, and it's possible he simply had
an attack.''

''Or that somebody deliberately brought him into contact
with something that triggered an attack. Do you have any
idea how easy it is to kill somebody with severe asthma?''

''That easy?'' she asked.

He nodded. ''And your boss? Was he anywhere near
him?''

''He was there where Jansen was being held last night.
He would be. It's Washington. Everybody's territorial as
hell. We'd lost an agent and nearly lost another one. Three
of our agents were in on it when the case cracked wide-
open, not ten minutes from our headquarters. So Tanner
would have been there. It would have been odd if he
wasn't.''

"Tanner?" Alex latched onto the name. "That's the man who did this to me?"

"I don't know. God, I don't know anything, all right? But my boss's name is Martin Tanner, and he fits the description you gave me. Dan's with one of the agents who was on duty when you were brought to the safe house that day, and she said Tanner delivered you to them," Geri said soberly. "I told Dan to try to get his hands on a photo of Tanner—something he could fax us. I want you to look at him. I need you to be certain, Alex. There's no room for error, here. I'm already out on a limb so far, I could get knocked off at any moment."

"I know," he replied. "Believe me, I appreciate it. All of it."

"For most of my life, my career has meant everything to me," she said.

"Look," he said. "If I'm wrong about your boss, you can swear I held you hostage all this time. Tell them I kept you drugged and chained to my bed. It wouldn't be a big stretch of the truth."

She laughed then. He'd finally managed to wipe that troubled expression off her face, just for a second, and then it was back, full force.

"We're going to get out of this," he promised her. God, he wanted to promise her so much. Everything. "I'm more determined than ever, now, Geri."

"Me, too," she said.

They picked up the photo from a little printing company in Wyoming with a public fax, and Alex finally had a name to put with the face of the man who'd betrayed him: Martin Tanner.

They rode for a long time after that, wanting more distance between them and any further communication they had with anyone involved in the case. Late that night, Geri was waiting for another appointed time to call her partner when they stopped at a deserted diner on the edge of a little town just off the interstate near Sundance, Wyoming.

Geri stood rooted to the spot, trying to take in the truth staring her in the face.

"I believe you, Alex," she said. "I believe that Tanner is the man you saw, that he did it. All of it. It's just... I've known him for years. I've trusted him. I've put my life into his hands, and I could have sworn he'd never betray me or anyone else at the agency like this."

"I'm sorry," Alex said. "Things happen. People change."

"I know. But if he set this all up... He made the assignments on this mission. He put Dan and me there. All this time, I blamed myself for everything that happened, but Tanner did it. He set it up. He set *us* up."

"It wasn't your fault, Geri. This was his doing," Alex said. "Somehow, we'll find him. We'll make him pay for what he's done."

"We have to," she said, more determined than ever now. Revenge was all she had to give the people who'd been hurt by what her boss had done.

Alex frowned. He'd thought a lot about possible ways out of this mess. "Geri, why don't you call your boss and tell him you're with me. Tell him I think you and I are the best of friends and that you're on my side. Tell him you know where I've stashed the formula, and ask him to meet you tomorrow to take me in."

"Alex—"

"We've got to end this," he insisted.

"And what do you think's going to happen by ending it this way?"

"I think your boss won't tell anyone he's heard from you. He'll either show up alone to take me in—in which case, I'll never see the inside of a jail cell—or he'll show up with some goons like the two who showed up at the cabin the other night.''

"You want to set a trap for him?" she asked in disbelief. Alex nodded.

"And get yourself killed? After all this?"

"Tanner's the one. This is the way to make him tip his hand."

"And how do we go about keeping you alive in the middle of all this?"

"That's where you come in," he said. "I trust you, Geri. And you have friends you can trust, don't you? Friends who will help us?"

"It's still too dangerous."

He fought for a wry smile. "I told you—I live for danger."

"Well, I've been trained to minimize all risks, and this is not a good risk, Alex."

"Neither's what we're doing right now. We have to flush the man out. We have to take him down."

"If you're right about this, Tanner can't afford to take you in alive."

"Then we won't let him take me in," Alex said. "Think about it. This is the only thing that will end it, right now. You and I have to stop running. It's too risky with so many people looking for me. And your boss has to be caught."

"Tanner will come armed to the teeth."

"So will you."

"It only takes a second, Alex. A split second. You could end up dead."

"Are you a good shot?" he asked.

"Not as good as I used to be before I took a bullet in my right shoulder. There was some nerve damage. Nothing works the way it used to," she admitted. "And even if I wasn't injured, this is still too risky."

"I trust you, Geri."

"God, don't do that," she begged.

"What? Trust you?" he asked, amazed. "How could I not trust you now? After all we've come through? After the risk you take every minute you stay with me? After the damage you've done to your career by being with me and not taking me in? Of course I trust you."

"Alex?" She looked stricken.

"What?"

"Don't."

"Why not?"

Her head dipped low, her hands raked through her hair. When she faced him again, he saw anguish in her eyes. "The last man who put his life into my hands ended up in a wheelchair," she confessed.

He stared at her, only now beginning to understand. "Dan? You blame yourself? For Dan?"

"Yes," she whispered.

Alex put his hand over hers, squeezing it. He gave her one of his patented smiles. "I thought that was my fault."

A quick rush of tears came to her eyes. "Don't," she said. "Don't be nice to me right now. Or kind. I couldn't stand it."

"So, I should be annoying again?"

"It's so much easier when you are," she said.

Alex whistled, despite the pain in his lungs, and shook his head, desperate to remove that look from her eyes.

"That's a helluva way for a man to treat a woman. I annoy you, and you're happy. I try to be nice to you, and you beg me to stop. I've got to wonder what kind of men you've been hanging out with, Geri."

"Thieves, mostly," she admitted. "Terrorists. Cowards."

"I would think I'd look pretty good to a woman after that."

"Fishing for compliments now?" she responded with a bleak smile.

"Well, you've got to admit, my ego's taken a real bruising with you."

"Your ego's colossal, and I can't believe it's possible to hurt it. But it doesn't matter, Alex. We don't have time for this—"

"This?" he interrupted. "You mean for *us?"*

"Yes."

"Geri, this may be all the time we ever have," he said. She paled. "Don't say that."

"Okay. I won't. Let's talk about you turning me over to your boss."

"It's a lousy plan, Alex."

"It's a great plan. He's probably desperate right now because you haven't checked in, because those two thugs at the cabin are dead. He's got to be scared that you and I are together, and that we might figure out some things between the two of us. Plus, he's got that whole mess in D.C. coming to a head. He's had no time to plan. This is our chance. We need to move. Tomorrow."

"We have no plan."

"We'll make one. Tonight. Call your buddy Dan. See if he'll help us."

"I don't like it," she insisted.

"Baby, neither do I. But there aren't a lot of ways out of this. I know. I've had a long time to think about it, remember?"

Her eyes took on that bleak look, as she softly confessed, "I don't want anything to happen to you."

He clasped a hand to his heart, as if he'd taken a blow, and grinned. "Careful. That's about the nicest thing you've ever said to me. I might start thinking you actually like me a little bit."

"I do," she said simply.

No smart comebacks. No denials. No pretense. It was amazingly gratifying and frustrating. They had maybe twelve hours before he walked into all kinds of hell, and finally, he was getting somewhere with her.

Determined not to think about that for every bit of the time remaining, Alex took her chin in his hand, kissed her gently on the lips. "You know, you're not half-bad yourself, babe. Let's get out of this mess, okay? We've got a lot to figure out between the two of us, as soon as this is over."

She had the dream again, fought it, tried to outrun it, tried to push it away, but she'd always been powerless where it was concerned. She woke up screaming, crying, trying to break free of a hold that had her nearly paralyzed.

She pushed up against a man's far superior strength, executed a neat little twist that had her on top of him in seconds, her hands around his neck a split second later.

Then she opened her eyes and looked down and saw Alex.

Immediately she backed off, taking her hands away. He coughed and grabbed for his throat, then lay there flat on his back, breathing heavily.

"Geri," he said, when he could, "we're going to have to talk about this bloodthirsty streak of yours where I'm concerned."

"God, you really can joke about everything," she said, leaning back, breathing heavily herself. "That's the second time I've almost killed you without even realizing who you were, and both times you've managed to joke about it."

"What do you want me to do? Yell?"

"Most men would."

"I'm not most men," he insisted.

Geri sat down on the bed beside him, disjointed sounds and images from the dream flitting through her head, like a movie that hadn't been spliced together properly. Blood. Darkness. Her own voice screaming, begging.

She shook her head. "I'm sorry."

"You're quick," he said appreciatively. "You think you could teach me that neat little twisting thing you did?"

"Alex." She started to laugh then—the laugh of a woman pushed too close to the edge one too many times. "You're the only man I've nearly strangled who's lived to talk about it, and then asked me for pointers on the technique I used."

He shrugged. "A man needs to know how to look out for himself. Especially around someone as dangerous as you. If you won't give me a lesson, how about telling me what's wrong, instead?"

She shook her head, trying to push the memories away. "Bad night."

"Come on, Geri. Tell me about the nightmares. Tell me about the night you got shot."

"I don't talk about it," she said, drawing her knees up to her chest and wrapping her arms around them.

"Well, I don't know how you came up with that plan, but it doesn't seem to be working. Do you think that you're just going to keep assaulting any man who happens to be in bed with you when that little nightmare comes around?"

"There hasn't been anybody in my bed, Alex. Not for a long time."

"So you just suffer through, all by yourself? I don't think that's going to cut it anymore, Geri. It's tearing you apart."

She nodded. "I'm just nervous about what's going to happen tomorrow. You're going to walk into the middle of this god-awful mess, and I'm scared you won't come out alive."

"I think I will. Otherwise, I wouldn't do it. It's not like I have a death wish. In fact, I've got a lot to live for right now. There are a lot of things I want to do, once this is over.''

She wanted to take the conversation on to the next step, wanted to hear about all the things he wanted to do—with her. That was the ludicrous fantasy that had been floating around in her head these last few days—that Alex was everything she thought he was—devilishly smart, determined, responsible, brave. If everything he said was true, he was a hero, and she'd always been a sucker for a hero. Her father had taught her to admire bravery, dedication, someone who wasn't afraid to make the tough decisions and to carry them out.

Alex had done all that, she suspected. Which made her even more susceptible to him than before, and it had her thinking all sorts of foolish things about what might happen if they got out of this alive. It had her thinking this might be all the time she would ever have with him. And then she thought about honesty. She'd blamed him for things that weren't his fault. She'd hurled accusations at him left and right and sworn that she hated him, because it was so much easier than the alternative—hating herself.

''What about you, Geri? What do you want to do when this is all over?''

''I just want it to be over,'' she said.

Alex rolled over onto his side, reaching out and wrapping his hand around her ankle, teasing at the back of her leg with his thumb. ''Just tell me. Close your eyes and just say it. The worst part of it. Say it.''

''I haven't talked about this with anyone,'' she said. ''Except when I had to, as part of the investigation after the shootings.''

''You got into trouble? Because of me?''

''The whole agency was in trouble, and when that happens, they always want an explanation. They want someone to blame.''

"And they blamed you?"

"No. My partner, mostly. I... He was trying to protect me. I wasn't hurt as badly as he was. Everybody thought I could make it back to active duty, that he wouldn't. I think he didn't want this to ruin my career with the agency, and he took responsibility for what happened."

"For what? What did you do that was so wrong?"

She pushed her hair back from her face, but then she could see him looking at her, and she couldn't have that. So she went to turn around and face the other way, but Alex grabbed her first. He drew her down to the bed beside him, pushed her head down to his shoulder, wrapped his arms around her and said, "Try it now. Tell me all about it now."

"Is this supposed to make everything better?"

Alex swore. "Something tells me you have been sorely neglected by the men in your life."

"There haven't been all that many," she said. "And the General wasn't exactly the nurturing type."

"I don't think I'm going to like the General all that much." Alex tightened his arms around her. "But go ahead. Just tell me, babe. Open up your mouth and let it all come tumbling out."

Could it be that simple, she wondered? Could anything ever be that simple? He held her, and everything was better? She told him all about her problems, and they magically got better? Even Alex wasn't that good.

"Geri?" he said. "I know what it's like to be alone. And I know that after a while, it just doesn't work anymore."

"It did for the longest time," she replied. "I don't understand how I could be fine one minute, and just...lost the next."

"It wasn't ever working for you," he said. "You just managed to kid yourself about that for a while. At least, I did. Give it up, Geri. Let me in. Just a little."

She closed her eyes, concentrated on the feel of his body

pressed against hers, so solidly, with such strength. She felt so safe with him, always had. Irrationally safe, even with all those people coming after them.

That was a big part of it. She was scared about the next day, scared she was going to let everyone down, especially Alex. And she had to be honest with him now. She owed it to him.

"Remember all those times I said I hated you?" she began.

"Vividly."

"I told myself I did, Alex. But I was lying. I hated you because it was either that or hate myself, and it was so much easier to hate you. But it was me. All that time, I hated myself even more than I hated you."

His smile was gentle, understanding. "What do you think you did that was so wrong, babe?"

"I know it was wrong."

"Tell me."

"I knew something bad was going to happen that night. Dan did, too. Right from the start. You can feel it sometimes, and still you can't stop it."

"What happened, Geri? Who shot you? Who shot your partner?"

"A kid," she said. "He was just a kid. And I could have stopped him. I had a shot. I just couldn't make myself take it."

"What was some kid doing in the middle of this?"

"It was a setup. We know that now. Dan knew it that night, and he tried to stop me, but I wouldn't listen," she said. "It was the middle of the night. Dan and I heard a commotion on the street—a car stereo turned up way too loud, and then shouting from inside the car. It stopped at the corner, and all of a sudden the door came open, and somebody pushed a girl out of the car."

Geri had to stop to take a breath. She could still see the

girl's face, too. "The girl was so afraid. One of the guys got out of the car, and the next thing I knew, he was screaming at her and holding a gun to her head. He was going to kill her. I was so sure he was going to kill her."

"God," Alex said, his arms tightening around her. "Tell me nobody else died that night."

"No. I should have stayed right there. We had orders. We weren't supposed to leave our post, no matter what."

"So you were supposed to stand there and watch somebody put a bullet in that girl's head?"

"We had a job to do, Alex. Protecting you and what you were working on. We had reports that people had been trying to get to you, that we should expect trouble."

"A setup like that? A girl getting shot in front of you?"

"Anything. We were supposed to be ready for anything."

"And not react, you mean?" Alex swore again. "You're still human, Geri. They can't expect you to stop being human."

"Oh, I don't know. I think they do. Dan knew it was a setup. He told me to stay put, and I didn't listen. I pulled out my gun and took off, and I put him in an impossible situation. To back me up or to follow his orders."

"He chose to back you up?"

Geri nodded. "If it happened the way you said, that's when Tanner got inside. He would have been monitoring our radio transmissions. We'd had a few glitches in the signals earlier that didn't seem important at the time. You always hit static and places where the signals are blocked. But looking back on it now, Tanner could have been listening. He could have engineered a little problem, just when he needed it. He'd know the instant we left our post at the front of the building. He could have kept us from telling Doc what was happening. Tanner could have gotten inside. He would have set up the security system. He'd have all the codes. And Doc wouldn't have been surprised to see him. Tanner could have walked right up to Doc and shot him, with a gun with your fingerprints on it. It would have been easy for him.''

''So you believe me? About all of it?''

''The more I think about it, the more it makes sense. None of us was comfortable with the story we pieced together of what happened that night. Dan and I both insisted the two boys and the girl looked like D.C. gang kids, and you can imagine how eager we were to believe we'd been bested by some punk kids. Nobody wanted to believe this could be random gang violence, although there's certainly a lot of that in D.C. But everything we came up with pointed to that—a random act of violence. But this—Tanner being involved. It all makes sense if he set this up. He would have access to every psychological profile ever done on me. Civilians caught in an operation have always been a problem for me.''

''And this is supposed to be a failing of yours? That you have a conscience? That you don't like it when innocent people get killed? It sounds like it's a lousy world you live in, babe.''

''A lousy job at times, but somebody's got to do it,'' she said.

He sighed. ''You're right. I'm sorry. There was a time when I was damned glad to have people like you looking out for me,'' he said. ''I'm still grateful to have you. And for what you're going to do tomorrow. God, Geri, be careful. I'll never forgive you if you get shot twice trying to save me.''

She almost smiled. ''You won't forgive me?''

''No way. Now finish your story.''

''Well, if Tanner was looking for a way to get me away from the front of that warehouse, he couldn't have come up with a better scenario than an innocent girl about to get shot. Any psych profile on me would have shown him that.

He could put me on duty that night when he needed me, when he knew how I'd react," she said. "I'm sure you're right about it. I'm sure it was Tanner."

Alex nodded. "So you think he hired these people? To put on a show for you? And get you out of the way, so he could get to me?"

"We'll know soon. Dan said they picked up the two guys who shot us both, and the girl, yesterday. That's what led them to Rob Jansen."

"You think Jansen was working with Tanner?"

"They knew each other. Jansen was engaged to Tanner's secretary, and he did some work for the agency last year. It fits, Alex."

"Now we just have to prove it," he said.

"We will." She was going to make this right, no matter what it took.

"Okay, tell me the rest of your story. You took off after the girl?"

"Yes. And Dan came after me."

"His choice, Geri. He had a choice, just like you, and he made it. You can't blame yourself for that."

"That's what Dan said."

"He's right. You trust him, don't you?"

"Yes."

"Then believe him about this," Alex insisted. "What happened next?"

"I ran toward the girl, caught the guy by surprise. He let go of her for a minute, and she ran into the alley. I grabbed the guy, had him facedown on the pavement. Dan took off after the girl and walked right into a trap. He put his gun away, to try to reassure the girl that she didn't have to be scared of him, and then a second kid walked out of the shadows with his gun in our faces." She sighed. "God, they just looked like kids, Alex. Fifteen? Sixteen? It's obscene to see a kid that age with a gun—one he's ready to use."

"It is," Alex said.

"So, there we were. The girl took off. Dan had a gun pointed in his face, but I had time. I had my gun in my hand, and I sighted it on that kid's chest, and then I looked into his face, and I couldn't do it. I couldn't pull the trigger."

"And you hate yourself for that? Because you couldn't shoot a kid?"

"That kid shot my partner a split second later. He very nearly killed him, and I do blame myself for that. I could have kept the whole thing from happening."

"If you'd let them shoot that girl? Or killed the boy yourself?"

"It was a setup," she said. "The whole thing was a setup, and it worked. Perfectly. Because I did just what Tanner expected me to do."

"Geri?" Alex shook his head. "You need to get the hell out of this line of work. You don't want to be good at something like this. Do you?"

Geri laughed then, until she was crying. "No," she admitted. "I don't want to do this anymore. It's too hard. Too ugly."

Alex held her tighter. "How did you get into this? Trying to impress Daddy?"

"I guess. He wanted a son, somebody to carry on the family name—somebody who'd be a soldier he could be proud of. And at first, I think I wanted to do it just to prove to him that I could. And then it just drew me in. The agency—"

"Wait. What agency?"

"We're a counterterrorism agency primarily. We go in where the U.S. doesn't want to send the military, so the government can claim it isn't officially involved."

"You're a spy?" he asked.

"An agent."

"And you get off on the challenge of it? The danger?"

"I guess I did. For a while. I'm good at languages, and growing up with my father, we lived all over the world, so I know a lot about different cultures. I'm good at blending in, at taking on a personality that allows me to blend in lots of places. It's more mental than anything else. Being quiet and careful. Planning things to the nth degree. Executing the plan. Our goal is always to get in and out without anyone knowing we're there, without drawing a weapon. And usually it works."

"And sometimes it doesn't," Alex said.

"Yes. Sometimes it doesn't. And then it's bad. Horrendously bad."

"So what happens in those nightmares of yours?"

"I see that kid's face down the sight of my gun. I know I should pull the trigger. I know what's going to happen if I don't, and I still can't do it. I just freeze up. I see Dan get shot. I see him fall. I see me lying on the ground, feel the bullet drilling into my shoulder, and then I'm crawling down that dark alley. One of my arms has gone numb, and I'm so dizzy I can hardly see, and I finally get to the spot where Dan is, and he's so pale, so still. There was so much blood, Alex. All I could do was sit there and beg him not to die—and know that it was my fault, that I could have stopped it.

"You need to think about that," she warned. "You're going to walk into that trap tomorrow with me guarding your back, and who knows what I might do. I might freeze up all over again."

"I'll take my chances with you."

"No, I mean it. Think. The other day, when you walked into the motel room and I had my gun drawn, it wasn't your face I saw. It was his. That kid's. I've begun to think I'll see his face every time I draw my gun."

Chapter 13

Alex looked at her for a long time, his gaze steady and sure. "Geri, you already saved my life once, remember? When those two men broke into the cabin, you did what you had to do."

She hesitated. In all that had happened, she'd almost forgotten that. Two nights of that dream, and the men at the cabin had been the last thing on her mind. "It's no guarantee I'll be okay tomorrow," she insisted.

"Hey, there aren't any guarantees anywhere, are there?"

"Alex, can't you ever be serious about anything?"

"What do you want me to say? That I don't trust you? I do. You want me to tell you that you're an awful person because you looked down the barrel of a gun and saw a teenager and couldn't fire? No way I'm going to do that. I don't want the robot, Geri. Or the agent, although she does have her moments." He grinned. "The one I'm concerned about right now is Geri, the woman. And I like her just fine."

"You don't even know her," she argued. "Most of the time, *I* don't even know her. I've buried her so deep inside, she may never dig her way out."

"Oh, I think I can find her." He gave her a roguish grin. "I think I already have. She went on this wild ride with me one day on the bike, had her hands all over me. Had me so turned-on, I could hardly see straight."

"That's because I drugged you into unconsciousness," Geri said.

"No, that was your evil twin."

She laughed, then shook her head. "I'll never understand you. I'll never understand how you always manage to make me feel better, to laugh."

He cocked his head to one side. "Somebody's got to do it. You desperately need to laugh."

"Nobody's ever done that for me, Alex."

"Never?"

She shook her head, thinking that she knew why. Nobody had ever cared enough to work that hard to make her smile, make her laugh.

She wondered if he was always like this, if he took such good care of all the women who came and went from his life. There had been a lot of women. She knew that from the background material she'd seen on him. Obviously, he knew exactly how to handle women—which was something she didn't want to think about tonight. Tonight was all they'd have, and she didn't want to waste it. She was suddenly desperate for every moment she could have with him.

Nervous, she knew she'd have to go to him, knew he felt responsible for her having been shot and that he seemed to think that meant he had to keep his distance from her. And maybe he felt guilty about the bit with the handcuffs, too.

Geri smiled. Odd how that was getting easier, the more time she spent with him.

He had rolled onto his side, propped his head up on one bent arm, and was watching her. "What was that look?"

"I was thinking about— I think you called it our little foray into bondage."

He fought a smile of his own, and she could swear she saw the heat flare in his eyes. "I brought the cuffs with me. You said you never know what might prove to be useful, so…"

"Alex!"

"Am I supposed to apologize for that whole scene again? Because I'm willing."

Geri knew she wouldn't ever forget being handcuffed to his bed. "I guess that depends," she finally managed to say. "Are you sorry?"

"Define 'sorry.'"

"Come on, Alex. Use that world-class brain of yours. You know what it means to be sorry."

"Do I regret handcuffing you to my bed? Well…"

Geri laughed again. "You're not sorry at all."

"I'm not proud of what I did. I was mad, and I knew you were going to be furious. I just wanted you to listen to me, and when I couldn't do that, I wanted to prove something to both of us. And I guess I pushed too far." He reached out for her, cupping the side of her face in his hand. "Did I scare you?"

"You've always scared me. Everything about you."

"But in a good way, right?"

"Sometimes," she said.

"I'm sorry. I never intended to take it that far with the cuffs, but…"

"What?"

"You know what," he insisted, running his thumb along her bottom lip.

"No, I don't. I know what I'd like to believe happened, and I know what I want to happen tonight."

He brought her hand to the middle of his chest, pressed it against a mountain of soft, warm skin above a thundering heart, then smiled again. "What do you want tonight, Geri? I'm all yours. I'll give you anything you want. Anything I have to give."

"I want this night with you. I want to feel the way I did that day we spent riding through the panhandle. Hot and urgent and free. I felt absolutely free that day. I didn't ever want us to stop riding. I didn't ever want to have to face all the lies and all the danger. I don't want tomorrow to ever come, because I don't know how I'm going to let you walk into the trap we've set—"

"Shh." He sat up quickly, kissing her softly. "I can't stop tomorrow from coming. Even I'm not *that* good. But I can give you tonight. If there was anything more I could promise you right now, I would. But that's all we've got. Tonight."

"I know," she said. That made it all the more urgent, although honestly, she didn't think her need for him could get any more urgent than it already was.

He put his hands on her arms, running them up and down from shoulder to wrist, just looking at her for the longest time. She felt the heat seeping into her cheeks. Alex leaned down to her and kissed her one more time—a slow, hot, wickedly sweet kiss that left her head spinning.

"It's been hell trying to keep my hands off you from the first minute I saw you," he confessed. "I looked across the bar and thought you must have come there after me, that I'd been caught, but what a way to go. I've been aching for you ever since."

"That wasn't me, Alex. In the bar, I mean. That was somebody else entirely."

"No, it wasn't. All those other women, the ones you pretend to be? They're all you, Geri. They're all coming from somewhere inside you. You can twist yourself into knots trying to deny it, but all of those personalities you put on come from you. All the things that happen to you on the job really happen to you.''

"Alex?"

"Shh." He stopped her with a kiss. "We won't settle this tonight. Let's not argue about anything tonight."

"Okay," she whispered.

"I think we should take a little ride."

"Alex?" She blushed, remembering what she'd told him about wanting to get on the bike and keep riding forever, remembering that other wild ride of theirs. "It's the middle of the night."

"So?" he demanded, perfectly serious.

"It's freezing out there," she protested. They were in the mountains now. There was still snow at the higher elevations.

"Just a little ride. Remember how good it felt to ride that day?"

"Yes," she replied. She'd never felt so free; had never wanted any man the way she'd wanted him.

"I want that day back," he said, seducing her with the memories. "And I know just how I want it to end."

She hesitated, the coming day and what it would bring telling her she should refuse. "We're going to need to be alert tomorrow."

"We'll sleep like babies," he said. "We'll be exhausted, sated, and very, very happy."

Oh, she wanted that. Every bit of it. "Alex—"

His hands closed over hers. "I'm going to put myself in your hands tomorrow. Put yourself in mine tonight."

"I want to," she said.

"Then let's do it. Get dressed. Grab your coat. It is going to be cold."

"This is crazy," she said, liking the sound of it all the more.

He grinned. "You've always said I was insane. Just wait."

In the end, she did exactly what he wanted. She threw on her clothes, her coat, her gloves, and hopped on the back of the bike with him.

It was a beautiful night. Cold, unlike the other day, but beautiful. The road he took was narrow and lined with towering trees, the mountains in the background, a million stars overhead. Geri had to stay close to him to have any hope of staying warm. She buried her nose against his back, and he took one of her hands and pushed it up under his shirt. She tugged off her gloves a second later, needing to feel his skin against hers.

The bike's engine roared beneath them. She had her thighs spread wide to either side of his, his hips nestled against her, her breasts flattened against his back, and she could touch him, could reach almost all of him from this position. She pressed a hand over his heart, took comfort in its hard, heavy rhythm. She didn't want it ever to stop.

And then she pushed that thought away, as well.

Her hands had a mind of their own. They roamed over his chest, his shoulders, down that narrow band of hair in the middle of his abdomen. She felt him suck in a breath, felt her own heart kick into overdrive. She wanted him. She wanted to touch him, to stroke him, like she had before.

As she looked around, it seemed they were the only two people in the entire world—just them and the stars and the ribbon of road, the trees, the mountains, the cold night air. There was no one to see them. Bringing her hand to his jeans-covered thigh, Geri felt the muscle contract beneath her touch, and stroked up and down.

He turned his head to hers. "You're driving me crazy."

She smiled and gave him a quick kiss, then let her hand slide farther up, finding that he was every bit as aroused as he had been that day they'd spent riding through the panhandle. The bike lurched forward once again. Every muscle in his body seemed to tighten even more, and once again she pressed her palm against that intriguing bulge in his jeans, the heat of him seeming to blast right through the material separating them.

She'd never explored a man this freely, this wantonly, had never done anything so decadent as riding down some deserted road in the middle of the night as foreplay. Only Alex, she reflected, would think of something like this. And she loved it. She loved touching him, loved knowing he was this aroused and imagining what he was going to do with her when they got back to the motel.

She was surprised when he pulled off the road onto a wide spot on the shoulder. He jumped off the bike, pushed her forward on the seat.

"You know how to drive this thing?" he asked, pure wickedness in his eyes.

"I can drive anything," she bragged.

"Good." He settled himself behind her on the bike. "Because it's my turn."

"Alex," she started to protest, even as excitement was building inside her. He *was* wicked.

"Take off," he said, already working on the buttons of her jacket.

"I'll kill us both," she argued.

"Yeah? Well, life's full of little risks, isn't it? Let's chance it tonight."

Geri laughed as she gave the bike the gas, the cold air assaulting her now that she didn't have him to block the worst of the wind. He left his gloves on at first, and still he was incredibly adept at undressing her. Who would have thought ice-cold leather could feel so erotic against her skin? Laughing, she squirmed away from his touch and then sucked in a breath.

"It's freezing," she protested.

"Give it a minute," he insisted.

But she didn't need a minute to know that being with him was going to be unlike anything she'd ever experienced. Already, her body warmed to his touch. His wicked hands were beneath her shirt, beneath her bra, cupping her breasts, teasing at her nipples, which were already so tight they hurt.

"Alex," she gasped.

"Hmm?"

"Your hands. I want your hands."

He brought one hand to his mouth and tugged off a glove with his teeth, shoving it into his pocket, then did the same with the other. She trembled at the touch of warm flesh against hers. She already knew he had magic hands—gentle, slow, teasing, magic hands. No one had ever touched her the way he did, stroking, soothing, searing. He could make love to her with nothing but his hands, and she would be happy.

Then he started with his mouth, finding the delicate skin at the back of her neck and pressing hot, openmouthed kisses there, turning her entire body into liquid heat.

He held her tighter, his strong arms wrapped around her, and she could feel his arousal—so big, so strong—against her bottom. He was holding her by the waist, thrusting easily against her. She was desperate for him by the time he pointed out another clearing at the side of the road.

She brought the bike to a stop beside a thick stand of majestic fir trees and turned to him. "You'll drive us back?"

"Not yet," he said, leaning back on the long seat.

He grabbed her by the waist, lifting and turning her, pulling one of her legs over until she was straddling the seat once again, but facing him this time.

"Alex?"

It was all she got out before his mouth came down on hers. She'd been dying for that kiss, she realized. Desperate for it and for any connection she could have to him. She wrapped her arms around him, and he did the same, pulling her flush against him—all those beautiful muscles of his against her soft, yielding flesh.

It wasn't long before he had a hand between them, yanking clothing out of the way, before she felt his hot breath on her breast, his mouth closing over her nipple, teasing at it with his tongue. It was crazy and so very cold, but his body was so hot, and she loved it. She absolutely loved it, would have let him do anything in the world to her right then.

But she didn't think they were actually going to finish it right there.

She almost stopped him when his hands went to the button and zipper of her jeans. But he pushed her back until she lay against the curve of the bike and placed a string of kisses on her belly, right above the waistband of her pants, and she found her hands tangled in his hair instead, holding him to her.

He slid the zipper down without a whimper of protest from her, and the next thing she knew, he was pulling down her pants, her underwear. His hand came foraging up her thigh, dipping into the liquid heat between her legs. She saw a hard stab of satisfaction on his face as he discovered how very ready she was for him.

He slid one finger deep inside her, then two, stroking, teasing, always pushing her just a little bit further, making her a little more desperate, until nothing mattered. Nothing but him.

He pushed her nearly over the edge, building the tension to the breaking point. She was right there.

"Alex!" she cried.

"Not yet," he insisted.

"Alex, I want you inside me. Please. The first time...I want you with me."

That did it. He sat up, his eyes dark and glittery.

He took off his jacket and threw it onto a pile of leaves behind the bike, then lowered her down, tugging off her jeans and her panties before she could so much as utter another word.

"You are crazy," she said, so excited she could hardly stand it.

"Crazy for you," he replied, pulling something out of the pocket of his jeans and tossing it to her. "Open that for me, would you?"

His hand went to work on his own clothes, unbuttoning the shirt completely. She remembered the way her bare breasts felt against his chest, remembered those springy little curls and those muscles against her skin. He ripped at the button of his jeans then. She watched as he lowered the zipper, shoved down his jeans and his briefs at the same time.

"Geri?" He nodded toward what she had in her hand. "I need that, babe."

It was a condom, she realized, once she'd dragged her eyes from the sight of him, standing there with his clothes all undone in the cold night air. He'd brought a condom. Had he meant for it to happen just this way? This wildly? This dangerously?

She laughed, feeling every bit as free and as wanton as she had on the bike that day. He'd brought it all back—all the magic, all the hope.

He grumbled impatiently and took the condom from her hand, ripped open the package with his teeth and rolled it on. She watched, her mouth going dry, the ache between her legs intensifying.

"You're not scared, are you?" he asked, lowering himself into the cradle of her thighs.

"No," she said. "I'm not scared of anything with you."

He smiled at that, tugged his shirttails out of the way and pushed her shirt up, until they were skin to skin, heat to glorious heat. He kissed her once, deeply, wickedly, and then she opened to him, arching against him.

She wanted him so badly, could feel the big, blunt tip of him at the opening of her body.

"Alex?"

"Hmm?"

"Are you going to make me beg?"

"I could do that. But not tonight, okay?" he said, bracing himself, sliding inside with one, smooth, powerful stroke. They both gasped in unison, and then he laughed a bit, his forehead coming down to hers. "You're incredible, Geri. You've taken me half out of my mind from wanting you."

He kissed her again and again, barely moving, just sinking a tiny bit deeper with every little thrust of his hips against hers. At first she wasn't sure if she could take all that he had to offer, but her body was slowly easing, adjusting to the breadth of him.

"That's it," he said. "You can take this. All of me. Just relax."

"It feels so good," she said.

"For me, too, babe. Me, too."

She put her hands on his hips, urging him closer, urging him to move, finding she needed that. His body was lying heavily on top of hers, his head and his shoulders blocking out the sight of nearly everything else, and she found she liked this—liked being utterly surrounded by him and vulnerable to him. Everything was different with him.

Alex groaned against her ear, pulling her earlobe into his mouth. Then he laughed again—a low, wicked sound—and she shivered.

"I know you're not cold," he said.

"No, I'm not," she admitted. "Not at all."

She felt as if she were flying, with the wind streaking past, and she didn't feel the cold at all. And at some point, they just took off—flying. Being with Alex was like flying.

A new tension came into her body, a need that came from so deep inside, it frightened her. She clutched at him with her hands, because he was the only solid thing in her world. She wrapped her legs around him and arched against him and moaned as he kissed her once again. He was thrusting deeply now, moving powerfully, faster, harder.

"Alex!" she cried.

"It's okay," he said. "I promise."

"I need you. I need this. So much."

He pushed his hands beneath her hips, palming them, pulling her to him, the fit so tight, his body so deeply inside hers. "Let go, Geri. I'll catch you. I promise."

And she did. She let go of everything.

"Just feel," he urged. "Feel how good it is to have me inside you. I don't ever want to leave."

Her hips bucked beneath his, straining to get closer still, and he seemed to swell inside her. He groaned, and she felt a hot pulsing between her thighs. Him, she realized. That was him. He shuddered against her, holding her so tight, and she wanted to take it all in, to absorb him into her in a way she could never, ever lose him.

Her own body started to tremble. It was as if she'd lost all control—lost herself, as well, in him. The feeling shot through her like a blast of heat, again and again. Her body gripped his, tighter and tighter, and then they just went soaring, flying. She cried out his name and clung to him, gasping for breath.

A minute later, he collapsed on top of her. She could feel the smile spread across his lips, because his face was buried against the side of her neck. She shivered when he kissed her there, teasingly, the smile still on his lips.

For a long moment their hearts were in perfect rhythm,

pulsing in a hard, heavy beat, pressed together, slowing ever so gradually. She loved that—their hearts beating together that way.

She had her hands in his hair again, loving the way it felt, needing to touch him, and then she opened her eyes, looking up into the sky, a smile spreading across her face.

"Oh, Alex," she said. "You've got to see this."

He barely lifted his head. "See what?"

"The sky. The stars. Look."

"You want me to leave *this* spot for stars?"

"Yes." She laughed.

"I like *this* spot. I worked damned hard to get here."

"Trust me, Alex."

He grumbled a bit, but slowly, carefully pulled away from her. He made a show of collapsing onto the ground beside her, then settling her against his side.

The night air curled quickly around them, until there was blistering heat where she was pressed against him, skin to skin, and cold everywhere else. But the view… The view was incredible.

"Isn't it amazing?" she said. "It's like we're on top of the world."

He tilted his head down to hers, until they were cheek to cheek. She could feel his smile again.

"Now, you're going to think I'm turning all sappy on you," he warned, rolling onto his side, so he could see her and the stars. "But I think we are on top of the world. I think you took me there."

"No, you brought me. Right here. It's perfect. So good it scares me."

"Don't be scared," he said. "Not with me, remember?"

Then he kissed her again, and they looked at the stars. The night was so dark, the stars so dazzling, it was as if they could almost reach out and touch them. A second later one of those stars went spinning out of control, shooting off toward the east.

"Make a wish, babe," Alex said.

She did—a wish, a heartfelt prayer. *Keep him safe.*

And they lay there, side by side, on top of the mountain, alone on top of the world, until the cold chased them away.

Chapter 14

As Alex had promised, she slept deeply, dreamlessly. They'd made the cold ride back down the mountain, climbed into an equally cold bed and huddled together for warmth and then made love again. She'd fallen asleep naked in his arms and had barely stirred for the rest of the night.

She woke sometime after nine, to find Alex's hard, aroused body next to hers. He'd kissed her awake, and was inside her almost before she realized what was happening, moving urgently and powerfully against her. They both tried to make it last, holding back for as long as they could, but it was impossible that morning. Her climax ripped through her. She cried out his name, and he smothered her cry with a kiss.

Afterward, he didn't say anything, just held on to her tightly, and when she couldn't stand it anymore, she felt tears slip from the corners of her eyes.

He kissed them away. "Don't," he insisted. "Please, don't."

She fought to bring her emotions under control.

"Geri?" he whispered.

She turned her face up to his. "Hmm?"

"Remember when I told you women have a nasty habit of leaving me? Of dying on me?"

"Yes."

"I don't want to lose you today."

She forced a smile across her face. It was one of the hardest things she'd ever done—to find a smile for him that morning. "I'll be fine, Alex," she lied.

They waited until the very last minute to shower and get dressed, throwing their things into the bag and then getting back on the bike, to find a pay phone. Dan was waiting for her call. He was ready. He had people with him who were ready. All Geri had to do was make the call.

"Do it," Alex said.

"Once we do, there's no turning back," she warned.

"Geri, there's never been a way to turn back, not from the very beginning."

She sighed. She realized she had tremendous faith in him. She drew strength from him. If he'd shown any hesitation at all this morning, any doubts, she couldn't have gone through with this. But he hadn't. He'd made his plan, and he was sticking to it.

"We're going to end this today," he insisted.

Geri picked up the phone and dialed Division One headquarters, asking for Tanner. He came on the line immediately, roaring at her.

"Where the hell are you?"

"Somewhere in Wyoming," she replied.

"We're still sorting through the ashes in that damned cabin, Geri. We thought you might be dead."

"Hathaway blew it up," she said, letting her nervousness come through. "He's crazy."

Alex grinned at that and flashed her a big thumbs-up.

"Listen," she said hurriedly when Tanner started asking questions, "I don't have much time. This is the first time he's let me out of his sight in days."

"You're still with him."

"Yes. His ego's tremendous. It wasn't hard to convince him I'd do anything for him."

Alex grinned at that, too.

"Tanner, just listen," she went on. "We're on a motorcycle. A red vintage Ducati." She read him the tag number. "I know what he's doing now. He's going home to Chicago. We're taking a northern route along I-90, and we're still about eight hundred miles away. There's no way we'll make it today. He'll find a cheap little motel on the interstate. He'll let down his guard there. You can take him then, okay?"

"Where are you, exactly?"

"About an hour from the South Dakota border. He's being careful, sticking right to the posted speed limit. The last thing he needs is to get pulled over by a cop. You can pick up our trail along the way today and follow us in. Don't try to overtake him on the bike. He has a laptop computer with him, and he hasn't worried about anything in his possession but that. The formula for the explosives has to be on it. If he tries to outrun you on the bike, anything could happen to it. Take him at the motel tonight, okay? He always stops around seven."

"Geri—"

"Listen, he's got a gun in his duffel bag, but he doesn't carry one on him. He's a lousy shot, anyway. You shouldn't have any trouble."

"Okay, but—"

"Here he comes. I've got to go."

She slammed down the phone, shaking by the time she was through. "Well," she said to Alex, "it's done."

He hugged her to him, and she took a deep breath, hanging on to him tightly.

"I hate this," she said.

"It'll all be over tonight," he told her.

She nodded, never dreading a single day more in her life, never more anxious for one to be over. She reached up and kissed him—hungrily, greedily.

"Alex, there's no telling when we'll have a moment to ourselves again. I just want you to know, crazy as they've been, the last few days with you have been...the best." The best of her life, she realized soberly.

"Hey." He held her face in his hands. "No talk like that. And nothing about goodbyes."

"Okay," she said.

"We've got to go, babe."

"I know."

He finally turned serious on her, looking uncharacteristically stern. "No heroics on your part. Promise me that."

"Alex—"

"Promise me, Geri."

"I don't know if I can do that."

"Your boss wants me and that damned computer of mine. And you're going to let him have us both. Promise me."

"Okay, I won't try to stop him from taking you from the motel," she said. But that was all she'd promise, and even that was going to be hard for her.

Alex kissed her one last time. They set off on the bike, this time knowing they'd be followed for sure, and at the end of the line... Geri sighed. There was no telling what would happen at the end of the line.

She never spotted her boss, but she trusted her instincts. He was there. Dan, too. Geri felt a heavy sense of dread that started out in the pit of her stomach and built as the day wore on, threatening to choke her, when they finally pulled off the interstate in southern Minnesota.

She'd talked to Dan earlier. He'd traveled ahead of them, selected a motel and checked into three rooms, side by side. She and Alex would be in the middle one—surrounded, but far from safe. They jumped off the bike, went into the motel office and picked up the key Dan had left for them.

Geri dreaded the walk to their room, every step of the way, just as she'd dreaded every mile that had passed that day. She kept thinking there had to be another, less risky way, of doing this. Not that it mattered. It was already done. They couldn't undo what they'd set in motion, much as she'd like to.

They got to the door of the room. Alex put the key in the door, then turned to her and gave her a world-weary smile, one she would always remember, always treasure.

I love you, Alex, she thought, her heart seeming to break apart at the realization. She'd never said those words to a man—had never said them to another human being in her life.

Her father certainly hadn't wanted to hear them, and there simply hadn't been anyone else. She'd never been the kind of girl to fancy herself in love with every boy who showed the least bit of interest in her, the kind who fell in love at least once a week. She'd never come close to that as a grown woman.

Until Alex.

He'd broken down all the barriers she'd so carefully erected, and she felt more vulnerable than ever, knew she had more to lose than ever before.

"Let's go," Alex said, charging ahead.

She lost her chance to tell him. There was no more time, not even for regrets.

Alex stepped inside. Geri followed him, locked the door behind them and then clicked on the lights. The door at the back of the room—connecting it with the room next door—slowly opened, and Geri found her partner standing in the doorway.

Standing.

"Dan?" She could hardly believe it.

Braced against the wall, holding up a black cane in one hand, he said, "I'm not going to win any races any time soon. But I'm on my feet."

"Oh." Her mouth fell open. She was amazed and so relieved. It was an incredible burden lifted from her shoulders, to see him standing. "I'm so glad. I'd hoped, but—"

"We don't have much time," he reminded her.

"Of course," she said, turning to Alex. "Alex, this is my partner, Dan Reese. Dan, Alex Hathaway."

She didn't know anyone else in the room, except Jamie Douglass, who introduced them to a tall, dark-haired, lethal-looking man she claimed as her big brother, Sean Patrick Douglass. He was obviously a military man, and he'd brought along some friends, also military. Geri shot Dan a questioning look.

"Don't ask. Let's just say we've been busy since you disappeared, and Sean and his friends have been...helpful."

Sean Douglass stepped forward and offered his hand to both of them. "I have friends in high places." He grinned. "Dr. Hathaway, we're going to have to take you in when this is over, no matter what we get on Tanner. But I think I can convince some people to listen to what you have to say. Hopefully we can get this straightened out quickly."

"Thank you," Alex said. "All of you. I appreciate the help."

Sean shrugged. "Hey, it's got to be better than spending another three and a half months hunting you down."

Alex grinned. Geri wanted to scream. How could he be smiling at a time like this?

Dan came forward with a tiny radio transmitter for her

and one for Alex. She took them both, slipped one inside her right ear, and the other into Alex's.

"Okay," Dan said. "Tanner's been right on your tail all day. He's across the road at that truck stop right now, watching this room. We've got our own person working behind the desk at the motel. He's going to slow the man down as much as he can." He touched a finger to his right ear. "We're all on the same radio frequency. You're both picking it up?"

Geri nodded. Alex did, too.

"Okay. We'll be able to talk the whole time. We have mikes in the room. A camera there." He pointed to a space at the base of a photograph. "We can see nearly everything that goes on in this room from the rooms on either side, and we have sharpshooters over there, and there." He pointed to small holes drilled into the wall. "We'll leave you alone with him as long as we can. You've got to understand, we don't have much in the way of hard evidence, except that he told people at headquarters that Geri's mission to Texas was a bust. He didn't say anything about a certain cabin being blown up or about the two dead bodies in it. He claims Geri's taking a few days off. That's all we've got. So you need to get him to talk as much as you can."

"I will," Alex said.

"Tanner's in a beige Ford Taurus. I doubt he came alone, and we'll be on the lookout, but we haven't spotted his backup yet. We didn't want to get too close today and tip him off."

"We won't let anyone else in this room, except Tanner," Sean said.

"Good," Geri replied. "We're set."

"You're armed?" Dan asked her.

She nodded.

He turned to Alex. "You're not?"

"No."

"Do you want to be?"

Alex hesitated, then said, "No."

"Okay," Dan said. "We're set."

A voice came across the radio, informing them that Tanner was approaching the motel office. Geri took a breath and tried to calm down. Dan was looking at her. As he left the room, he got her into the corner and warned, "Watch your back."

"I will."

"If Tanner's here to take Hathaway anywhere but Division One, he won't be leaving any witnesses behind."

"I know," she said. It was a risk she was ready to accept. She wasn't leaving Alex now.

"Okay. It's up to the two of you."

Everybody else backed out of the room. Geri sat down on the edge of the bed, wondering if the mikes could pick up the thundering beat of her heart, wishing she had one more day with Alex, one more night, one more minute. He was standing in the middle of the room and looked over at her, giving her one of his patented, award-winning smiles.

She had to fight the urge to scream, to grab him and shove him out of harm's way. Instead, she settled for saying in a deceptively calm voice, "Don't turn your back on Tanner."

"I won't," he promised easily.

"And don't get between him and the sharpshooters in case they need to take him out."

Alex nodded, and then it was time. The voice on the radio told them Tanner was walking across the parking lot toward their room.

Alex had been waiting for three and a half months to confront the man who'd betrayed him. The memory of the downed guard's face had been fresh enough in his memory at first that he'd feared the inevitable confrontation when someone found him. But later, the memory had faded. Anger had taken over. He'd become recklessly angry, so much so that he'd been eager to confront the man responsible for tearing his life apart this way.

But now that the moment was upon him, things had changed. He was concerned about the woman by his side, the one who'd come to mean so much to him in so short a time. He didn't care how well trained she was; he didn't want her here in the middle of this, and had thought of a half-dozen ways he might have kept her out of this today.

"God, what are you thinking now, Alex?" she asked.

He smiled a bit. "That I should have taken off and left you by the side of the road somewhere in South Dakota today."

"What?" she retorted.

Alex could hear someone—her partner, he guessed—laughing in his earpiece, and he cursed the fact that they weren't alone, that people could hear everything they said from here on out.

"It would have kept you out of this, Geri."

"I would have been furious. More furious than I've ever been at you, and that's saying a lot."

"Yeah, but it would have kept you out of this," he repeated.

She looked at him, a wealth of emotion in her eyes. He would have given anything for just a little more time alone with her. But all he had was a moment or two in front of an audience.

"Oh, hell," he muttered, and pulled her to him, dropping one too-brief kiss on those luscious lips of hers.

"Alex!" she protested.

He shrugged, not letting her go. "You're supposed to be smitten with me, remember? And naturally, with my colossal ego, I bought it."

She frowned, took a breath and turned serious. "When he comes through the door, don't make any sudden moves. Don't act like you're reaching for anything inside your pockets or behind your back. He'll think you're going for a gun. Don't give him an excuse to shoot you."

"Scared that somebody besides you will get the pleasure of doing that?" he teased.

"Oh, yes. That's my main concern right now."

He winked at her. "I'm going to miss you, babe," he said. One way or another, they'd be spending some time apart after this.

He read the words on her lips. "Me, too."

And then he had to look away. He couldn't stand there and look at her any longer and pretend that everything was okay. It wasn't. He was scared. Somebody was going to come bursting into the room any minute with a gun in his hand, and if the bullets went flying, there was no telling what might happen.

From the radio, he heard, "Subject's at the door and armed."

Alex watched the doorknob, barely picked up the sound of someone jimmying the lock.

"So," he said, turning back to Geri, his heart in his throat. They weren't supposed to know anyone was coming. They should probably be talking about something. "Ever been to Chicago?"

"Once," she said, watching the door. "In the middle of winter. It was minus ten degrees, and there was an insane arctic air coming off the lake, whipping through the buildings downtown."

"It's not always like that," he said, noting that she'd put herself between him and the door now. *Damn.* He took her by the arms and turned her around.

"Alex!" she protested.

"Oh, hell." He leaned down and kissed her once again.

It was a desperate kiss, an I-might-never-get-a-chance-to-do-this-again kind of kiss, and he put this whole heart and soul into it. She slid into his arms, wrapped her arms around him and held him tight, kissing him just as desperately in return.

"Oh, this is touching," a cynical voice said from behind them.

They broke apart. Alex shot around and found himself face-to-face with a man he'd like to strangle with his bare hands, a man he truly despised. Unfortunately, the man standing in the open doorway had a gun in his hand.

Remembering the role he was playing, Alex turned back to Geri and with as much venom as he could muster said, "What did you do?"

She gave him a brilliantly cynical smile. "You didn't really think I'd just take off with you, did you? You're practically a dead man."

"This man," Alex began, pointing an accusing finger at Tanner. "I told you, this man—"

"He's my boss," she interrupted. "I've worked with him for years, and you... Well, everybody knows what you are. What you've done."

The motel-room door slammed shut behind Tanner, and she and Alex both turned back to face him. "If you two are done," he said, "we'll wrap this up."

"I can just imagine how you're going to wrap this up," Alex countered. "The way you wrapped up that little mess at the warehouse?"

"You killed one of my best operatives," Tanner accused.

"Sure I did," Alex replied.

"Your prints," Tanner said. "Your weapon."

Alex nodded. "I really appreciate that little lesson in fire-arms you gave me that day."

Tanner sighed. "We'll have to be going. Pat him down for me, Geri."

Geri did so, quickly running her hands up and down his body, producing nothing but a pair of handcuffs. Tanner raised a brow at that.

"His idea of fun is a woman in handcuffs," Geri explained.

Alex fought the urge to smile.

"Cuff him for me," Tanner said.

Alex turned around obligingly and put his hands behind his back. "I know you've been dying to get me in these cuffs again."

"Dying to see you behind bars, too," Geri quipped.

Alex shrugged as best he could. "I try never to disappoint a woman."

Geri ignored him and turned to Tanner. "Where's everybody else?"

"We have people outside, a helicopter standing by."

"We're taking him to D.C.?"

Tanner nodded. "But I wanted to do this part of it myself." He came closer to Alex. "You've caused me a great deal of embarrassment, Dr. Hathaway. Not to mention the death of a friend. I'm not happy."

"You're not going to be any happier any time soon," Alex promised.

Tanner frowned. "We need to be going. You'll need your computer, Doctor."

"Why? There's nothing in it that would interest you."

"It's got to be there," Geri said. "It's the only thing he has worried about on this whole trip. The only thing he kept from the cabin before he blew it up."

Geri pulled the laptop out of the bag sitting on the bed and handed it to Tanner.

"You'll need me—alive—if you're ever going to find anything in my computer," Alex said.

"He's right," Geri added. "Anytime I've gotten a look

at that thing, the only thing I can call up are games. He's like a child with his little games.''

Alex didn't move.

Tanner brandished the weapon menacingly, dead center in front of Alex's heart. ''There are a lot of ways to hurt a man without killing him, Doctor. Why don't we take a little ride, and you can think about it.''

Alex thought that was it—that they'd be on their way, see exactly where Tanner was going to take them. He didn't like leaving this room, but he didn't see that he had a choice.

What he didn't expect, ever in his wildest suppositions, was to see this man he absolutely hated, turn around and raise his hand, his weapon, toward Geri. *Geri.* One of his own people.

He was going to kill her, Alex realized. Right there. Without a word. Without one twinge of regret in his eyes. Just kill her.

Of course he would, Alex realized. How stupid could they have been not to have figured that out before. Tanner had already killed one of his own people. He couldn't leave any witnesses, and Geri was supposedly the only person who knew where Alex was, and who knew Tanner had him.

The whole scene moved in slow motion. Alex fought it, but he couldn't move any faster. Tanner's hand with the gun was coming up, aimed at her. One look at Geri's face told Alex that she'd known. *Dammit,* she'd known. She wasn't surprised at all, and she was going for her gun, but he didn't think she was going to make it in time.

Alex screamed out her name, and then he did the only thing he could—he jumped between her and the bullet.

The gun hardly made a sound as it fired. He heard a strange little pop, a series of them, actually.

His head and his shoulder connected solidly with the floor. Tanner crumpled to the floor beside him, bleeding and swearing, the gun slipping from his useless hand—or what was left of his hand, Alex noted with great satisfaction.

Instantly Geri was there. She went for Tanner's gun first, taking it and tucking it into her pocket, then leaned over Alex.

"God, what did you do?" she demanded, rolling him over.

He thought his whole arm and shoulder had gone numb, maybe when he hit the floor, and it hurt like the devil. He couldn't move, either. Then he remembered the cuffs. She'd cuffed him at her boss's order. No wonder he couldn't move.

Then he remembered what he'd seen in her eyes the moment before he threw himself between her and her boss.

"You knew," he said. "Dammit, Geri. You knew he wasn't going to let you leave this room."

"I knew it was a possibility," she said, pulling at his clothes.

All of a sudden, he realized they weren't alone. There were people flooding into the room. Someone handed Geri a wicked-looking knife, and she slit his shirt open because he was bleeding.

Alex was furious. His brain was stuck on the fact that she'd known. "You came into this room anyway? Knowing what he was going to do?"

"I knew that if all the other things we believed about him were true, it was likely he couldn't let me leave this room alive."

"And you came here anyway?" he asked.

"It's my job, Alex," she said, her face tight with worry.

"Damn you," he snapped.

"God, do you ever shut up?" she cried. "Can't you even bleed quietly?"

He saw a piece of cloth in her hand, which she pressed

down hard on his shoulder. He growled at her and sucked
in a breath. "Careful. That hurts."

"It usually does when you get shot," she said. "Why
the hell did you do that?"

"I guess I've gotten a little attached to you, babe. I
wasn't going to stand here and watch him shoot you."

She gave an exasperated sigh and kept working on his
shoulder. "You couldn't just leave it to the professionals in
the next room? They had rifles on him the whole time. They
practically took off his hand."

"Not before he got a shot off at you," he retorted.

"Dammit, Alex. They could have handled it," she said,
her voice breaking for an instant.

"I couldn't take that chance."

She looked straight at him, and he could have sworn that
everything—absolutely everything—was right there in her
eyes in that instant, and then it was gone, and she was
growling at him again.

"Just shut up and let me do what I can to stop the bleeding, okay?"

She was scared, he realized, and for once, he did what
she asked. He was feeling decidedly light-headed, anyway.
All of a sudden, the room was filled with people armed to
the teeth, radio transmissions zipping back and forth in that
little earpiece they'd given him, and Geri muttering under
her breath, most of it obscenities directed at him.

She moved quickly, competently, as she did everything
else. There was worry in her eyes, strain showing in those
little lines at the corners of her mouth, and she was mad as
hell at him right then, but he couldn't help but be impressed
by the way she handled herself.

He could smell the blood now, feel the wetness against
his shoulder and his arm, which had gone totally numb, and
he didn't think he could lift his head from the floor if his
life depended on it.

"I can't believe you did this," she complained again.

Obviously, she wasn't a woman who appreciated the signs of undying devotion—like a man throwing himself in front of a bullet for her.

"Do me a favor, Alex." She was trying to free his arm, which was lying under him at an awkward angle and still caught in the handcuffs. "The next time I lift a pair of cuffs from someone, remind me to steal the damned keys."

"I will," he said. "I promise."

"Does anybody have anything we can use to cut these cuffs off him?" she yelled, so determined, so sure of herself now. She turned back to him. "You know, we're even now."

"Hmm?"

"This is almost the exact same spot where I got shot."

And she'd survived. Good. As far as he was concerned, that meant he would, too. Not that he was ready to think about that. He was still struggling to accept *why* she'd been shot.

"For me," he said. "I hate that you went through that for me."

"Forget it," she insisted. "We're even. And no more of this, Alex, okay? Paybacks are just hell."

Alex just lay there and watched her work over him with a lazy smile on his face.

"What?" she said a moment later. "What could you possibly find to smile about at a time like this?"

"You," he whispered. "You're amazing."

"You're going to flirt with me now? Alex, you really are insane."

"And you're beautiful," he insisted, then got worried. "Did I ever tell you that, Geri? How beautiful you are?"

"No, dammit, you didn't," she said, tears in her eyes as she looked down at him. "Don't go to sleep, Alex. Okay? I'm going to slap your face if you even try it."

"Really?" he said.

"Yes."

"I love it when you play rough, babe."

He was working hard to distract her, because she looked so worried, and sparring with her had always come easily. So had baiting her.

But it wasn't working anymore. She looked really and truly scared. He had to work hard for a smile then. He felt like there were so many things he should tell her, but they were all things he just hadn't sorted through in his own mind yet, and maybe he'd never get the chance. He didn't want her last memory of him to be like this.

"It was fun, wasn't it, babe?" he whispered, because it truly had been, and he wanted her to be able to remember there had been good times in all of this.

"Fun?" she said, fighting for control. "You mean, while it lasted?"

"Well..." he considered.

That wasn't what he was trying to say, but she was right. One way or another, it was done, wasn't it? Granted, this wasn't the way he'd hoped it would go. But all good things came to an end, and he didn't want her to feel bad about the way this turned out.

"It was fun," he said. "I wouldn't have changed a thing, babe."

She nodded, her tears falling uncontrollably. Alex didn't know what to say, and he could hardly think anymore. He was still trying to figure it all out when the whole world just went black.

Geri slapped him twice, right across the face, but it didn't do any good. He barely stirred. She checked for a pulse with a trembling hand and found it. Checked that he was still breathing, as well, then tried to look objectively at the wound.

It *was* almost identical to the one she'd received, and hers had bled a great deal, and she'd been weak and shocky, but she'd pulled through just fine. There was no reason to think he wouldn't. Of course, there was no way, either, to tell exactly what the bullet had done after it had torn into that spot on his shoulder. All she could see was the point of entry.

She checked the caliber of the weapon. A .38. At nearly point-blank range. She swore, seeing him jump in front of her one more time. She still couldn't believe he'd done it.

She'd known what Tanner was going to do. She'd had her hand on her gun, could have jumped out of the way, she thought. Probably could have gotten a shot off. But no. *He* had to try to save her.

Dan came in and stood beside her. "You okay?"

"Yeah," she lied. "Hell, I'm lucky I didn't shoot him myself when he jumped between me and Tanner."

Odd that she'd joked about that so often with Alex. About shooting him. Killing him. Hating him. Why had she told him so many times that she hated him? And never found a moment to tell him that she loved him?

"Chopper's on its way," Dan said. "It's two minutes out."

"Thanks," she said.

She'd ripped her earpiece out a minute ago, unable to listen to all the noise coming across the channel.

Dan put his hand on her shoulder. "He's going to be fine."

Geri nodded, holding pressure on the wound that stubbornly refused to stop bleeding.

"Sounds like you two had a good time," Dan said.

Geri almost started to cry then. "We did," she said, hardly able to breathe. "It's the craziest thing. We had a blast."

Right up until the moment he'd jumped in front of that bullet. *For her.*

And until he added that little zinger at the end, right before he passed out, about this whole ~~thing between them being nothing~~ but fun while it lasted.

Damn. She couldn't let herself think about that now. It hurt too much.

Everything hurt right now, and there didn't seem to be anything she could do about it except sit there on the floor beside Alex, alternately swearing at him and making vile threats about the things she was going to do to him if he didn't pull through.

Chapter 15

Things had to be bad before Geri turned to dear old Dad for help. Four weeks from the day she'd stood watching as Alex was loaded into a helicopter, she was entirely out of patience. She'd been lying awake nights imagining a dozen different scenarios to explain why she still hadn't heard from him—all of them bad—and she was willing to go to the extreme lengths of having dinner with her father at his current home base—his town house in Georgetown—to find out where Alex was.

Geri didn't hate her father. She'd simply never been that important to him, had never been that important to anyone. *Except Alex.*

She'd truly believed at one point that she was of elemental importance to Alex Hathaway, but all indications were that she'd been wrong about that, too.

"Damn," Geri muttered.

She'd told herself to be careful, the way she always was. She'd told Alex she was so much better off alone, so much safer that way, and what had he done? He'd talked her out of it; talked to her about reaching out to someone, about trusting them, about taking the risk.

Surely he'd meant with him. She didn't want anyone but him.

Now she was thinking it simply hadn't been real, any of it. A few crazy, intense days on the road with Alex. One extremely wild ride. What did she know about men, anyway? About the way their minds worked? Or about relationships?

He'd said his never lasted because he didn't trust women. Well, she didn't trust men. Which made it crazy to think they'd ever find a way to trust each other, especially while the whole world went spinning out of control around them. But that was exactly what she'd done. She'd trusted him, fallen in love with him.

But what did she really know about love, either? Except that it hurt. It left her scared and vulnerable and needy, which she hated. He'd called her "needy" once, and she'd absolutely hated it.

Groaning, Geri thought he should have left her alone in her drab, colorless little world. Should have let her build her shell and keep everyone and everything out, and maybe she would never have felt a genuine emotion in her life. But nothing would have hurt her, either.

Right now, she just hurt. And she was mad at her father for letting her down her whole life, and mad at Alex for being just like him. For making her think he cared about her and then showing her how unimportant she was. She'd taken years of hurt and silence between her and her father, but she'd be damned if she'd take it from Alex.

Which was why she'd called her father. He was on the Joint Chiefs of Staff and golfed with the president at least once a month. If anyone could find out where Alex Hathaway was, it was the General. Geri had asked him about

Alex two days ago and now found herself invited to dinner. She had taken a taxi to the town house and was left cooling her heels in the sitting room, her father nowhere to be found.

The last four weeks had been difficult, and she'd been busy, which was probably the only thing that had kept her sane this long. She'd had a great deal of explaining to do. There was her boss, the traitor. Her own flight across the country—quite willingly—with a man wanted for murder and treason. The two men she'd killed in the cabin in Texas that Alex had then blown to bits. The incredible jurisdictional haggles involved in three Division One agents teaming up with Jamie's brother Sean—she'd never gotten a straight answer on whom he worked for—plus whatever covert military team he'd commandeered to help them that day. They'd also commandeered an impressive array of military equipment and Division One gadgets that they'd used in a totally unauthorized exercise, which resulted in her boss and a couple of motel rooms in Minnesota being shot up. The locals had had a field day, with them whisking two shooting victims out of their jurisdiction with nothing but the barest of explanations.

If it hadn't resulted in hauling one Dr. Alexander Hathaway into custody and bringing down the real criminal in the whole mess, Geri was sure they'd all have been courtmartialed. Division One had been created by a bunch of exmilitary men, and they'd kept several of the military's longstanding traditions, including the court-martial.

Not that it would be so bad. Alex was right about the job, at least. She hated it. She'd gone after it in the first place to finally impress her father—something she'd never managed to do. And while the job had been a challenge she'd enjoyed for a time, that time was over. She didn't want to be shooting at anybody anymore, didn't want anybody shooting at her. She had no idea what she wanted, except she wanted it to be real. No more pretend woman. No more lies.

Sometimes, when she missed Alex so much it hurt, she thought maybe she'd be better off if she could go back to the way it had been before she'd learned to laugh and to smile and to feel with an intensity that left her heart aching. But she couldn't go back, couldn't be that coldhearted robot of a woman. Geri wanted to be utterly alive and free and happy, wanted to experience everything the world had to offer—but she wanted to do it with Alex.

She didn't have any experience at all with love, but she thought deep down that what Alex had shown her was the real thing. She just didn't know whether it meant anything to him. If it did, his heart should be breaking right about now. Either that or he should be with her.

There was a shred of logic inside her that said he could very well be as busy as she was. That likely he had been taken into custody the minute he was conscious. Someone had probably been standing over him in the emergency room reading him his rights. But that was logic, and Geri had used up an excessive amount of it during her first twenty-nine years of life—maybe a lifetime's share—which meant she was now running on sheer emotion.

She'd spent her nights alone and weepy—needy—and her days answering questions for a bunch of bureaucrats and military men, the low point of which had been a grilling before the Senate Intelligence Committee. Everybody had wanted to know what had gone so wrong at Division One, and how to fix it.

Next, they'd spent even more time trying to put Division One back together after figuring out exactly what Tanner had done and why and how he would be punished. It had been a gut-wrenching process for them all, and she knew the agency would never be the same after this.

Even worse, the entire division was in the doghouse

again. At first, no one could be sure that Tanner was the only traitor, so Division One had been taken totally out of the loop where Alex was concerned. Some other agency was handling him, and information was available strictly on a need-to-know basis. As far as Geri was concerned, she definitely had a need to know, but she doubted anyone up the military chain of command would agree.

All she knew was what the public knew—that he'd been taken into custody and was being held at an undisclosed location pending the outcome of an investigation into Doc's death. Nothing about the explosives formula had come out.

Geri drummed her fingers on the mantel and looked up at the antique clock. Twelve excruciating minutes had passed since the appointed time for dinner. It was totally unlike her father to be anything but punctual. She was still pondering the oddness of that when the doorbell rang. Hastings, her father's most proper English butler, conscientious to a fault regarding his duties, was nowhere to be found, which was odd, too.

Shaking her head, Geri went to the front door and flung it open without a thought, only to find Alex Hathaway standing on the General's doorstep, a familiar, wicked-looking red motorcycle parked behind him on the street.

Geri blinked at him, thinking he had to be an apparition—the figment of a stressed-out, sleep-deprived, half-crazed mind. For a minute, she could only stare.

He was wearing a crisp white shirt and a pair of disreputable-looking jeans—frayed at the knees, faded to the palest of blues—which hugged his body every impressive inch of the way from his waist to his feet. His hair long enough to brush his collar, lips twisting into a wry smile, he looked just the way she remembered—when she could block out those awful last few minutes they'd spent together. When she could keep from closing her eyes and seeing him as he lay on the floor of that motel room, bleeding and pale and utterly still, refusing to respond to any pleas she made, any curses she uttered.

She watched now as that wry smile stretched into a full-blown, thousand-watt Alex Hathaway smile, one that had her feeling a little light-headed and simply incapable of speech.

"Hi," he said. "The General said you wanted to see me."

"He did?"

Alex nodded. "Think I could come inside, Geri?"

"Uh... Sure." She stepped back to let him pass, drinking in the sight of him. He had a small ponytail at the nape of his neck. She remembered burying her nose in that spot to keep it warm, that crazy night they'd gone riding at two in the morning and made love on the side of a mountain in the cold, cold air, without even feeling the chill at all until they were sated.

Had they truly done that? Had she?

She'd wake, achingly lonely, after dreaming of him, her body soft and warm and needy. Sometimes she could swear she remembered everything about him, and other times, she thought she'd imagined it all—the magic, the exhilaration, the laughter.

God, she hadn't laughed since she last saw him.

Which had been four excruciating weeks ago, she reminded herself.

It hurt to even think how he'd changed her life so fundamentally, for the better she'd thought, and then had disappeared, leaving her more alone than ever, showing her how unimportant she was to him.

It was even worse than with her father, because she'd never felt the General really loved her. But Alex... She'd believed in Alex. She'd thought him some truly magical creature who was going to transform her completely into someone who could find joy in every single moment. Which was sheer nonsense, really. He was just a man. A man who'd left her, forgotten her. She felt utterly deserted.

It reminded her of the times her father used to parade her for show, when he needed to look the part of a family man, and then he would tuck her back into some convenient corner with a nanny or a tutor, or at boarding school. That had hurt. But not like this. Rationally, she knew they weren't the same things—she and Alex, she and her father. But she wasn't the calm, rational woman she'd once been. She'd been profoundly changed by Alex Hathaway, whether she liked it or not.

Taking a breath, squaring her shoulders, she demanded as coldly as possible, "What do you want, Alex?"

He frowned. "You know," he said, rocking back on his heels and digging a hand into his pocket. "I was thinking we could either do this the easy way or the hard way."

"Do what?" she asked.

"Talk."

"We never talked," she said defensively. "We argued."

"But we did it so well," he countered, smiling a bit. "God, I've missed arguing with you. I've missed *you*, Geri."

Hell of a way to show it, Doctor, she thought, refusing to let herself say it aloud.

"I can tell it's going to have to be the hard way," Alex said.

"And what exactly is 'the hard way'?"

He moved faster than she'd ever seen him—except when he'd been bound and determined to get himself shot. The next thing she knew, he'd slapped handcuffs onto her right wrist and his left one, binding them together.

Then he stood there waiting, that devilish smile on his face.

Geri raised her manacled wrist, which in turn brought his

up as well, and shot him a venomous look. "Have you lost your mind?"

"According to you, I lost it a long time ago, babe."

"Alex, this isn't funny," she whispered, her throat tight.

"I'm sorry," he said, honestly seeming contrite. "Believe it or not, I'm not trying to do anything except make sure you hear me out, that you can't get away until I've said what I came to say."

"I could hurt you," she threatened, raising her cuffed hand. "We're talking serious bodily harm. I suggest you get me out of these. Now."

"I couldn't, even if I wanted to. Haven't you noticed? These are *our* cuffs, and *you* forgot to steal the key."

She blinked at him in disbelief. "*Our* cuffs?"

He nodded. "They were still attached to my wrists when I got to the hospital in Minnesota. I had a devil of a time convincing the nurse I wanted them back. She thought I was joking. I finally told her they were evidence in a crime, and eventually somebody gave them back to me. I welded the links on the chain back together one day in the lab, and here they are. Our cuffs."

"What is this? Some variation on 'Our Song'?" Geri shook her head. "'Our Handcuffs'?"

"So you're not the sentimental type?" He shrugged. "I am. I enjoyed sparring with you, Geri. I enjoyed having you cuffed to my bed and riding on the bike with you. I enjoyed just about everything about our time together."

"Really?"

He nodded.

"Oh, I remember now. Fun while it lasted."

"I said it was fun, Geri. You jumped in with the other part."

"I thought I might as well save you the trouble. You told me it wouldn't last. You told me nothing ever did with you."

"I know, babe. I'm sorry."

She shrugged with as much nonchalance as she could manage, as if to say no harm done. She'd survive. She always had before.

"You know," Alex said, "believe it or not, every now and then even I'm wrong about a few things."

Geri laughed, a short, cynical sound. "Imagine that."

He was annoyed. She could tell. Not that she cared.

Then, as she watched, he seemed to take every bit of that anger and shove it aside, as if it were nothing at all. He smiled again, warmly, tenderly. She didn't think she'd ever seen him smile quite that way before.

He leaned a bit closer. "I missed you," he said.

She swallowed hard, a lump in her throat giving her all kinds of hell, and said nothing.

"I'm sorry it took me so long to get here," he said. "I've been a little busy."

"Really?" The General had always been "busy."

"I went from the hospital to a holding cell to something labeled 'protective custody' that felt a whole lot like jail."

"Really?" She closed her eyes, wanting to believe him. Wanting to believe he wouldn't have left her if he'd had a choice all this time.

"Did you miss me a little bit?" he whispered.

Lie to him, she thought. Just lie. But she'd found herself in the odd position of being unable to lie anymore. It was as if everyone had some preset limit on the number of lies they could tell, and she'd simply run out. There were none left inside her. Which meant she couldn't say much of anything to Alex except what she did. "I missed you. I tried very hard to forget you, but—"

He reached out, touching his hand ever so gently to the side of her face. "I've hurt your feelings," he said, looking sadder than she'd ever seen him. "I'm sorry. I assumed that with your security clearance, you'd have been kept up-to-date on what was happening. In fact, I wouldn't have been surprised if you'd come to break me out of that hellhole.''

"My boss betrayed you," she said. "Division One hasn't been anywhere near the case."

"I'm sorry," he said again. "They honestly didn't let me see or talk to anyone—except to answer their questions—for the longest time."

"I know. I had some of that myself."

"Are you in trouble? Because of me?"

"No. Not anymore."

"I don't want you in any kind of trouble because of me."

Geri grimaced. She had trouble, all right. Trouble sleeping. Eating. Concentrating. "Alex, you're been nothing but trouble since the moment I laid eyes on you."

He frowned, his eyes narrowing, his gaze locked on her face. "You're not trying to tell me it was all bad, are you?"

Geri faltered, no lies coming to mind, no quick retorts, no wise-ass remarks. *Damn.* There was only desperation and a too-tight throat and all that aching need.

"What do you want me to say, Alex?" she managed.

He shook his head, his look so tender she nearly started to cry.

"You don't have to say anything right away," he replied, his free hand settling against her arm, then sliding up and down in a soothing motion. "I'll go first. I missed you. I've been worried about you. Are you okay?"

She nodded, thinking it was mostly true. Then she asked, "Are you?"

He nodded, too.

"Your shoulder?" she said. "Your arm?"

"It's fine. A computer keyboard's more forgiving of a slightly unsteady hand than a weapon."

"I'm glad." She bit down hard on her lip, drowning. That was what it was like, drowning in an unfamiliar mix of churning emotions brought on by just the sight of him.

And then she looked for some foothold, some rational thing they could discuss. "Is it over? All the trouble, I mean?"

"Yes. I'm getting a formal, public apology from the president, in fact."

"Good. And the explosives?"

"That's the other thing that's kept me away," he said. "We've been building and testing a modification to the security systems in use now, and it's working. They're going into airports ASAP. Even if the formula did get out now, the security systems would catch them."

"That's what you were doing the whole time? Besides trying to figure out who Tanner was? You were trying to make your own explosives obsolete?"

"It seemed like the logical thing to do. If I could make an explosive virtually invisible to current security systems, I should damned well be able to modify the security systems to pick them up. After all, I knew exactly what I'd put in the explosives to change the chemical makeup in the first place."

"Of course," she said. He could do that. He would think to solve the problem that way, would feel a responsibility to do it. He was a hero, at least in her book—a brave, determined, dedicated man. And she'd been raised to respect heroes.

"So," he said, taking a breath, "how are things at Division One?"

"We're...coping. Tanner will be court-martialed for this, and Dan Reese is coming back to the agency. He's taking Tanner's place."

"You must be pleased. About Dan," Alex said.

"Everybody is. Even Dan. I never thought he would be. It's a desk job, after all. But we need him now. Dan trained at least half of the agents who'll be reporting to him. He's someone we all trust implicitly. I think he sees it as his duty to pull the agency back together now, and Dan's the kind of man who's always appreciated things like duty and honor.''

Alex gave her a sad smile. "I still feel terrible about what happened to him."

"Don't. He's fine. In fact, I'd say he's better than ever. Still limping, and he probably always will, but he's a different man now. The whole situation changed him—for the better, he says. He's getting married soon, in fact. I've never seen him this happy."

Alex nodded. "And what about you?"

"I'm, uh... I don't know how I am," she said honestly.

He touched her face, brushing his thumb across her cheek. "Are you mad at me, Geri?"

Suddenly it was hard to breathe, and very, very hard not to cry. "I don't know, Alex. There's this awful mix of feelings inside me where you're concerned, and I honestly don't know what I'm feeling right now."

She sighed heavily. Her chest hurt.

"Wait. That's a lie," she said. "I seem to have lost my ability to lie. It's the oddest thing. I keep waiting for my nose to grow an inch, every time I try. I feel like I'm so obvious about every little lie I attempt, that everybody must see right through me. So I don't even try it anymore. Or, if I do, I end up confessing right away. Odd, huh?"

He nodded. "Is it so bad? Being unable to lie?"

"I guess most people wouldn't think so. But I've never been most people."

"No. You never will be," he said. "What did you just lie to me about, babe?"

"I'm all mixed up. I feel like I'm choking. Like all these awful feelings—"

"All of them awful?"

"No. There're just too many of them. I cry all the time. I never used to cry, Alex. Even when I was a little girl. I just didn't do it, but now I do. And ever since you've been gone, I think I've forgotten how to laugh."

"No," he said softly. "Not forgotten. You just needed me for that. I can make you laugh again."

"Oh," she said, as the feelings welled up inside her again. "I'm scared, Alex. I went nearly my whole life without being scared. Until now."

"What are you scared of?"

"That I'll never see you again."

"You don't have to be scared of that, Geri. I'm not going to let that happen."

"Thank you," she said, feeling utterly ridiculous.

"You're welcome," he replied, and she didn't feel so bad anymore.

"You know, the worst part is that I feel like some silly little girl. I feel like I used to when my father had hurt my feelings again. When he showed me one more time exactly how unimportant I was to him. Every time I needed him, he just wasn't there."

"Well, obviously he's not as smart as he likes to think he is."

She laughed at that. Her father considered himself a brilliant man. But then, Alex thought the same thing of himself, and in his case, she'd seen the test scores to back it up.

"It's his loss, Geri. If it helps, I think he regrets it."

She went still at that. "You talked to him about me?"

"A little. He's a real character."

"Yes. He is."

"He's also very proud of you."

"Oh, Alex, don't. You don't have to say that."

"I'm not just saying it. He told me so himself. Said his little girl graduated at the top of her class at Annapolis, that she ran circles around a hundred men for the job she has now. He may have been a lousy father. He may not know how to say it now, but he is proud of you."

Geri swallowed a hard knot of emotion and blinked back tears.

"Now," Alex said, "what did I do to remind you of your father?"

Heat flooded her cheeks. She didn't want him to know this much about her, didn't want anyone to. She wouldn't have told anyone else but him, either. "God, I feel so stupid. It's—"

"Geri? It's not stupid." He tilted her chin up so he could look at her. "If it's enough to bring you to tears, it's very, very important to me."

"Is it?"

"Yes," he groaned.

"That's it," she said. "That's what I wanted. To be important to him. To be the most important thing in his life, and I never even came close. I've needed that all my life. I've been waiting for it. Isn't that silly?"

"No. Everybody wants that. To find one person who'll put you ahead of everybody else, who'll always be there for you, no matter what. So," he went on, "did you think I was out sunning myself on some island, sipping pretty little frozen drinks with umbrellas and flirting with some other woman?"

"No," she said.

He frowned at her. "You sure about that?"

"I think so. I had an idea what Uncle Sam might put you through, but much as I hate to admit it, I'm not always rational where you're concerned, Alex."

"No!" he retorted in mock disbelief.

"You bring out the worst in me. And the best. How can that be?"

"I made you happy, Geri. Tell me, as crazy as it was out there, that I at least made you happy, just for a little while."

"You did," she said.

"I was coming to find you," he said. "I just had to take

care of a few things first. I hadn't even seen my family. They kept them away, all this time. My sisters have been raising hell. I finally got to see them today, and then there was only one other person I needed. You.''

Geri started to cry then, like some silly, needy woman.

"Oh, babe," he said. "Don't."

He went to wipe at her tears, but the cuffs got in the way.

"I'm sorry," he whispered, drawing her into his arms as best he could, settling her against the unrelenting heat and solidity of his oh-so-familiar body. "I was going for symbolism."

"'Symbolism'?" She got her second wind and managed to quip, "You're going to hold me hostage, or what?"

He raised a brow at that. "It's something to think about, assuming we can't come to an amicable agreement."

"About what?"

"You and me."

"What about you and me?"

"You've got your little hang-ups with your father, and I guess I've got mine, too."

"I remember. You change women about as regularly as some guys change the oil in their cars."

"That's not true."

"I've seen the reports, remember."

"I explained that to you," he said. "Remember?"

"Women have a nasty habit of leaving me. Of dying on me." She remembered.

"It gets old, you know? Watching women who've become important to you disappear. Thinking you weren't important enough to them to make them stay."

Important enough? "Oh, Alex."

He nodded. "We're not that different, Geri. I used to lie in bed at night and think if they really loved me—my mother, my sisters—they would never have left me. I used to think, by definition, love didn't hurt, but it does sometimes. It's part of the risk we take. I know that now. I'm ready to risk everything with you. I'm not afraid of it any longer. And I'm not looking for any kind of guarantee, except that you love me, every bit as much as I love you, and that you'll fight with everything you've got to stay with me, to make this work, no matter what.''

"Alex—"

"Shh." The pads of two fingers came to rest against her lips. "Let me get this out before I kiss you. Because once I start, I'm not going to stop. Not for a long, long time. I had a lot of time to think in those months I was gone. All that time I'd been telling myself I was playing it safe not letting any woman be that important to me, and I'd just been plain lonely. Being in that shack in Texas, living in front of my computer, wasn't that different from my normal life. Pretty sad, huh? Pretty stupid for a supposedly smart man."

"You're a brilliant man," she said.

"I'm gettin' there," he said. "I made a promise to myself back in Texas. That if I ever got out of this mess, I was through with pushing people away. I was going to take a chance. I think love is worth the risks, Geri. I didn't intend to dive in headfirst like this, but there you were. I've never met a woman like you. I've never met a woman I admired more or one I need more. Are you ready to talk about how important you are to me?"

Tears rolled down her cheeks. "We could talk about that."

"I can't breathe without you." He smiled. "I get this odd little feeling in my chest, like my rib cage is shrinking or something, like I'm suffocating, and I think, *I just need to see her.* I need to be in the same room with her. I have to know she's all right. I need for her to need me, every bit as much as I need her."

"You really do?" she cried.

He nodded. "I think that's the real thing. I think that's love. When you can't even breathe for fear of losing someone, of imagining being forced to endure life without her. What do you think? You think that's it?"

"You need a definition?"

"You know, I didn't think to check the dictionary. There are probably whole books about this stuff. Love, relationships, feelings. There are probably tests and things we could use. I'm really good at tests."

"So you're proposing some kind of test project here?"

"No, I'm proposing, period. I'm proposing that we hop on that bike. The one parked at the curb." He nodded toward the front window.

"I saw it," she said.

"I have fond memories of that bike. And I've developed a real affinity for cheap motels with orange-and-lime-green bedspreads and some kind of bars on the headboard we can hook the cuffs around. I'll bet the whole road between here and Wyoming is lined with those places."

"Wyoming?" she echoed.

He nodded. "They sprang me loose from jail about nine o'clock this morning, and I've been busy. I made an offer on some real estate today. I haven't seen the owner in person, but I picture him as a crusty old rancher who was born there and is about a hundred years old now. He didn't want to sell an inch of his place. But I told him all about you. Told him I just needed a little bit on the side of a mountain, for purely sentimental reasons, and he gave in."

"You're buying that mountain in Wyoming? *Our* mountain?"

"A little bit of it. I told him a certain woman in my life thought it was a magical place, shooting stars and all, and I just had to take her back there. Someday soon, I hope. I'd like to be able to take her there anytime I want. We could lie there on the fallen leaves and count all those stars, make all kinds of wishes. We could even take a blanket next time. What do you say, Geri?''

She couldn't say anything. She only cried harder and held on to him.

"Can I take that as a yes?" he asked gently.

"To going back to Wyoming with you?"

"Well, Chicago's on the way. I thought we could make a brief stop there. You're going to have to meet the family. Wait till you meet my nieces and nephews. They're amazing. We probably should do the thing with the rings and the minister there. We'll hurt their feelings if we leave them out of it. And then we'll hop back on the bike. I want to spend our honeymoon on top of our mountain.''

"*Our* mountain?" She went to put her left hand against his cheek, forgetting once again that they were attached. Metal clinked together, and she felt a huge grin spread across her face. "With *our* handcuffs?"

"Well, it is a honeymoon." He smiled. "What do you say, babe?"

"I think it sounds like a brilliant plan."

"Did I mention that I love you?"

"You were backpedaling, wanting to consult some scientific research on that point."

He shook his head. "I do, Geri. I love you. I always will. And you're already the most important person in the world to me. I won't ever let you forget that."

"I love you, too, Alex. I love you for working so hard to teach me to laugh, for caring about whether I have a smile on my face. For taking me on moonlit rides on cold, mountain roads and for dragging out all my secrets, for refusing to let me put the walls back up. I love you. And I promise, I'll never, ever leave you."

He gave her one searing kiss and wrapped his arms around her as best he could, considering the fact that they seemed to be permanently attached by a short metal chain, then said, "Hop on the bike with me, babe. Let's go."

"Aren't you forgetting something?" she asked, raising her bound hand. "You think you can ride with these on?"

"I can do anything." He grinned. "And the cuffs don't come off until I get a wedding ring on your finger."

* * * * *

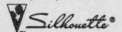

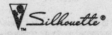

THE FORTUNES OF TEXAS

This BRAND-NEW program includes 12 incredible stories about a wealthy Texas family rocked by scandal and embedded in mystery.

It is based on the tremendously successful *Fortune's Children* continuity.

Membership in this family has its privileges…and its price.

But what a fortune can't buy, a true-bred Texas love is sure to bring!

This exciting program will start in September 1999!

Available at your favorite retail outlet.

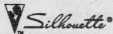

Silhouette®